No Man's Land

Volume 1
Sarah A. Hoyt

Goldport Press

DEDICATION

To my beloved,

Daniel Hoyt, without whom I'd never have written any book, much less this one.

For all the years, all the books, all the cats, all the kids: the real ones and those we duct-taped to the family line temporarily or permanently. For all the love, all the nail-biting moments, the career issues, the small triumphs (and the big ones), the four interstate moves (so far), the inadvisable real-estate purchases, the tears and the laughs. Thank you for sticking with me. It's been the best adventure, ever.

You've been waiting for this to be published since I told you about it — under duress! — forty years ago. I hope its final form is worth it.

Acknowledgements

Special thanks my editorial team, without whom this would be a confusing mess:

My structural editor, D. Jason Fleming, my editor Laura Schroeder, and my copy editor Sarah Clithero.

Also thank you to the encouragement and beta reading team:

(Uncle) Lar(ry Bauer), Amanda L., Amy B., Holly F., Ian B., Padre, Daniel A., (Lady) Eleanor Celtic, Brenda D., Holly C., Nathan B., Caroline F., Linda P, and the remaining Hoyt's Huns who prefer to remain anonymous.

Thank you, guys, for late night pep talks/threats/demands/extorsion of "just one more chapter." Thank you for all the times you said, "that makes no sense whatsoever" and forced me to figure out why my characters were doing whatever crazy thing they were doing. And thank you for hitting me with the chancla of perseverance and the chinchilla of hope, not to mention the carp of chastisement whenever needed on the long path to publication. For all the smileys, the questions, the prodding... I'm more grateful than I can say.

Of all the first readers in every possible world, I'm very glad I have you guys.

HERO

SKIP

Everything was going fine until my father stopped giving orders.

Okay. No. So everything was not fine. For one, we had been ambushed.

Which was the problem.

There are no ambushes in space battles. My father had dinned the theory and practice of space battles into my skull before I entered the Academy at twelve.

This is as good a place as any to say I was a child prodigy.

Or maybe I wasn't. There isn't really any way to tell. Late born son of a brilliant father and a demanding mother—my father named me Publius Cornelius Scipio Africanus Kayel Hayden, for crying out loud!—it was clear enough what I was supposed to do. What I was supposed to be. I wasn't genetically improved—or not so that anyone would ever admit to—so it was just... Look, I had to be what I had to be. And that meant I was a young boy admitted to a private but prestigious military academy five years earlier than everyone else there. Which meant I had to graduate as fast as I could.

This is how I ended up as my father's second-in-command at the battle of Karan. At seventeen.

And we were ambushed. But there are no ambushes in space. Just like there are no ambushes on the high seas.

You see the enemy approach for days on end. The best you can do is conceal your strategy or your capabilities from them. But you can't hide. There's nothing to hide in or behind. Certainly not with a Schrodinger-drive ship. You can't port near enough to a planet that would hide you. And you certainly can't port close to the enemy. Or rather you can, but then the risk of porting to the same space as the enemy and achieving the most pyrrhic victory of all time is high.

And we had intelligence—we had intelligence!—from the Nivirim side. They had no technology we didn't have, and their ships had a tendency to fall apart because, well, forced labor doesn't build good ships. And there was no way to hide a ship in space.

There was no way.

So my father, commanding five battle cruisers, the entire war fleet of Her Royal Majesty Queen Eleanor of Britannia On High, empress of the Star Empire, had ported to a nowhere convergence called Karan. Oh, there was some reason for it, including the fact that Karan gave access to other port points, which gave access to other port points which would put our colony worlds of Eire and Hy-Brasil and Prester within reach. Which meant if we let the Nivirim fleet port there and hold it, with no contest, those colonies would be vulnerable, or call it actually enslaved, given the Nivirim system of government.

That's the high-level version of the situation, which was all I knew at the time.

The trip to orbit in order to port to Karan took a day, and then we were there. There was the middle of nowhere in space. In full view of Nivirim vessels. Ten of them—an unusually large force—but Father said not to worry. "Battles in space aren't a matter of ship count, Skip," he said. "They're a matter of capabilities, of maneuvering, and of training. And we're better at all of those." He said it after dinner, leaning back in his chair. His blue eyes crinkled at the corners, the way they did when something amused him. "Always remember, Skip: free men fight better than slaves."

I believed him. I still believe him. My father, you see—my father never gave me any reason to doubt him. Not even then.

Before I tell the story, something must be rightly understood: I look like my mother, Lady Harcaster. Her ancestors, who had financed the colonization of and ruled over Aeris, all looked like me: colorless, narrow-nosed, thin-faced, tall and spare, the kind of people who grow older by getting thinner and dryer and harder, like aged wood. There are 'grams of them going back to the time of colonization and they probably look more lifelike than the originals.

Growing up with Mother, I always knew exactly what she expected of me. And what she expected of me was always impossible. So, of course, I did it.

Father, on the other hand, was my anchor. From my earliest memories, I knew Father loved me. So I did what he wanted me to do, not because I feared him, but because I didn't want to disappoint him.

I suspect that's why I accepted the appointment as his second-in-command aboard the HMS Victoria, commanding Britannia on High's space fleet. Because I got to spend time with Father and away from Mother.

Was it stupid? Oh, yes. My stupidity or his? Who knows?

"Look, Skip, your rank is largely ornamental," he said. "And temporary and probationary. The only reason for you to be Vice-Commodore, fresh off the Academy, is that you stick close to me and you learn. You learn, Skip. That's all. That's all you're doing here. You're learning."

I learned. Oh, the blue uniform with the half cape was pretty nice, too. But mostly, I learned. Because sure, I'd be the Earl of Harcaster when Mother died, and have full rule over Aeris, which I loathed because it was not Capital City. But that was a function of being born to Mother, who'd brought the title into the marriage. Being called Lord Harcaster wouldn't mean anything. Being called Viscount Webson, the junior title of Mom's family, made me feel stupid. It wasn't something I'd earned. And I wanted to earn something.

When I was at the Academy, people kept quoting Father and talking about the victories he'd achieved. I wanted to learn that. I wanted to earn that.

The next three days of the ambush-that-wasn't, while Father maneuvered, and the enemy maneuvered, and he planned for every eventuality, was like being back at the Academy. There was a hollo table, and the ships on it, floating in air. Father moved them. And firing capabilities, and where the weapons were in each ship were discussed, as well as the shielding capabilities, though these consisted mostly of turning the proper points to where we knew the enemy weapons were.

It was on the third night, with Father and the eight captains and vice captains of the other ships, all assembled, that I asked the stupid question.

They'd just gone over the plan, and something that was constantly mentioned at Academy hadn't been mentioned at all. I cleared my throat and before I could stop myself, heard my voice say, "Sir, what about boarding? What about preparations for boarding or to prevent boarding?" My voice sounded young, wishful, naïve. In fact, much like the voice of a student. Or a child. I was momentarily glad I hadn't called him "Father" or—as in childhood—"Daddy."

Look, that was the reason that ships carried each a complement of some five hundred men, each at enormous cost. Because ships got boarded. At the Academy, we'd studied five battles where defending your ship from boarding had turned the tide of the battle. One of those was the first battle my father had fought as commodore: the Battle of Ryrr.

But all nine men stared at me as though I'd lost my mind.

"It never happens," Father said. "Not these last thirty years, Skip. It doesn't happen. We board. They don't. Their ships aren't that agile. They have outmoded maneuvering."

"But," I said, feeling that if I'd already made a fool of myself, I might as well go on. "Why do we have infantry on alert aboard, then? And why do we wear sidearms into battle?"

Father patted my shoulder. He actually patted my shoulder. "It's the Force, Skip. Things change very slowly. It's just tradition."

All the captains had smiled indulgently, and I wasn't even mad that Father had called me Skip and not Vice Commodore Hayden. Because I knew it was from an excess of feeling and not a desire to humiliate me.

It was the last time he called me Skip.

Because in the night, while we all slept, we were ambushed.

You probably read about it in the history books, but here it goes: our intelligence was faulty or suborned. Which one, it doesn't matter, and it wasn't ever established, although investigations and interrogations ran for years.

Until Karan, boarding between spaceships had been done with boarding sleeves. So a lot of maneuvering went on, until you could be in the right place where you knew the ship shielding was weak enough that the piercing machinery at the end of the sleeve could attach and make an entry.

Our propulsion and navigation systems were better than theirs. Which is why it hadn't happened in thirty years.

But you know what those extra five ships apparently contained? Lots and lots of small vessels, each of which could carry twenty-five infantry troops. Ships equipped with an explosive prow.

I woke up to the sound of alarms. Our ship had been penetrated. Every officer and serving man were fighting with our utterly inadequate sidearms.

I put my uniform on in the dark, only because I was so fresh from the Academy that waking with an alarm and dressing in the dark, without thinking, was second nature.

But the hallways were choked with people fighting and dying, and only the enemy was in uniform. Our people were in pajamas, in their underwear, or very against regulation, mother-naked and rocking holsters, or in one case that sticks in my mind, dripping wet and with a towel wrapped around himself, Roman-style, with a blaster in each hand and one between his teeth. He was making good work, too.

I remember that. I remember snapshots of the battle in the corridor. I remember blood. I remember dismembered bodies, mostly ours. I remember people, their bodies torn, pouring out blood onto the glassteel of the floor. Many still fighting, even as their lives ran out in red rivulets and pooled in dark patches on the floor.

I remember sweat, shortness of breath. I remember the stink of blood and death. I remember running out of charges on my weapons, and picking them up from corpses without stopping.

All through it, I knew one thing: I should be in the command room with Father. Father would know what to do.

And then my mind becomes clear as I entered the command room. It was filled with dead. Dead in piles.

In the middle of it, Father. He was also in his uniform. He was getting up. There was a gaping wound in his chest, and he was lurching up, trying to reach the com.

"Son," he said. "Son." It was a bare rasp. "They knew. They had— They came here first."

He didn't need to say it. I could see the path from the outside, through a protected wall, through two adjacent storage rooms. It was plugged with the Nivirim ship, or we'd be leaking air into space.

"Father," I said. "Commodore, please don't talk."

"I must give orders. I must warn—"

But even as he spoke his voice got fainter, and his knees folded under him, his body toppling. And I, with my Academy training, got on the com and called, ship by ship, for status.

Our ship was the only one fully breached, though one of the small ships had attacked the Belcaria. Sentinels had seen it in time, blasted the disembarking attackers as soon as I called out.

I got on the coms. I screamed into them, my voice by turns hoarse and shrill.

Did the captains understand this was Vice-Commodore Hayden? Did I even tell them? Was it even true? Technically, Father was hors de combat. I was in command. I was the Commodore.

I roused the ships. I gave them instructions. Textbook instructions. It's all I knew. But the hollo of a man in uniform bellowing instructions to the just awakened can be effective. The ships spun, and fired on the small would-be intruders before they got near. The few that penetrated were met with a full complement of wakened-in-time, in-uniform, in-their-right-minds infantry.

Me? I stayed at the coms. I stayed with it, calming, cajoling, ordering.

Do you know I don't remember firing my sidearm even once, while I was at the coms? But I must have, because Father was unconscious, and there was no one else there with us but the dead. So unless the dead got up to fight—I don't know. It's as plausible as anything else—while I talked, I fired and fired and fired, and accounted for about thirty-five of the enemy, which effectively choked the door, so they couldn't come in anymore from inside our own ship, to stop the commands going out to the fleet.

They must have been working on breaking through the barrier of corpses when our people, commanded by me at a distance, and mostly from the Belcaria, took the Victoria, cleaning up as they went.

When it became clear the people trying to enter were our people, I got off the coms. I had the vague idea that if I could only keep Father alive till the medics got there, the regen would make everything all right.

He was on the floor where he'd lain down. His eyes were closed and his hands were cold, and I thought he was dead.

I have no memory of all the orders I gave in combat, but I remember what I cried, then: "Father! Daddy!"

His eyes opened. I lifted his head. I babbled about medics, about regen.

Father stared at me and smiled. He said, "Good man, Scipio. Well done, son." And then he died.

My father had the most amazing eyes. Blue, sure, but a very dark blue, so that from across the room they looked black. But up close, you saw them blue and deep like the night sky in summer, blue and deep like the whole universe.

One moment, they were looking at me, shining, deep blue. The next, they were black.

I looked into my father's eyes and I lost myself.

I forgot what I'd been meant to be, what I was.

They came in. They pronounced Father dead. I was wounded, they said. Nothing vital hit. Or nothing vital that couldn't be re-gened.

I didn't want to leave Father. If I didn't leave him, perhaps he would come back? They had to tranq me to drag me away to the infirmary.

When I woke two weeks later, they told me that Father was dead, but I already knew.

I wore the blue uniform with the half-cape once more, on a freezing winter day, in blowing snow, as I stood in the family cemetery next to the Earl's palace of Aeris, and watched Father's coffin lower into the grave, while space force captains and countless infantry stood at attention, wedged awkwardly between statues of angels and spacemen, of kings and imperious women holding aloft wreaths of victory.

There, in a deep hole, they buried what remained of the most important person in my life to that day.

When it was done, they let loose a twelve-cannon salute, Earth cannons, the kind not used in battle since Old Earth. Then a military band played the sweet, haunting "Home of the Spacer," consigning Father's memory to the stars.

I stood at attention there, and then I stood beside Mother and received the condolences of a grateful Empire. The Queen herself, with frost-blued fingers, pinned the Wreath of Valor upon my chest, the big one, in gold, with the replica of the first colonizing ship in the middle.

I removed it after the funeral. And then I removed my uniform. I sent my resignation to Her Majesty.

And then I lost myself in the fleshpots of New London, the Empire's capital city.

THE KING IS DEAD

EERLEN

As he'd feared, the cries and screams echoed, even up in the guarded family wing, at the top of the ancient palace.

Eerlen Troz had rushed up five flights of stairs, the screams and baying of grief accompanying him every step of the way, as he climbed up and up and up.

Sometimes a fresh note broke in, and he could almost follow the progression of the news through the various parts of the building. "The king is dead" was spoken, and the screaming started.

Visiting city and league dignitaries in the guest quarters, traders and nomad clan ambassadors, also in the guest quarters, some muffled sounds that might be from the guard quarters, and he surely hoped the military commanders staying in the palace weren't howling like peasants who'd lost a child, like nomads who'd lost a lover.

Up and up and up, rushing and breathless, nodding to the guard at the bottom of each flight of steps, ignoring their pointed looks of enquiry, Eerlen held up his long, ceremonial tunic so as not to trip on it and cursed that he'd not been prepared for this.

He'd not been prepared for any of this. He'd expected nothing more than a dinner with Myrrir and the commanders, a discussion of forces and schedules of shield holders. And then a quiet night with Myrrir in the royal quarters. Perhaps a game of Etarresh before bed.

Maker's womb, this was the last thing he'd expected. But he must get to the child before someone else did. And it wasn't even because the child was young and the shock would be great. There were far worse outcomes in play, when the heir to the throne was only sixteen.

By the time he reached the top floor, where the royal family slept, he knew the child—his sireling—would be awake. Eerlen was also out of breath, panting, cursing that he was too old for this. Much too old for this. And that it had been far too long a time since he'd crossed Erradi with his bedroll, hunting for his keep. Much too long since even his last ceremonial partial route to check on the Troz clan, of which he was titular head.

He opened the door to Brundar's room and rushed in, freeing his arm from the guard's hand which had gone so far as to clutch at him. The guard couldn't think he was protecting the heir or that Eerlen meant the child harm. It was curiosity. Mere curiosity.

The child was awake and sitting in the middle of the bed that was still too big for him, even now that he was adult height. He sat, his eyes wide open, staring at the door, giving every impression he expected an attack. Which meant his instincts were good, at least.

He was tall but not yet filled out, a sketch of an adult without the shading, his eyes too large in a too-thin and pale face. His green eyes turned towards Eerlen. Surrounded by the child's disheveled red locks, that face had something not quite real, or at least not quite tame. It was a face one expected to see peeking from the shadows of trees in the deep forest, a face that disappeared as soon as seen. The mouth worked. "The screams... The..." Brundar said, his voice too thin, as though he were much younger. "Was there a breakthrough? Is—"

Oh. That. The historical Draksall breakthrough that killed everyone in the palace four hundred years ago, and gave the throne to the infant saved by his nursemaid.

Well. When there were tapestries and paintings of that catastrophe all over, how could the child not think of that?

Eerlen shook his head, more hoping than sure that it was reassuring. His breath had almost steadied. He took a big swallow of frigid air. These walls didn't keep the heat in, no matter how big the fire in the ornate fireplace.

The palace might be made of something they no longer had a name for, in shapes stone could not copy. But whoever the ancients were, they had been more resistant to cold than even Erradians or had something other than fire to keep them warm. He was grateful for the air's coolness, at any rate. And for the need to do something, to keep the horrible aftereffects of the death of a ruler from swallowing all, before he could stop and think he'd lost his lover, he'd lost his sworn lover, he'd lost his best friend and helpmeet and support. Because if he stopped and thought of that, he'd break down and cry like a nomad at a funeral.

But I am a nomad. At least, at heart. And this is a funeral. Or a wake, he thought, but didn't say. Instead, he stepped towards the bed and knelt so as not to tower over the child. Stretching his hands, he took hold of Brundar's and held them in his. "Brundar," he said, and hesitated for a moment. "Your parent came home... Was brought home. He was wounded. He has...he has died. You are the ruler of Elly."

He meant to swear his fealty then and there, but he should have known better.

It is not like he doesn't come by his wildness naturally.

When that thought came, it was already too late, and the child had leapt from the bed, running on bare feet, wearing only a knee-length nightshirt.

Eerlen got up and followed. He didn't waste his breath in calling.

Brundar was running like a scared colt. And he'd been running towards what scared him since he'd learned to run. Perhaps not the best survival strategy, but he came by that naturally, too.

Brundar knew where to go, of course. It wasn't the first time that Myrrir had been carried in wounded. Warrior king. Eerlen could have spit. He had tried to argue for moderation. In vain. Given the age of the one heir, given the multitude of others who could have claimed the throne sideways, by right of siring, and given that some of those had troops in their following, Myrrir should have had more care for his life.

For the sake of the child, Eerlen had begged.

He'd been told, He's my child. He'll survive.

Yeah, well, he thought, as Brundar, far faster, vanished around the last turn of the last flight of stairs, and into the ground floor receiving room that had too often served as an infirmary. The guards on the last three flights of stairs had been crying. The news spread.

The bottom floor was a bedlam of people crying, and wiping noses to sleeves and hems of tunics. Eerlen ran past them without even really looking, registering only that there were groups and couples, and people standing alone, pale and crying. Crazy brave, heedless, and often far too willful. But loved. Myrrir was loved.

Tears prickled behind his eyes, and he shook his head as he hurried. No time. Not now. He could always howl later.

He noted without pausing that the yelling in the death chamber—the heated argument that had seen drawn swords—stopped dead as Brundar ran in, and lifted a short prayer to the Maker that the child not be run through by those swords, thereby clearing the way to the more ambitious of the arguing people.

By then, he was mere steps behind and erupted into the room in time to see the five adults in the room standing, frozen in the poses they'd obviously held when Brundar ran in.

Khare Sarda of Karrash, his sword still drawn, his blue eyes flashing, and Parnel Haethlem of Erradi, wearing his bloodstained tunic, his face almost as pale as his pale hair, standing beside him, while facing them were Guinar Ter of Lirridar and Kalal Ad Leed of Brinar. Ad Leed appeared to have put his sword flat over the others' swords, as though trying to bring them down. Lords of the four subdomains of Elly, and two of them Brundar's crossiblings and used to ruling. All of them either with drawn swords or about to draw them.

But worse in that respect was the person by the bed, who had not drawn his sword. He was muscular and somber, the biggest person in the room overtopping the others by a head, his dark battle leathers stained with blood—how much of it Myrrir's, Eerlen couldn't guess. He'd carried Myrrir in—his lips clamped firmly together, his face an unreadable mask. That would be Lendir Almar, commander of the royal guard and over-commander of all the armies of Elly, the second-in-command after Myrrir. The child of the last commander. And Myrrir's sireling, who had always seemed to loathe Eerlen and therefore Brundar, for reasons not quite clear.

The only one of the recognized heirs not present, Nikre Lyto, Eerlen's adopted child, Myrrir's adopted sireling and heir to the role of archmagician, was holding shield at the battle front. Without that, he'd have been killed by now. Nikre neither wanted the throne nor had defenses against the court's intrigues.

You couldn't have arranged things more disastrously if you'd meant to, lover, Eerlen thought, looking to the hasty pile of cushions and furs on which Myrirr had been lain, and which had become his deathbed.

Myrrir had never been beautiful. Too many Erradians, too much

Draksall in his ancestry. A jaw too square, a mouth too strong, and the uncompromisingly direct glance that had flashed from beneath those too-straight eyebrows. Of course, if he talked and moved, everyone forgot his plainness. But he'd talk and move no more. Someone had closed his eyes. His hair was still bound for battle, braided and tied and securely pinned to his head. He still wore his battle-leathers, slashed and soaked in blood.

They said the dead looked like they were sleeping. Myrrir didn't. He looked dead.

It was nothing too horrible, though his lips had contorted and remained in a final twist of pain, refusing to cry out. And he was pale. Deathly pale. But most of all, it wasn't Myrrir. The shape might be the same, but something had left. Something was not the same. What was on the bed might be the same form, but it wasn't Eerlen's lover. Not his sworn. Perhaps because Myrrir had never been able to stay completely still, even when asleep.

There was blood, a pool of it, under the body on the furs. Some of it dripped from the edge of the furs onto the floor, but sluggishly, starting to congeal. The child should not have seen that. The child—

Brundar stood very still. A statue in the shape of an adolescent on the edge of maturity. Arrested where he'd stopped in his flight, two steps from the corpse, one hand forward, as though to touch Myrrir and wake him—if anything could!—one foot advanced, bare against the age-darkened oak, his nightshirt looking flimsy and far too short, even his hair seeming to have frozen in place, a mass of curls thrown back by his flight. He was so still, he might not have been breathing.

And the other five watched him, their eyes intent. Eerlen would feel better if he could swear the look was not that of a wolf staring at a rabbit.

He didn't dare touch Brundar. Almost afraid to break the moment, which would break, inevitably, the minute the child started to wail, Eerlen reached under the hem of his tunic for his ankle knives, one worn on each ankle, and that against etiquette and risking Myrrir's laughter—Are you afraid a dire wolf will jump you in the palace, or a Draksall, sweetling?—and fuck the settled habit of not carrying swords except in battle. He was a fool to have complied even minimally and outwardly. Now he wished for his sword, his lance and his bow. And all too little.

His considerable magical power for defense or attack couldn't be used in the palace. The shields would not allow it. It was old interdiction, designed to stop Draksall breakthroughs, but it put the throne at risk now.

Eerlen had a feeling the minute Brundar wailed, the tableau would break and minutes later, the child would be dead, leaving the throne of Elly to be fought over by the three half-siblings remaining in that room. Eerlen bet on Lendir, who outmassed both Sarda and Ter and was more battle-hardened than mere governors. But that wouldn't matter to Eerlen, because he'd be dead before they cut down his sireling, his daggers broken against those swords.

Brundar took a deep shaky breath. It sounded too loud in the absolute silence of the room. He wheeled around, standing, square-shouldered and crossing his arms on his chest, looking much like Lendir Almar, probably without knowing it.

The voice that came out was controlled and even, with an edge of offense. "Why wasn't I informed before it came to this? Why wasn't I called before the news went out?" The two questions flew like slaps at Lendir, whose eyes opened wide, startled, and then Brundar turned to the four across the deathbed. "And what is this? Why are swords out in a death chamber? Is this the behavior of the Lords of the Land of Elly?"

For a moment, it hung in the balance. Eerlen didn't know but could suspect how fast the child had thought and judged the re-actions of those in the room, and taken advantage of his moment of absolute quietness to plan. It probably wouldn't work, but if he had one chance, it was that: sound as much as possible like Myrrir, assume authority and carry it through on that. Myrrir had been loved. For all his faults, for all his errors, he had been loved. And three of the adults in this room were his sirelings. And vassals of the new king. If they'd own it.

Eerlen became aware of his heart thudding so fast, his head spun. And he hardly dared breathe. The daggers felt cold as he gripped them, one in each hand.

Lendir broke first. The look of surprise passed. For a second, something like laughter fled behind his eyes, and then left his features impassive again.

He fell to kneeling without grace, the sound of his knees hitting the floor resounding on the wood. "King of Elly," he said, looking up at Brundar. "Defender of the lands, Lord of the people, receive my fealty."

If Brundar was surprised, he didn't show it. He nodded and waved his fingers at Lendir, without lifting his hand. "Stand, Almar. Commander of my guard." The off-hand acknowledgement and confirmation of post might have been done by Myrrir himself. Absolutely sure. Certain of his own authority.

Brundar looked inquiringly at the four governors, tilting his head to the left. He said nothing.

Eerlen, weak with relief they had Almar and his sword, and by extension, the armies behind Brundar, swallowed hard, because he would not cry, not even with relief. He caught the edge of a glance from Almar, a minimal lift of the corner of the commander's lips, and wondered if he was being mocked or consoled, but it didn't matter. He wiped his sleeve down his face, to hide his expression. Nothing mattered as much as Brundar's survival.

Ter tried a protest. He would. He was the oldest of Myrrir's sirelings, thirty-eight, and he had thought himself the heir to the throne for half that time. "Almar, you cannot be serious," he said. "Brundar Mahar is a child. His sire, who will reign behind the throne, is an ice nomad, barely broken to civilization! Unless you mean to rule behind the throne yourself."

Lendir knew better than to answer. Brundar wheeled around on his half-crossibling, snapped, "No one will reign behind the throne, Ter." It was said in the tone of an adult correcting a child. No real anger, though plain irritation. And no defensiveness.

Kahre Sarda, Myrrir's youngest, best beloved natural sireling, put away his sword in measured gestures, and Haethlem slid his into the sheath at his waist. Small, dark and lithe, Sarda fell to his knees first, with the gentle drop of a dancer upon a rehearsed movement, inclined his head and pledged his fealty and his domain of Karrash to Brundar. Haethlem, tall, blond and square-shouldered, dropped to his knees behind Sarda, before Sarda stood, and pledged fealty and Erradi—for what that was worth with war raging and invaders at its core and Haethlem's own household more often threatened than not—and then Ad Leed gave Lendir Almar a quick glance. Was there an imperceptible nod from Almar? Why? What would a Lord of the Land owe Almar?

Ad Leed pledged. Leaving Ter standing, looking sullen. To be fair, he always looked sullen. Or at least peevish. The force of

Myrrir's features had been softened in the Lirridarian, but he compensated for it by scowling.

"Ter," Brundar said, once more the adult in the room. "We do not have the time or resources for a civil war, while the enemy has broken through into Erradi and occupies a good portion of it." Just that. Not so much a threat as a statement. The implication being that but for the invasion foothold in Erradi, he and his forces would wipe any resistance Ter could mount off the map.

Ter let out his breath in a sort of sigh of impatience, and shoved his sword, with force, into its sheath, so hard that the clang of guard hitting metal trim rang like a bell, raising echoes from the high ceilings. He knelt measuredly, and said his oath like spitting.

Brundar looked at Eerlen then. "Archmagician?" he said, lilting. And for the first time in the whole wretched evening, Eerlen remembered he was more than Eerlen Troz, out-of-practice-ice-nomad-and-fur-trader, and the sire of the...of the new king of Elly. He felt the weight of the silver chain around his neck and the ancient jewel it held, the red jewel of the Archmagician, the chief of the magicians of Elly. The one who must remove its complement from Myrrir's dead finger and slip it onto Brundar's, before he was de facto as well as de jure king of Elly.

He bowed, slipped his knives back into their sheaths, noting Lendir's amused look at that—he really was mocking Eerlen!—and, bowing, stepped past his sireling, now his king, to the royal corpse. It helped to think of it as the royal corpse, and not Myrrir's remains.

He had to remove the blood-darkened, worn leather gauntlet from Myrrir's right hand to get at the ring, at the ruby of kingship.

Unbidden, in his mind, he remembered twenty years ago, being the newly-minted archmagician and making his bow to Myrrir, king of Elly. The chain was unaccustomed at his neck, the ruby of office shone on his chest. He was still in shock, feeling ill-awakened as the ruby muddled his mind with a sense of immense power and a confusion of impressions of his predecessors.

He remembered thinking it would have been easier to swear fealty to Mahar in battle, where Myrrir Mahar would be dressed in leathers and look much like the other commanders. But of course, he'd had to do it at the palace, in a formal reception. The ruby informed him that was how things were done.

He could see himself in his mind's eye, just seventeen, wearing his nomad furs: tunic and pants of white fur, homesewn and crude, his magician's blue cloak still new. He'd been initiated less than a year before that. He could feel the stares of the dignitaries and courtiers, and hear that one person—he'd never figured out who, either—laughing in the corner.

And Myrrir—in green silk with gold embroidery, a long, formal tunic and court slippers of gold-embroidered leather that kept tapping rapidly beneath the hem, even as he sat on his ancestors' gilded throne—looked impatient and bored.

Had Eerlen not noticed the king's diadem laid askew on his hair, and that the hair was bound at the back, like a warrior's, as though the king had rushed in from battle, gotten hastily dressed, and dropped the diadem on his own head as he ran down the stairs—which was exactly what had happened, with an added swear word at the need to formally meet the new archmagician—Eerlen might never have found his voice.

But he'd smiled at the diadem and whispered his oath about laying his magicians: healers, illusion spinners, spell makers, portalers and shield holders and all at the king's disposal.

And Myrrir had looked amused and also as though he were thinking the words that he had whispered into Eerlen's ear much later after the celebratory banquet, the intricate dancing and the obligatory music. "Never mind the magicians and healers. Can one lay the archmagician?"

Remembering, Eerlen swallowed hard. Smooth, really smooth, my love, he thought as he pulled the ring from the stiffening finger.

He turned and knelt before slipping it onto Brundar's finger. Brundar instinctively closed his hand. Later, a goldsmith would have to be engaged to make an insert to conform it to the new king's finger. Stupid to cut it to size before Brundar stopped growing.

Eerlen bowed his head. "I, Eerlen, head of the Troz line and the Troz clan, Archmagician of Elly, swear its brotherhood of Magicians and all its functions, its healers, shield holders, illusion weavers and judicial magicians and all creators of portals and spells to the command of Brundar Mahar, King of Elly."

Not for the first time, it occurred to him to think that Brundar was an odd name. Who called his child Vengeance? The child would grow to ask the same question.

But Myrrir had done it, and Eerlen was honorbound to answer the question when it came. Not that Myrrir's name—Blood Oath—was any better. The Mahars were strange people. And kings for thirty unbroken generations. One more. Let there be one more. No, two more. Barren of a line-child himself, the end of his long, storied line, Eerlen wanted to see his sireling's children.

"You may leave," Brundar said, waving his hand at the four governors. "Almar, keep watch at the door, please."

Eerlen turned to leave. He could do with some kind of privacy. Tears were going to overwhelm him at any moment, and he'd promised himself a good howling. Not that there was ever full privacy for the royal family. There would be an ear at the door, a valet's intrusion. Just enough to allow him an unguarded moment.

But Brundar said, "Stay, Troz," calling him by his line name for the first time in Brundar's life. And Eerlen stayed. He heard the door close, by Lendir Almar's hand, softly, as if he feared disturbing the dead.

Brundar turned a desolate face to Eerlen and opened his mouth as though to speak, but before Eerlen could so much as move, he closed his mouth, turned away, took the remaining steps to the bed, fell to his knees, buried his face in Myrrir's shoulder and shook.

Well, at least he isn't howling. Nothing that can be heard outside.

At length, he heard the word Brundar whispered: "Emee." It was the baby word for parent. And there, in the silent death chamber where the fate of the whole world had just been decided by the child on his knees by the bed, it made Eerlen Troz's hair rise at the back of his head.

Because it was Murder

Eerlen

It was the morning after Myrrir's death, and Eerlen Troz had felt better. He was almost sure he'd slept, for at least a couple of hours, or at least lost consciousness for a couple of hours, after the good howling he'd promised himself and indulged in.

It hadn't been very satisfying, as it had happened in his room, a small chamber adjacent to the royal quarters and with his face pressed on the pillow to deaden the sound.

The chamber and the bed felt strange to him—he'd almost never slept there—and the royal apartment next door too empty, too cold. In the back of his mind, he kept waiting for the sound of footsteps, for Myrrir's voice calling, "Len." No more.

He'd give his life for that, even to hear the revolting pet name which might have been appropriate when Eerlen was very young but certainly wasn't now.

This room had once been used by a valet or a body-servant, but it had been changed into his own room when it became obvious that he'd be living in the palace. Not that he ever slept in it if Myrrir was in residence or expected. Then he shared the royal bed. Which was almost every night.

This room was narrow, long and sparsely furnished, with a single bed, two large trunks for his clothes and a writing desk with inks and brushes enough for a business letter, or a complex dispatch. There was in fact one of those started, which he'd been working on when summoned by Myrrir's mind-touch, saying he'd been wounded and was being carried into the palace.

It was a business letter and opened with "Greetings and salutations to Kalal Ad Leed, Lord of Brinar—" It had been meant as a formal request for cloth for the army, bureaucracy since Ad Leed knew very well what was needed, and it fell under "doing Myrrir's

work for him." Because Myrrir couldn't be everywhere, and he
trusted Eerlen like his own self.

With a pang, Eerlen realized he didn't know if he'd ever take
on those duties for Brundar, if Brundar realized those duties even
existed, and that he would probably have to find another room
within the palace, if Brundar should want him to stay and not
decide that Eerlen should, instead, return to his nomad route in
frozen Erradi, hunting fur bearing animals, sleeping in ice caves.

Not that Eerlen would mind. In many ways, it would be better to
escape the palace and the settled life of a courtier, not to mention
the constant reminders of Myrrir. He'd never been suited to the
palace. And he kept expecting Myrrir's voice. Craving Myrrir's
company. Imagining Myrrir calling him.

His eyes were drawn towards the only ornament in the room,
the only thing not strictly utilitarian. It was a life-size portrait of
himself and Myrrir, painted a couple of years before Brundar's
birth. It was a copy of the one in Myrrir's workroom on the other
side of the royal bedroom. It had been painted in one of the
chambers that Myrrir used as a workroom: a vast room, with a
vaulted ceiling, soft rugs and enveloping nomad-style floor cushions, which Myrrir preferred to chairs or sofas.

Myrrir was dressed in a dark blue silk tunic, ending just above
the knee, pants of the same material falling in soft folds beneath,
and court slippers in dark blue leather engraved in some kind
of floral motif. He wore the swearing belt Eerlen had given him:
composed of heavy squares of silver, engraved with passages from
Missa's Confession. It was quite the most elaborate and expensive
thing that Eerlen had ever commissioned the making of—ten bear
pelts. Enough for a small house—and utterly inappropriate to
Myrrir, who probably would have preferred red leather tooled
with Eerlen's name.

But Eerlen had been young and over-impressed with the idea
that the king would accept his swearing and swear to him in
return. Myrrir's dark blond hair, the color of ripened wheat, was
pulled back on one side and fell over the other shoulder, straight
and smooth. It had been Myrrir's despair that his hair shed ties
and binds, so he had to work double hard at it to keep it out of
the way in battle. He'd once cut it short when he was very young,
and the story was still a scandal at court.

By Myrrir's side, Eerlen looked—to his own eyes—insignificant and much too young. He was about Myrrir's height, and as with Myrrir, there was too much Erradian and too much Draksall in his ancestry for him to ever be pretty, much less beautiful. But there, the resemblance ended. To Myrrir's laughing green eyes, his counterposed a dull grey. And where Myrrir's features gave the impression of mobility and inner joy, as though he were about to burst in laughter, Eerlen looked grave, as though he were pondering some deep matter. In fact, in those days, he'd lived with a near-crippling fear of saying the wrong thing. But it could pass as serious thought in some lights.

He wore—against Myrrir's protests, he remembered—an ankle-length dull-white silk tunic. Silk had been Myrrir's insistence, but the white had been Eerlen's. And while it might be Erradi's color, Myrrir had been right that it washed out Eerlen's pale skin and hair, till the whole looked like a shadow, except for the ruby, which Eerlen had cupped in his left hand for the portrait. It hadn't even been on purpose, to showcase his status, but he'd put his hand up and the painter had liked the gesture and told him to hold.

His other hand reached forward, almost meeting but not quite, Myrrir's hand, that reached back. He, at Myrrir's insistence, wore Myrrir's swearing belt, a thing of gold and diamonds, with Mahar spelled out in garnets in the middle of it.

Eerlen remembered being uncomfortable and feeling out of place and stupid when the portrait was painted. Right now, he'd trade all his self-assurance, all the knowledge that twenty years as archmage and the king's sworn had earned him to be there again, when the portrait was painted. To reach fully forward, to feel Myrrir's warm battle-calloused hand engulf his. To have Myrrir look back, laughter in his eyes. To know he had years ahead with Myrrir.

He'd endure everything—the stillbirths over the years, the seventeen children who'd breathed for no more than a day, if that long, the one he'd almost hoped, and whose graves dotted the royal cemetery, at Myrrir's insistence whose headstones read, Much loved sireling of Myrrir Mahar, the blighted hopes for his own line, Myrrir's voice, on a rare sad note: Too much Draksall on both sides, sweetling—the comedy of errors of learning how the court worked, the days of missing the ice and solitude so much he felt he'd die, the weeks of holding the magical shield over the battle against the might of the enemy with barely any time to eat or sleep... He'd endure all of it for twenty years more with Myrrir. Truth be told, for twenty days more with Myrrir. Or twenty hours.

He sat up. For one, because if he knew; if he'd been forewarned, he could have kept Myrrir from being murdered.

The word in his mind shocked him and he shook his head. War deaths weren't murder. Not that way.

He dragged himself to standing. His eyes felt gritty, perhaps from crying, perhaps from not having cried enough.

He'd got so far as to think he must choose clothes for the day and bathe when there was a knock on his door.

"Come," he said, while ready to reach for his dagger under the pillow. No, it shouldn't be anyone hostile, not when enemies would have to get past guards, but who knew? Technically, as the king's sire he had no power and no status—certainly far less than as the king's sworn lover and helper, which he'd been until yesterday—but someone might decide Brundar loved Eerlen too well, and therefore Eerlen must be removed.

But the person who came in would know all about the guards. Because he led them. Which wasn't to say he was tame or safe. Lendir Almar stood just inside the door, his bulk projecting a strange echo of Myrrir's more gracile form, his serious eyes a shadow of Myrrir's laughing ones, and said, "Troz."

"Almar." What followed, Eerlen guessed, could be anything from a request to vacate the premises to a request to accompany him to a tidy cell, to— No, there was no good outcome here, not when Almar was frowning thunderously, an expression that made him look like Myrrir in his worst moods.

"I need help and the king is asleep. I don't want to wake him, and the archmagician should have authority in this, because it is judicial."

Eerlen started. This was not at all what he expected. His hand flew to the ruby as it did when he wasn't sure. "The archmagician? My authority?"

Almar took three steps into the room, and stopped, his hand extended towards Eerlen but just short of touching him, a plea, lifted, half-folded, palm up. "Milord," he said. "As head of fourth circle, I beg you to stop my sir—to stop Myrrir Mahar's preparation for burial until a quorum of the circle can examine the corpse." He paused a breath. "If you don't, he will be washed and dressed and the traces will be gone." Another pause. "I'd say you do the examination yourself, but you'd still need a quorum of fourths before it were taken as official, begging your pardon, milord. But your being his sworn, you'd need corroboration."

"Yes," Eerlen said, curtly. And was shocked to hear the word, because his mind was spinning madly: Of course Almar was the head magician of the fourth circle. A justice bringer; an examiner of scenes of death; a determiner of guilt.

Ridiculous for Eerlen to have almost forgotten in the mess yesterday that Almar was under his control. He could have brought him to heel with— No. He could not. Almar was Myrrir's and Myrrir's sirelings were as stubborn as their sire. He couldn't have made Almar do anything short of breaking him, and that's not what the archmagician did. But Almar was a fourth, as Myrrir had been, of all things, a third circle—a healer—as Brundar would likely be when fully grown. Fourth circles were judicial magicians, judgers of guilt and foul play.

"But the traces of what?" he asked, confused.

Almar bit his lower lip, not so much in frustration as in surprise. He looked at Eerlen in utter surprise or perhaps in suspicion, as though he couldn't believe Eerlen was asking this in earnest. "Of my sire's murder."

He could prevent Myrrir from being murdered, ran through Eerlen's mind, in recollection of his earlier unbidden thought. Had he picked up something from the scene? From Myrrir's mind-touch? Sometimes his magic knew things he didn't know. "It was a death in battle," he said aloud. He scrubbed his hand across his face, as though it would make the whole thing go away. "Those aren't murder."

"It feels like murder," Almar said. "I could feel it in the room last night. The murderer was there, too." And then his eyes widened, apparently in shock at Eerlen's long and fluent cursing. It surprised Eerlen, too. He'd never been profane, certainly where anyone could hear him.

In difficult situations, faced with recalcitrant traders, or a shortage of food for the army, or a new shield-piercing spell by the enemy, he'd been known to say "Rotten ice," but that was it. In fact, servants and secretaries knew that very mild swearing was a sign of extreme displeasure.

He stopped in shock the third time he mentioned the Maker's

Balls and the Maker's Empty Womb, and sighed. "Shall I try it first? Then call a quorum?"

"Milord, your being the archmagician—" Almar didn't quite say that given his command of power, its strength and his experience and abilities, Eerlen could create traces of murder or erase them, even if there had been the opposite. But he made it clear.

Eerlen almost swore again. "Very well," he said, almost with venom. If Almar vocalized his suspicions, Eerlen could challenge him to a duel for it. But he hadn't. That reticence, that pause insulted while not providing the remedy of covering the insult in blood. "Is the chamber guarded?"

"I left two of my best with instructions to let no one through."

"Very well. Go and wait there," Eerlen said, as he put out a call for all fourth circles within reach of Eles city, and why they should come.

Then he rushed through bathing. He remembered when the ever-running warm water pools of Eles palace had been a sybaritic delight, but that day, he rushed through dipping and soaping and rinsing, half-dried his hair and braided it still half-wet. He slipped on undyed linen pantaloons and short tunic, Elly peasant attire for the Northern temperate area, pulling the ruby to sit over the tunic. He owned better clothes and as the archmagician, he was entitled to better clothes, had often worn them, for effect. And as the king's sworn—

He heard Myrrir in his mind, saying, "Oh, please, Eerlen. Stop trying to pretend I seduced some hapless illiterate! Put on something the court won't gawk at."

He frowned at Myrrir in memory. Myrrir wasn't good at treading the very fine line of palace politics. He'd been born the child of a royal parent, after his full-grown sibling had died childless. Myrrir had known himself a ruler from the time he was born. He'd never needed to dissemble and excuse, to apologize or beg. He'd always been at the pinnacle of society, either destined to become ruler, or the ruler.

Eerlen, as half-Draksall from a parent the brotherhood had cut off, sensed his position, both archmage and king's sworn, as precarious, like a floorboard that turns under your foot.

Yes, he was the Archmagician. Yes, he'd lived in the palace for twenty-three years, and been the king's sworn for twenty-one. But it was important just now not to give the impression of lording it over people, or that he still had a role in the palace. It would give rise to the idea he intended to control Brundar, and would rule behind the throne.

Because he knew he stood on fraught ground, he dressed humbly and eschewed palace slippers for his own moccasins with the rough soles: better for running.

He ran out of his chamber and down the five flights of stairs.

To his surprise, Brundar, looking ill-awakened and too young in a long tunic of heavy dark fabric, was waiting outside the door. "They won't let me in," he said, his voice less the king's and more the bereft child's. "They say they're examining my parent."

By the far wall, knit in the shadows, Eerlen glimpsed Nikre Lyto, his adopted child. Though he was likely the next archmagician, and though he was by law and right a member of the royal family, he was shy and unassuming, and Myrrir's death would have made him more skittish, fearing the fight of succession might reach for him. Myrrir had fondly nicknamed him Archmouse for his retiring ways.

Eerlen started towards Nikre, but the door opened, and Almar, pale and strained, stood in the doorway. "You must come in, Archmagician," he said. His eyes flickered to Brundar. "And you, my lord. Distasteful as it is, both of you must come in."

Brundar's eyes widened. He swallowed audibly, but he inclined his head and stepped into the death chamber ahead of Eerlen.

Myrrir had been stripped and turned on his stomach. There was a sheet covering him to the small of his back, where the marks of several dagger stabs were visible.

"He has wounds in the front, too," Lendir said. "More grievous, perhaps, though these..." He paused. "These were poisoned. And came from the back, where only his trusted stood."

"His trusted?"

"Ter, Sarda. My half-siblings. Their seconds-in-command. They were the ones behind my sire. I was... I was further back and only rushed forward when I saw him fall. I have witnesses. The dagger stabbed him in the back, several times, making it impossible for him to back away when the shields failed and he was slashed from the front. But even so, he'd have survived, only the dagger was poisoned. Plant poison, probably from gaern. We can't tell for sure, but though it was slow due to small dosage, it was the poison that killed him." Almar seemed to anticipate Eerlen's protest that daggers were not good means of poisoning someone. "There was a spell on it, Archmagician. You're welcome to study it, but once the skin was breached, the poison would find its way to the blood. It's no spell we know."

Eerlen felt for the spell, could sense the threads of it. They were incisive, effective, and utterly alien to Ellyan spell work.

"The spell is not... If it's Ellyan, it's wholly invented by a genius." He didn't say he only knew one genius who could create such innovative work. Because that genius was Brundar, who wasn't even a full magician yet, who had no reason to kill his parent, and whose mind at any rate ran to healing spells, not this type of dark subterfuge.

Aloud, Eerlen said, "It's very effective. You are correct. From the moment Myrrir was cut, no matter how small the pinprick, the poison would find his blood, and the poison is strong enough, it would kill in any amount."

"We judge he got four or five times the lethal dose," Lendir said. "The king was murdered."

"Why?" Brundar asked, startling Eerlen, who'd forgotten his sireling was in the room. "Why would anyone murder my parent? While he was fighting to defend Erradi and all of us?"

And suddenly, with a feeling that his world had sunk beneath him, Eerlen thought that they should never have done this. They should have let it be a secret. They shouldn't have certified the royal murder.

If they didn't find the murderer, it would make both brotherhood and crown seem ineffective and unimportant. Better no one knew a crime had happened.

...But would the murderer or murderers not try to kill Brundar? If they thought they'd gotten away with murder, unpunished?

His mind thought of the death of Myrrir's firstborn. They'd proclaimed it an accident, and while guarding Brundar, had never let it be known the royal family's security had been breached.

Had that been the right thing to do? Or had it led by steps to Myrrir's own death?

THE HUSKS

SKIP

I turned half-awake, between sleep and consciousness. For some reason, the image of a starfish turning over and over, frictionless, in the eternal dark void of space came to me.

Cold, I thought. I'm cold. Which was nonsense, as I was awake enough to know the bed was soft beneath me, the blankets perhaps too warm, my left leg protruding from under them, seeking cooler air.

But the sense of cold persisted, and I tumbled deeper in sleep, as my mind fell into the command room of the Victoria. Father was there, looking into my eyes. He knelt next to me, but I was the one on the glassteel boards, and cold radiated from my chest through all of me.

"He's bleeding out," Father said, to the shadowy figures behind him, in the bright yellow of medics. "He's bleeding out. Stop him bleeding out."

His eyes shone very blue. And he whispered to me, as though it were some kind of secret between the two of us, "And when he had spent all, there arose a mighty famine in that land; and he began to be in want. And he went and joined himself to a citizen of that country; and he sent him into his fields to feed swine. And he would fain have filled his belly with the husks that the swine did eat: and no man gave unto him."

My teeth knocked together in cold. "Father?" I managed to gasp, feeling as if each breath would be my last, as my heart sped up, and I couldn't understand—

"And when he came to himself, he said, how many hired servants of my father's have bread enough and to spare, and I perish with hunger," Father said, and patted my shoulder, as though he were saying something very consoling. And then, very intently,

"Forget the husks, son. Forget the husks." He shook his head and got up, and I heard him tell the shadowy paramedics. "Bleeding out, I tell you. This has to stop."

The paramedics knelt and worked on me, their hands cold and hard. They injected something into my veins. It only made me feel colder, and my heart beat faster and faster and faster.

And then I died.

I woke up with a scream caught in my throat, choking me.

Sitting up, surrounded by soft white blankets, pillows at my back, I heard the hum of the air system. And realized I hadn't screamed.

I couldn't have screamed, because the man sharing my bed was asleep, turned on his stomach, his right arm under his pillow, his left arm bent around the pillow, his head turned so his face was towards me, a classically handsome face, almost too handsome and too perfect, like the faces of some statues that don't look quite real. His skin had a light tan. There were no wrinkles around his closed eyes. But grey threads in his light brown hair shone in the scant light coming from the wrap-around windows.

I'd been his—friend? diversion?—companion for three months, and for the first time, it occurred to me that one or the other wasn't real. Either his youthful skin and looks or his greying hair had been worked on. And I had no idea which.

His name was Loshian Jordain, and he was rich. We'd met at an interesting party in a club few but the very rich knew existed. But I had no idea why either youthful good looks or grey hair would matter to him. And there was no possible reason I should know. How he wanted to look was entirely his business.

But for some reason, my ignorance disquieted me, as if the dream returned in a confusing sense that perfectly mundane things had immense significance. I got up, dragging the topmost blanket from the bed and wrapping it around me, toga-style, but dragging on the floor. I still felt—no, not cold. The temperature in the room was perfect, both heat and humidity. But a ghost-cold-ness clung to me like a memory of being naked in the frost, and the feeling in the dream, when I'd been bleeding out.

I walked to the curved transparent glassteel wall that formed two sides of the room, and looked out.

This apartment—belonging to Loshian, not me—perched high in Star Reach, the tallest and most expensive residential address in

New London, outside—I guess—the Queen's palace. I don't know. It's not like the palace has been for sale. Ever. Since colonization. So its value was surmised and nominal. Not so this place, where condos went for sale regularly, and were quickly snapped up by people who considered their staggering price pocket change.

Star Reach climbed a hundred and fifty stories above the city. On this clear summer night, looking down was like standing above a plane of dazzling, multicolored lights, as though all the stars had fallen to the ground and taken on fantastic and diverse coloration. Fireflies caught upon a misty blue ground. I blinked, and identified the more sparsely lit area where the royal palace was. I mean, it was lit itself, a shining white-blue confection resembling the myths of fairy palaces. It had been sculpted into multiple towers, the central one composed of the original colony ship. But around it, there were no houses, or buildings. Only manicured parkland for miles around. Then to the extreme west, a ring of strange shimmering light against the sky showed the point at which spaceships took off from the Spaceport.

Every few seconds, ships took off: business ships, explorers, diplomatic missions. The Star Empire, ruled from Britannia, the second largest group of free worlds colonized by humans, was now fifty clusters of worlds and growing, each world ensuring the safety of the others, creating a mutual net of protection, before the horrors of the totalitarian satrapies and oligarchies consumed them.

Some of those explorer ships would be discovering lost colonies, most of which had been flung back in time by the early Schrodinger drives—before the time function was discovered—and which had been separated from civilized humanity for anywhere from three hundred to ten thousand years. Or more.

I watched the ships take off a long while, afraid to go back to bed, afraid to go back to the dream. Not sure what about the dream scared me so. My father's eyes—

"Skip?" Loshian's voice, from the bed, sounding slightly hoarse, as people do who've just awakened.

I looked back over my shoulder, but didn't say anything, mostly because I didn't want to say anything. I experienced his calling me as an interruption, though an interruption of what, I could not say. I'd just been standing there, staring out.

But I suppose at some deeper level, reasoning or something like it went on, because I realized my sense that Loshian had somehow altered his appearance, changing to appear either younger or older, disquieted me.

Look, he wasn't my first lover. In my close on to a year in the capital, there had been a lot of those. And I didn't think we were in love. Or did I? I didn't know anymore. He'd been the one who'd lasted longest, and we could talk. He understood me, or I thought he understood me. Not that I'd told him much of anything that mattered. I couldn't talk about my family and I didn't talk about myself. Mother's last communication had begged me not to involve the family in a scandal.

Homosexuality wasn't precisely frowned upon in the empire. We weren't that kind of prudish society. But transitory relationships were. As was a life of hedonism and promiscuity, which, if you squinted and looked at a certain way, was what I'd been using to forget the Victoria and the blood-soaked glassteel planks of that damned deck. And my father's dying eyes.

He's bleeding out, came out of my dream in my father's voice. And that bit of the parable of the prodigal son. Which made absolutely no sense in my situation. Or perhaps it did. I had been spending my heritage.

I shivered.

"Skip?" Now Loshian sounded alarmed. "You're not ill? Did you take—"

I had a feeling he was afraid I'd consumed some mind-altering substance. Not unusual in the circles I ran in that year. Only I didn't indulge. I liked to think my mind was my own. And it was odd he'd not noticed I never took hallucinogenics. Or maybe not. I'd gone to a great deal of trouble to pretend I was a party boy, up for anything.

Then again, perhaps he feared I'd taken something lethal. Though why he'd fear that, I couldn't imagine. I didn't know what he meant because he cut himself off, and I said into the halted-breath silence, "No, I'm fine." My voice also sounded hoarse, and a little slow, as if it were echoing from somewhere else. Perhaps from those deep thoughts I was only dimly aware of having. And which I'd prefer not to acknowledge.

The truth was that my mind was adding things up, now, in full view of my awake self. I knew why I'd thrown myself into the sybaritic delights of the capital—not unknown to me, as I had experienced them over two very chaotic weeks, while on break from the Academy in my final study year—and it wasn't because I felt a great need to jump into beds all over town. I'd come out of the regen tank to a series of hellish nightmares, and to people fawning over me and my supposed heroism. I'd shed my all too-well-known identity and tried to overwhelm the horror with pleasure, the touch of the dead with the touch of the living.

But it wasn't working. In a way, the dream had been absolutely right. I felt empty and hollow. I was bleeding out. Only what I was bleeding out was not blood, but the years of my life, the energy of youth.

I was wasting myself. I couldn't forget the past. I could only forget myself.

"You're scaring me," Loshian said. "Are you sure you feel well? Can I get you something?"

"No," I said. "I'm thinking." He chuckled, which struck me as strange, but not worth stopping for.

The thing was, what was I supposed to spend my life on, if not waste it? My entire life, I trained and learned and planned for war. I had become a war hero, famous throughout the Empire, at barely seventeen. I—

"You're serious!"

"Yes," I said, wondering what was so strange about my wanting to think. And then I caught sight of the shimmer of a ship taking off the spaceport. Headed for orbit. Headed for a Schrodinger jump, perhaps to a new world, or a newly discovered world, or—

Suddenly, I knew what I wanted, with a surging desire that was like the wish for food or for air.

"I think," I said, having trouble saying the words because it still felt as though my thoughts were very far away, and I had to reach a long distance to get to them, much less put them in words. "I do think I've wasted enough time. I think I'd like to enter the Imperial Diplomat Service School."

His laughter cut off abruptly when I turned to look at him, and his mouth hung open in a singularly foolish expression.

My disdain must have shown in my eyes. He closed his mouth with a snap, and his upper lip curled. "I hope you're not angling for a recommendation! I'd have to pay your tuition. Even if I were willing to, it would be useless; they'd never take anyone who hasn't undergone a rigorous pre-education. And frankly, though that's not explicit policy, every spot ends up going to a nobleman, or noblewoman or the younger brother or son or sister or daughter of one. Even I would have trouble getting in, much less—"

"That," I said. "Is not a problem."

He laughed, then cleared his throat. "Skip. Catalea is not a noble surname. Not even on the extended list. I know. I do business with these people."

"Oh, that. Skip Catalea is a name of convenience," I said. I stepped away from the window, like a somnambulist.

Some sense told me I had to get out of here. I was done. It was time to move on. What did I have of mine in his apartment? For some reason, his reaction made everything feel even more wrong. He'd been decent for three months, hadn't he? We hadn't been in love, but we'd been friends. Friendly, at least.

He raised his eyebrows. Looked alarmed.

I'd remembered where I'd put my bag. In the closet. But first, I'd get dressed. I smelled of sweat, but nothing terrible. I could get a hotel for the night, and bathe there. And in the morning, I could apply to the IDSS. Sure, I could bathe here, but I didn't want to. I didn't want to stay any longer than I needed to. In fact, I felt a great urge to leave this place and start living my life again, not... Whatever I'd been doing here.

I wanted to be dressed. Being naked felt strangely vulnerable. I found my clothes in a pile near the bed, let the blanket fall and pulled on underwear, tunic and pants, quickly, as if I'd been awakened in the middle of the night and ordered to stand formation. My shoes were by the bed. Sturdy slipper-like walking shoes. I slid my feet into them.

I found my bag in the one closet I'd used, and started filling it, pulling the clothes out of the closet and throwing them in the bag, not caring overmuch for how they landed. They were practical fabric that shed wrinkles, anyway. At the end, the bag was half-full. I hadn't brought much with me. A few pants, tunics, shirts, one decent ceremonial full suit for occasions. And not the kind of suit I wore in real life. Because that was far too fancy for Skip Catalea, besides being uncomfortable as hell to wear.

The only jewelry I'd brought with me, I was wearing: the plain signet ring of Father's non-titled family. The signet, with the roaring lion on it and the odd engraved writing inside. His father's ring.

"Skip," Loshian asked, his voice very matter-of-fact. "What is your real name?"

I paused, in the act of putting the strap of the bag over my shoulder.

Should I tell him that? I had used a pseudonym for a reason. Mother didn't want there to be a scandal. But Loshian wouldn't make a scandal, because it would involve him, as well. At any rate, I'd lived here for three months. Even with automated cleaning, between fingerprints and shed skin and hair, there would be enough that someone of Loshian's wealth could have my name and entire history within hours. No, there was no point. I was no longer sure what we'd had was a friendship with pleasant interludes, but we had lived together for three months. He deserved to know.

"Publius Cornelius Scipio Africanus Kayel Hayden, Viscount Webson."

He seemed to settle lower in his sitting position as his whole body sagged. He said, "Son of a bitch." Which seemed to me unkind, though I'd thought it was true for at least three or four years now. He went pale as the blankets. He stared at me eyes wide, and repeated under his breath, "Son of a bitch."

"I hardly think that's germane. She does the best she can," I said, because if I didn't say it, I was going to start giggling, which wouldn't help anyone. But the situation was ridiculous, and I couldn't determine if he was infuriated at my deception or scared of my family name.

And then he made it all clear. "I thought you were— And from the casts—I —you're—your story. You were below the age of consent when I— When we—"

"We hardly need to worry about that," I said. "I don't intend to discuss it with anyone, much less bring an action. I promised my mother I'd not make a scandal. Mother doesn't want talk."

"But you can't apply at the school!" he said.

"I'm going to apply at the school." I was fairly sure I'd be accepted, too. I'd never been intellectually deficient and the tests they gave were mostly general knowledge and aptitude. My education prepared me for that and plenty. The Academy fed into the IDSS as often as into the military. But also, I was young, not naïve. Given my name, and my reputation as a hero, it would be a feather in their cap. I wasn't innocent enough to think the school or the Empire would pass a chance at publicity.

"Skip, this is madness." He got up from the bed. He was about my height, but more solidly built. He extended an arm, as though to detain me. I reacted the way I'd been trained to react, taking two steps back and getting ready to respond. Something about that must have made him change his mind. He had, after all, heard of me. Obviously. "Look, Skip, we've had fun. And I like you, I really like you. Come back to bed."

I can't explain it. I'll never be able to explain it. But I felt a deep certainty that if I acceded, if I went back to bed, if I waited a few hours, or even a few minutes, I'd never get up from that soft nest of blankets and pillows. Not alive.

It made no sense. It was not like Loshian was in any way connected with the underworld. And he wasn't an assassin. And New London was not lawless.

The whole reason I'd spent a year tumbling from bed to bed unharmed was because the law in Britannia protected the foolish and the anonymous young.

All the same, one of the first things my father had taught me was to respect that kind of deep intuition, and the fear that often accompanies it, even. Father said that humans were still animals, and still had a deep animal instinct that talked to us, though our civilized, tamed selves might refuse to acknowledge it. I'd never had occasion to test this wisdom. But Father had never led me wrong.

I said, "No," and rushed to the door, punched the programmed signal and went out, before he could get his clothes on.

Led by my deep instinct, by that inner voice, I didn't take the elevator, going into the emergency stairs, instead.

I heard the elevators go up and down and up, but thought nothing of it. Even after almost a year of no real exercise, I retained the good physical condition from the Academy. I didn't count the floors, but when I finally started breathing hard, I looked out, saw the elevator landing empty, and called an elevator to go up first, then down. The going up made it less likely Loshian would be aboard, if he was pursuing me. I had no idea why he'd be pursuing me. It wasn't like he could believe I wanted trouble any more than he did. I really didn't believe he would be coming for me, but I was in the grip of that inner, irrational fear, a fear too large and too inarticulate to argue with.

When I got in the—empty—elevator, I found I'd gone down

fifteen floors on foot via the emergency stairs, which was not bad. But going down the hundred and seven would be madness. Also take far longer than I was willing to invest. I wanted a bath, and a bed. One that I'd paid for and which belonged to me. I wanted to feel secure and safe.

Father's signet ring has a com built in. Oh, not original, but Dad had it put in, a thin veneer on one side, leaving the weird writing unimpeded. It made sense. If you had a ring, the ring should have coms. I'd had it transferred to my name.

As the elevator went all the way up, past Loshian's floor—the third down—and then down, I spoke the codes to call an automated cab into the ring, and gave the address.

When I got to the street level, the foyer was empty, but a bullet-shaped cab was waiting, one of the automated ones. I gave my credicode as I got in, and then the address of the only hotel that came to mind: the Alexin-Edam, where noble families stayed when they came to New London for a short stay that didn't justify opening their townhouses. Father and Mother and I had stayed there when I was young and we came to New London for a quick jaunt. I had memories of the vast dining hall, a magical sparkling land of crystal and glittering silver to my young eyes. I had memories of walking between Mother and Father, a hand holding each of mine, in the gardens of the hotel in spring, as the flowers fell from the cherry trees and perfumed the air.

Before I got to the Alexin-Edam, about two blocks from the hotel, from inside my cab with its safely darkened windows and flying at first floor level, which was the highest you could fly in New London, I saw Loshian. He was walking back towards Star Reach. He must have taken a cab also, but was now walking back...why? Because he thought I might be walking? Because he hadn't seen me from the air in ten blocks? He'd obviously dressed hastily in yesterday's clothes, and hadn't done his tunic up completely, so the long tails flapped forlornly to the rhythm of his walking. He looked upset and tired.

Well. Perhaps he'd felt more for me than I'd thought. Or at least I tried to tell myself that, but didn't quite believe it.

I didn't see him again for over three years and in quite different circumstances.

The Alexin-Edam looked exactly the same as I remembered. I felt safe from the moment I went in, comforted by a place that matched my memories, from the marble steps at the entrance, to the dark paneled wood inside, to the room I was led to, with thick red carpet, dark-wood furniture and a bed that could be programmed to my precise tastes.

I had a very hot shower, a blissful sleep, a vast breakfast.

After which I took another cab, this one to the IDS school, where I applied and which, after the formality of a day of tests, welcomed me with open arms.

Escape

Eerlen

The royal chamber's windows and doors had been tightly closed. The fire in the hearth burned high and too hot. The stench of sweat and acid vomit pervaded everything, like a living thing, clutching at Eerlen.

Eerlen Troz knew where the stink of sweat came from. He'd been at the battle front for six hours. He'd been in this overheated chamber for another three. He was covered in it, his tunic glued to his body, the linen feeling sticky, the leather over it unwieldy. He realized, through tension and headache, that he'd never removed his battle leathers. The various pieces were still tightly strapped over him, protecting him from arrows unlikely in the royal palace.

He'd been called from the front. From shield holding. No one called the archmagician from shield holding. It needed three shield holders to replace him and that if you could get second circles.

But he'd been called—impossible—by a mind-touch from Almar—even more impossible. A fourth circle, even the head of fourth, would not presume! Which had dispensed with formality and said only, "Brundar needs you." He'd withdrawn before Eerlen could ask any question or express his displeasure.

He'd wanted to scream from the moment of that touch. He'd wanted to scream because he worried for Brundar. Why did Brundar need him? He'd wanted to scream because he was furious at Almar's presumption. How dare Almar contact him? He'd wanted to scream because he'd had to call in three second circles—off rotation, not the strongest, ill-awakened, ill-prepared—to serve as shield-holders and make sure they were holding the shield as impregnably as he had before he could come to his sireling's aid.

And all the while, Almar hadn't answered any of his own mental touches, except for the general impression of "hurry." And an underlying sense of panic.

A fourth circle didn't have the right, didn't have the access to the power, didn't have the ability to block out the archmagician. And even the head of fourth had no right to summon the archmagician.

Eerlen half-expected to be lured to a trap. Always possible from someone at court. But that was not why he'd run to the back of the lines, back past the infirmaries, back, and behind that, to a deserted area, and opened a portal. Nor why he'd opened the portal to his chamber in the palace. Though, since no lower than a first circle would dare enter it past his protections and the palace shields, he supposed that would have circumvented any ambush. No, the reason he'd done all that was that sense of urgency in Almar's mind-touch.

As soon as he stepped into the narrow chamber, he heard sounds of retching from the royal bathroom.

Eerlen had never moved from the room Myrrir had assigned him. Brundar liked him close, and appreciated his advice for "the boring stuff," as he called it: the everyday negotiations and trades, deals and organizing Eerlen had done for Myrrir. Though Eerlen now used the guest bathing chambers down the hall, to preserve Brundar's privacy—not that he thought Brundar cared—Eerlen still had a door generally kept closed to the Royal bathroom. The sounds came through that door.

He opened it, to find Almar helping Brundar stand. The child looked spoiled-milk pale, his lips almost blue.

Standing by, near the door between the bathroom and Brundar's bedroom, looking as though he would bolt at any minute, through the room and screaming down the stairs and out of the palace, still in padded tunic and battle leathers, his hair bound up, his blue cloak around his shoulders, was Kalal Ad Leed, third circle magician.

Almar gave Eerlen a bare glance, filled with something akin to hatred, but he said nothing, not even, "Glad you came."

It was Ad Leed who spoke, in a confused, apologetic voice that wavered and broke. "I was in the healing wards, at the front. I was called— Almar—"

Oh, this was a fine thing. A fourth circle didn't directly summon a third circle. The brotherhood didn't preempt the archmagician's assignments to the wounded awards. Even in a matter of life and death, the query went through the lines.

How else would the archmagician know who was available and ready at a breakthrough?

Almar had the bit between his teeth, and it would have to be dealt with. Eerlen remembered his training. He remembered the importance of hierarchy, else the Brotherhood of Magicians was undone with no way to allocate resources or establish priorities.

But as he took a deep, shaking breath, ready to come over the archmagician and impose discipline, he realized it would be dealt with—later. Not now.

Before he could speak, Brundar had knelt again, shakily, and vomited once more.

Eerlen stepped forward, but stopped as Almar knelt to support Brundar. Almar growled, "It's poison. We're getting the poison out."

And Eerlen could do no more than nod mutely and help support the child through that and the following bouts of vomiting.

Later, they bathed Brundar—all of them, Almar, Ad Leed and Eerlen, in close contact and fighting for space, and Brundar too far gone to care for the violation of his privacy. They dressed the king in a night tunic and put him to bed, and Ad Leed used his power to repair whatever damages the poison had already done before they could force it out.

Eerlen and Almar had stood, in different corners of the room, like fighters claiming opposite territories, watching the third circle work.

Eerlen watched the power flow out of Ad Leed, who seemed to shrink and shake with the effort. Ad Leed had removed his leathers, but he was sodden and soaked in his linen tunic and underpants, standing, frowning, intent. He looked pitiful and pitifully young.

The power, like glimmering threads, plunged into Brundar. Brundar's power, third circle, overpowered and well-trained, would allow him to see the threads, and maybe he was doing so through his half-closed lids. If so, he was in a half-dream, because he neither moved nor spoke. Nor did he reach for the power.

When Ad Leed pulled the now-pale power threads back with a slight groan, Almar stalked out, towards the bathroom. Ad Leed turned and tried to speak. He cleared his throat, found Eerlen, looked him in the eyes and said, "He's out of danger. And I laid a sleep suggestion on him. He won't wake for...a couple of hours."

Which was when Almar stalked back in, carrying a blanket he draped around Ad Leed. Despite the caring gesture, Almar was furious.

Perhaps others wouldn't be able to tell, but Eerlen could. When Myrrir was in a similar mood, Eerlen had heard people talk of how controlled and calm he was. But Eerlen knew that expression from Myrrir's face: the almost too-hard lines of the features, the lips straight as the carved lips of Myrrir's statue, now in the garden memory, cold stone over cold body, for eight months.

The archmagician knew those eyes, unnaturally dark under lowered eyebrows, were bright lightning and rising winds, signs of an approaching storm.

He glared at Eerlen and made a sound like growling, then punched the wall near him, and said, "Poison. Maker's empty womb, poison! And the path obscured and I can't sense it!"

Eerlen raised his eyebrows. Why was the fourth circle glaring at Eerlen? Did he dare suspect the Archmagician of trying to kill the king, his own sireling? Because no one but the archmagician should be able to totally obscure a path from the head of fourth. What was this madness? He made his voice hard and cold. "Did you enquire what he ate, and when?"

Almar looked like he'd like to growl back, but cleared his throat and said, "Nothing." He gave a half-laugh and opened his hands, as if to show they were empty. "He was going over...cases. Justice cases that had asked for Royal clemency. I was with him in my capacity as head of the fourth circle. Also guarding him, of course. And then—he had water."

"Water? Who brought him the water?"

Almar shook his head. "It was in the room, with us, in a jar. He poured himself a cup. I might have done it— But he poured himself a cup." He closed his eyes, as though a headache threatened. "I sensed it almost immediately. It's why he's alive still. There was..." He frowned. "A compulsion of some kind. On the water. Aimed at him. It's nothing I've ever seen. Not a weaving I've seen. Like...the weaving on the dagger that conveyed poison to my sire's blood." He rubbed the center of his forehead. "I needed help. I could give him a compulsion to empty his stomach, but healing is beyond me. I never learned—I asked if Nikre was in the palace. He was not, so I called Ad Leed. As fast as the poison acted, I thought a high healer was best."

He met Eerlen's eyes, and looked puzzled. Eerlen guessed his anger showed and Lendir Almar couldn't imagine why Eerlen would be angry.

Suddenly, as though coming to his senses, Almar took a deep breath and spoke in a rush. "Forgive me, Archmagician. I shouldn't have— It wasn't a hierarchy thing. I called you because he is your sireling and you love him. Not because you are the archmagician. And I called Kalal—" A half-lidded look at Ad Leed, which for some reason annoyed Eerlen. "Because we are— Because he's my own—and I trust him as I trust myself."

Because they were what? Lovers? Not sworn. Eerlen would see the bond if that were the case. It was visible even among non-magicians, much less magicians and one inner circle. But what else had Almar refrained from saying? What else would he refrain from saying? And only your blood relatives or your lovers called you by your first name. This was very cozy. He'd called his lover.

Except you damn well didn't call a third circle without going up the line, without making it an urgent appeal to the head of third circle, who had the power to allocate his thirds as he best pleased, absent archmagician interference. Eerlen had seen Myrrir drop everything when the head of third called him—when that was Ad Leed's parent, Malin Ad Leed, Myrrir's subordinate, and later when it was Myrrir's own sireling, Guinar Ter—because even the king followed the discipline of the brotherhood, but apparently these two were above it.

He bit his lip, hard, to stop the anger. At least Almar had recognized Eerlen loved Brundar. He wasn't insulting Eerlen by suspecting him. Eerlen willed his heart to slow, willed the pounding anger in his veins to calm.

Yes, Almar and Ad Leed had broken protocol and hierarchy, and yes, Eerlen would have to deal with it and soon, but Maker's Balls, half of his anger was at another attempt against Brundar's life. Three in less than a year.

He wheeled on Lendir Almar, in sudden impatience. "And you can't tell? You can't tell who laid the compulsion? What the poison is? Whence it came? How could you be so utterly incompetent as to let the King be poisoned while with you? Are you ready to turn in your blue cloak and have your power perception shut and be

severed from the brotherhood? Are you, Head of Fourth? Should
I let someone else take your role?"

To his surprise, Almar only squinted and groaned. "Maybe you
should. I've tried everything." His eyes suddenly met Eerlen's, and
they were too much like Myrrir's. Except Myrrir had never looked
like he thought himself an utter and abject failure. The look in
those eyes tore at Eerlen. As did the deep, heartfelt, despondent
groan. "You'll suspect me of poisoning him."

Eerlen shook his head. "Don't pretend to be dumber than you
are. I've studied your power after...the first attack on the king. It is
not you. That type of weaving would leave marks in the seconds
after. And you don't shield." He frowned. "At least not from me.
That is why I told you to be with him at all times. Because I trust
you. That is why I removed you from battle roster." And they could
ill afford it. "It is not you. But why can't you read who it is?"

"Sir. Archmagician. May I—"

They both turned to the healer who still stood at the foot of the
bed and trembled, despite the blanket around his shoulders. Kalal
Ad Leed normally looked like the given name that his very young
parent had picked for him. Eerlen vaguely remembered the talk of
how young Malin Ad Leed had been. The shock of it. The Lord of
Brinar and head of third had been sixteen when he delivered his
line child. People tittered behind their hands that he'd called that
child Kalal because he was young enough to still play with dolls.
Now full-grown, the new Lord of Brinar was petite and pretty and
deserving of "sweet doll," if anyone was. Brinarian-born and bred,
he was tall and light for the region, but then he didn't spend his life
outdoors, so a golden, glowing tan, with intense blue eyes, dark
curly hair and perfect features fit his name.

If Ad Leed was Almar's age, as I've known him from childhood
seemed to imply, he didn't look it. And besides, Eerlen remembered the gossip around the time he'd become archmage. Ad Leed
looked closer to Brundar's age. Young enough to be Almar's child.
And Eerlen had a vague memory of Kalal Ad Leed being one of a
group of well-born children allowed to play with Brundar.

Right then, though still somehow beautiful, Kalal was pale and
shaking, and Eerlen cursed himself. How stupid was he? A healing
of that magnitude would near-kill a third.

Well. He could lend the child power. But that felt somehow too
intimate, too— He checked whether Ad Leed's pattern was near

critical enough to start feeding on his body, or if they had time. No. They had time. He could be fed and warmed without the violation of power contact.

"Pardon, healer," he said. "I've ignored your needs." In three steps, he went to the door and called the servant on duty down the hall. As he turned, Almar had steadied the healer, an arm around his waist. And it was stupid for Eerlen to look at that intimate touch and think, Ahah, lovers, as though he'd uncovered some grand conspiracy.

Lendir Almar, head of the royal guard, commander of the armies, could lay whom he very well pleased. It was none of Eerlen's business whom Almar took to his bed.

The magicians' lives, outside of power-weaving, were not any of Eerlen's business. And he paid no attention until or unless it was forced on him. Why would Eerlen care? Was he losing his mind?

Outside the brotherhood, as Myrrir's sireling, Lendir Almar ranked as high as the sire of the king at court. And they were close to the same age. It wasn't like Lendir was his child or his liege. Again, it was none of Eerlen's business. Eerlen had no right to violate Lendir's privacy unless Lendir gave him a reason.

As the servant appeared at the door, Eerlen gave orders in the most matter-of-fact way he could muster, to have Kalal Ad Leed taken to one of the guest rooms with bathing facilities, to have clothes brought to him and to feed him and make him comfortable.

Ad Leed gave him a crooked smile. "I presume," he said. "You'd prefer I don't leave."

But Almar answered before Eerlen could. "Not yet." Which was proper. For one, as exhausted as Ad Leed looked, Eerlen wouldn't trust him through a portal on his own. Even a public portal. That was how magicians got lost.

And then they were alone, Eerlen and Almar, with Brundar asleep. Color had come back into the child's cheeks, and he no longer looked dead.

Eerlen wanted more than anything to bathe, and remove the padded tunic, which served him well in frigid Erradi, but was slowly baking him here, and—

He started untying the battle leathers—leather protectors tied at chest, crotch, knees, waist, forearms, arms, chest and belly, and softly cursing himself, because he'd gone into the pool with battle leathers and boots. Both of which were probably now ruined for good. If he hadn't been so tired and so panicked, he'd have remembered to remove them.

The chest shield was easy to remove, the buckles on the side. He threw it down, and started unbuckling the belly one at the waist.

"We should take him and leave," Almar said, looking at Brundar. He chewed at the corner of his own lip. "He'll never agree to it if he's fully awake."

"Leave and go where? If, with the entire palace and your entire corps of subordinates he's not safe, where and when will he be?"

Almar was doing something with his hair. Either the tie had broken, or he'd loosened it, and his hair had become a golden cloud around his face, like Myrrir's used to do. Though Almar's, like Brundar's, had a tint of red that had never shown in Myrrir's hair. More brass than gold. And it was shorter, only below the shoulders. At that, Almar only had a bare hint of red in his hair, not the full bronze. And in Almar's case, a hint of curl, less than Brundar's wild bramble of hair.

And he'd apologized for breaking hierarchy. And— A strange, detached ideation, an imagining with full senses, of plunging his hands into that soft-looking mass of gold-red overwhelmed Eerlen. He guessed he hadn't groaned at it, because Almar did not react. He got his hair under control, tied it back and said, "Erradi."

"Erradi? Pardon me. You want to go to Erradi? Under-invasion-by-Draksalls Erradi? You want to take the king into practically enemy-occupied land?" Eerlen had removed all the leathers but his boots, and was contemplating being barefoot in front of Almar, because his palace slippers were in his room. Feet were not something indecent, but one didn't go barefoot except in the family, in front of siblings, parents, children or lovers. Bare feet meant intimacy. Family.

His feet were wet and uncomfortable. They hurt with cold, which was strange, considering how hot the room was. Tied too tightly for circulation, grown tighter with being wet. Maker curse propriety. He sat down, and started tugging the boots off. "Do you really want to take him to the ice lands?"

Almar smiled. "Yeah. Since I'm talking to an Erradian nomad, you probably understand that the breakthrough is in a tiny and contained area, and has been there your entire life."

His entire life. As a small child, with his parents, following a nomad route... His years in hell with the last archmagician as an apprentice... Unable to go to his own shelters because the last thing he wished to do was give Drahy access to Troz spaces.

"Do you have access to the ... Are there hereditary Troz shelters?" Almar stared at Eerlen, frowned, then shrugged, with an effect of giving up. He crossed the room in two steps, knelt at Eerlen's feet and and finished tugging the boot from Eerlen's left foot, then tossed it in the general direction of Eerlen's pile of leathers, with a look like it was a shame to waste good equipment. Which was true. And Eerlen felt guilty enough already. Then Lendir Almar pulled the right boot off and sent it to join its fellow. He glared at Eerlen's feet, and Eerlen half-expected him to massage them. Instead, Almar stood, turned his back, and walked to the fireplace, to poke the fire that didn't need poking. He spoke without turning. "You should put slippers on. Your feet look frozen."

Eerlen stood, the old floor cool under his feet, drew himself up and squared his shoulders. "They're in my room. As to shelters, Troz is one of the ten lines," he said, his voice as frosty as the icy Erradian winds. To his shock, Almar giggled as he turned around. It wasn't even a sound he could have imagined Lendir Almar, Commander of the Royal Guard, making. But he supposed the head of fourth was punch-drunk.

At what he was sure was his outraged look, Almar shook his head. "Sorry. I'm settled. My family has been settled for...centuries. We've been in the palace guard for over a hundred years. And my ancestor to first join the palace guard was the second child of a cloth merchant. Erradian, but settled. Lived in Tarkross. I still have distant cousins there."

Eerlen's turn to apologize. "I beg your pardon. I didn't realize the line pride was that fragile. Get raised in an ice cave. Memorize the genealogies. Remember the ten lines. Be proud you're one of them. Even when we were all poor enough to eat ice, we had the inherited shelters, the... Yes, I have access. But—how will it look, the king leaving the palace? Residing in no known place? And I'll have to delegate the archmagician functions. He'll have to delegate... And there's so much work both Myr—Brundar and I do and have to do."

"Can you? Delegate?"

At that moment, as though called by the question, someone came running in the door. For a moment, reacting, both Almar and Eerlen turned to the door, and Eerlen started to reach for his ankle knives, before it registered in his tired brain that the person who'd come in was family, his own adopted child, his own apprentice, his likely successor.

The person he loved most in the world after Brundar.

Nikre Lyto had been born the child of Brinarian fishermen, in a dirt-poor hamlet of twenty or so palm-roofed huts on the Southern coast of Brinar. The sort of place where people would have starved to death or frozen to death if the seas of Brinar weren't so full of life, and the climate so forgiving.

Even so, they lived one step ahead of annihilation, overworked, underfed. Getting a child to weaning with both child and parent healthy was a heroic struggle. And no one in the hamlet had even small power, not even enough to send a message to the brotherhood. But—

But someone had walked from the hamlet to the nearest village with a small power who could communicate with the brother-hood. Walked for three days in monsoon weather. The small power had, in turn, gotten hold of an eighth circle, who'd been alarmed enough to patch Eerlen through, because he couldn't reach the head of fourth, who'd been on battle duty. The garbled report Eerlen got was that there was a child with power there, one that the child's sire was trying to kill, so the sire's new lover could inherit the boat of his late sworn, the child's blood parent.

Eerlen had time. It chanced he had time on his hands that after-noon, something so rare that he still had nightmares of not having had that time, of having put it off for another day. He'd opened a direct portal, with no expectations and no hope of finding a real talent. Where would the power come from? Sometimes power surfaced after generations, but it was never high in those cases. It would be a small power, or eighth. Sometimes such rose as high as seven, but that was like finding a jewel in pig muck. And how would a hamlet with no power even know the child had power?

No one had ever explained the last, but the child did have power. High power. Archmage power. Eerlen suspected the child had done something to keep himself alive. Something strange, that the people watching assumed was magic. And might have been.

The attempt to drown Nikre that Eerlen's arrival had interrupted was not the first attempt to kill him. Nor the second. And that was without counting neglect and abuse.

Eerlen had dealt with it the only way he could. There, in front of the child and the whole hamlet, he'd dueled and killed the culprits both at once, but not a fair fight because Eerlen was both larger and better fed.

Then he'd taken the trembling child in his arms and opened a portal. Nikre had been three years old, filthy, starved. His so-called sire had been denying him food for the two years Nikre's birth parent had been dead. Nikre had been living from handouts and probably from the village refuse heap.

There were things Eerlen could have done, even then.

Oh, he'd seen the child's pattern. He knew that beautiful, even strength in all the circles, even if a little stronger on eighth, was rare. He knew the child had archmagician power. But the child hadn't said a word or made a sound, and the villagers, scared, eager, had told Eerlen they thought the child was mute. They'd not heard a sound from him.

The sane thing to do would have been to take the child to a farm. One of the Mahar farms, where food was plenty and people gentle. Hand him over to a kindly couple. Eerlen could think of several off the top of his head. Pay them to look after the child...

Eerlen had lost his one pregnancy. The child had died within him at full term. He'd not caught since. His sireling, the king's only born-alive child, had been killed months ago at two years of age. Eerlen held the trembling child in his arms, and Nikre had put his little, scrawny arms around Eerlen's neck and hid his face against Eerlen, tucking his whole head under the archmagician's chin.

Eerlen couldn't have let him go if he tried.

And so he'd dragged the waif to the palace and burst in on the dining hall, in front of a table full of merchants and clan heads, to tell Myrrir why he was late for supper. He meant to explain he'd have to go clean up, as he was covered in blood from a double duel.

Myrrir, whose only body-child had died, and who just then suspected maybe he might be with child again, had risen from the table in alarm, looked at Eerlen and Nikre. His eyes had rested on the child, and his gaze softened.

He'd appeared to only half-hear Eerlen's poured-out explanation. While the rest of the court at table gasped or tittered, the king had extended his arms to the waif, gathered him in his arms. The filthy, seawater-soaked child snuggled close, ruining the royal robes, and neither waif nor king cared.

By the time Eerlen said, "I need to clean up," Myrrir was feeding honey nut balls to the toddler and murmuring endearments from which "Archmouse" stood out as the strangest.

Eerlen had refused to let Myrrir adopt Nikre. There had been a clash of wills over it, loud enough to make the palace shake, but for once, Eerlen had won.

By then, it was obvious that Myrrir was carrying again, the pregnancy that would give them Brundar. The child of the body should be the heir. And Nikre was older, muddling things. Also, barring disaster, Nikre would one day be archmagician. Archmagician and king. Wearing the double jewels was a hard path not to be wished on anyone.

So Eerlen had adopted him. Not as a Troz. The Troz of Troz couldn't be Brinarian-born. The clan would rebel. And at the best of times, the Troz clan was an extended feud with genealogy tables. Instead, they'd kept Nikre's body-parent's line name, Lyto, to honor the parent who'd probably depleted himself to death to take Nikre to weaning and leave him healthy enough to survive the next two years of neglect and attacks.

And Nikre had learned to speak or perhaps merely dared to speak after years of fear. He'd eventually stopped running from his nursemaid's room to climb into bed between Myrrir and Eerlen, crying and shaking.

In every way but blood and line name, he'd been Brundar's older crossibling, Eerlen's child, Myrrir's sireling. One of the two that commanded both their hearts. Kal—sweet—to Brundar's Kari—spicy—as Eerlen and Myrrir referred to them: their very own version of the famous Karrashan dish.

At twenty-one, Nikre was still sweet. He was broad-hipped and short. Full-grown, the top of his head barely cleared Eerlen's shoulder. His hair was dark brown, wavy and waist-long, as befitted a prince of the blood. He looked beautiful to Eerlen. He'd always looked beautiful, even when he was a starveling covered in dirt and scabs. But from the looks people at court and in the brotherhood gave Nikre, Eerlen didn't think it was just his perception. Nikre was golden-skinned, with dark amber eyes and lips disposed to rest in a suggestion of a smile.

However, the strongest impressions he gave were silence and kindness. Both of which were true. Coming of age, Nikre, fully trained as archmagician, fully ready to step into Eerlen's shoes should Eerlen die, had asked to move into a servant's apartment, a little independent residence that was part of the palace but also private. He had a small walled garden, which he'd filled with flowers and blooming trees. He kept to himself, unless someone needed him, when he would break himself in two to help.

He was also smart, shy and self-effacing.

Now, he stood at the door to the room, disheveled, his cloak off and folded over one arm, as though he'd removed it as he ran. His pattern looked...not depleted, but enough for him to be tired. "I was told Brundar was ill—" he started. "I came—"

"Nikre," Eerlen said. He resisted an impulse to throw himself in his child's arms. For one, he'd overwhelm Nikre, who looked tired enough. For another, it would alarm his kindhearted child. "Almar said you weren't here," Eerlen said. "He said you were called—"

Nikre shook his head. "I wasn't here, no," he said. "I was called to a public portal in Karrah. It was inexplicably blocked. Someone—" He shook his head. "It took me two hours to clear, and then I came in via the public portal and the guard told me you'd been called from the front. I was told Brundar was ill and Kalal Ad Leed was called." He looked toward the bed. "Is Kari...is he?"

"He'll be well," Eerlen said. "He was poisoned and there was magic used." Eerlen told Nikre what had happened with interjections from Almar, finishing with Almar's idea of taking to the nomad route in Erradi.

Eerlen looked at Nikre's face. As the plan was unfolded, Nikre's first reaction to Almar's blurted, "We should take the child to Erradi and follow the nomad routes. If he—" was to frown, then look at Eerlen.

But as Almar went on, "If he has access to Troz shelters, we can have the child...well, not hidden, but not to be predictably found. We can—" And explained the advantages, Nikre looked reluctantly impressed and nodded, slowly, as if thinking. Eerlen could tell from the look in Nikre's eyes that he wanted to come up with something against it, but couldn't.

After Almar finished, Nikre sighed. "It is a strange idea, but it might be for the best. All attempts against him have been in the palace. Though that might be because we don't let him go to the battle front, on a predictable schedule. Only as an emergency posting."

"No. I will not schedule him after Myrrir—" Eerlen said, and immediately regretted it, seeing the momentary stab of grief in Nikre's eyes. "I wouldn't risk that again."

"Sure," Nikre said. "But Erradi...unless everyone knows your route—"

"No one knows my route. Even I haven't followed it in twenty-one years," he said. "And I'm the Troz of Troz. There's shelters only I...and you and Brund can open. Only those of the blood. So it should keep us safe."

"Then I'd say you have to do it. We can't keep risking Brundar." He was looking at Brund on the bed. "He's well, isn't he? He'll not be affected? Maimed?"

"He's exhausted and threw up everything in his stomach till there was nothing," Almar said, then shook his head. "The brat will be fine."

Nikre nodded. "Good." He gave Almar a raised eyebrow. "Without him, you and I will end up in the soup, as factions form behind each of us and Ter and Sarda and a four-ended war will rage. Meanwhile, the Draksalls take all of Elly. We can't bet on another Amissar Mahar, either, to free our descendants. We'll be gone."

Eerlen realized he was very tired, because he almost laughed at Almar's startled look and muttered oath. "Stop the scary imaginings. Maker's tits, Lyto. I don't want the throne," Lendir Almar said.

Nikre nodded. "Does it look like I do? The child by adoption who looks not at all like his parent or sire? Even if I were inclined to the job—and I'm not—I'd live in fear. But I don't think us not wanting the throne would save us in the case of Brundar's death Should Brundar fall, there will be people who want us for king. Who'll push us to it. Being king might be the only alternative to being dead."

Almar made a face. He looked at Brundar, sleeping in his mage-induced stupor, and smiled, a crooked smile. "Thank you for the extra reason to keep him alive, Nikre, but I already didn't want him to die. He's a taking brat." A look at Nikre. "You both are. It's why I didn't kill either of you when you were little and climbing me to pull my hair."

Eerlen heard himself sigh. The sibling banter was a reminder of a more innocent time. These days, Nikre and Almar were more likely to treat each other as formal acquaintances. For that matter, Almar more often called Brund Mahar or Your Majesty. It was as though being family had died with Myrrir.

"Nikre, if we do this, if we go to Erradi, you'll have to do all the work of archmagician. And you will have to be regent, too," Eerlen said

Nikre's eyes went huge. His lips formed "No," but before he could vocalize, Eerlen said, "We can couch it as you relaying the orders from Brundar. We can't leave it to Ter or Sarda. It will have to be you. And the power of the brotherhood will give you some protection. You can reach me, through the ruby, of course, but... I suppose I can do battle-shifts, if ... Only the brotherhood will know. And only some of the inner circles will be aware of my schedule." Was he convincing himself of this? He looked up and saw Almar's eyes fixed on him.

"Not Ter," Nikre said. "Or Sarda. Or Haethlem. And I don't care if there's two heads of circle in those three." He looked mulish. "There's too high a chance one of them is the viratir in our midst."

Eerlen would have said serpent himself, but the huge, beautiful, sparkling, and hellishly poisonous Brinarian reptile was absolutely fitting. He turned to Almar. "Can you delegate the guard duty, including commander of all armies? Since Brund can't do that even now, much less while on the run? And can you do head of fourth circle at a distance?"

"In the guard, my underling is my sibling Malin Leemar. I'd trust him with my life. For head of fourth...they can call me. Through Troz, if nothing else."

At Eerlen's look of surprise, he grinned apologetically. "Malin is my half-sibling. Fifteen years younger. Kalal's age. They were born the same month."

Nikre nodded. "I can work with Malin. Malin is family. Or close enough. I, too, would trust him with my life, which is good because I'll have to. I won't move to the family quarters, though. I'll keep my place, so they don't start getting ideas I've usurped the throne."

He knelt by the bed, leaned and quickly planted a kiss on Brundar's cheek, as though afraid someone would notice. Brundar moved slightly and mumbled something.

There were tears in Nikre's eyes as he got up. He gave Eerlen's forearm a hard squeeze. "Keep him safe, Eerlen," he said. Then rose on tiptoes and kissed Eerlen's cheek, his lips cold and soft. "And yourself, too." He gestured with his arm that supported the folded cloak. "I'll go bathe and change. I'm filthy. I'll leave orders for them to bring you food before you leave. Leave me any paperwork I need for the regency. For the brotherhood, all I need is your backing."

When he was gone, Eerlen turned to Almar. "You are sure you want to go with us?"

Lendir sighed. "You'll need help guarding Brundar, honestly. And keeping him from doing the unadvisable, too. Because he'll get bored and stir-crazy. And you know Brundar. Too much of Myrrir in that one."

Eerlen tried to phrase his question twice, but couldn't find with a way to phrase it politely. The best way was to be blunt. "Won't Kalal Ad Leed mind?"

Almar had been staring at Brundar, but turned and frowned. "Mind?"

"That he can't...you know?"

Almar looked at Eerlen blankly for a moment. "Can't what? Take over for me? Troz! Kalal is governor of Brinar. He can hardly command the Royal Guard."

"No, not that. I don't think he'd want to." He wasn't close to Kalal Ad Leed, but the third had always impressed him as a breezy personality, caring but informal. It seemed whenever Eerlen needed him, outside the battle front or inner circle gatherings, he could be found with hiked tunic, fishing with his subjects or helping some merchant in Var Leed deliver, or perhaps barefoot, helping one of his farmers at planting time crunch. When he was not sitting in his garden working on new healing formulas or presumably his accounting books. He was the least military person Eerlen could think of, though he acquitted himself well in battle.

"But I wondered how he'd feel about this trip," Eerlen continued. "It will be three of us. A family group, following a nomad path through Erradi, and living off the hunting and the fishing. You and I and Brund. Won't Ad Leed mind? I would have, were it Myrrir. Though of course you aren't sworn."

Almar's mouth dropped open, slack. He looked utterly baffled, as though Eerlen had grown a second head. He closed his mouth. The softly muttered "Maker's thighs!" shocked Eerlen, and Almar's laughter shocked him even more. "I'm not an Erradian no-mad, Troz. I know what other people say about Erradian nomads, but I've never considered swearing to my half-crossibling. Any more than I'd consider swearing with Brundar."

Eerlen's turn to stare. "Half-crossibling. Oh. That's why you could mind-call him."

A nod. "And why I trusted him. I raised him, Troz. After my parent, his sire, died. Same as I raised Malin. Don't you ever see what's under your feet? Ad Leed is family."

Eerlen started to say something about the cloud of children always in the palace, and assuming Ad Leed was over because he was a future Lord of the Land. He realized it sounded bad. The truth was, he'd stayed out of Lendir's business. There were enough people who didn't like him. He didn't want to borrow trouble.

"I see why you looked so angry. I didn't call my lover, Troz. I called my crossibling because I'd trust him with my life." Lendir sighed. "The head of the third circle is Ter. And he's on my list of suspects. I routed around him. Like Nikre intends to. Like all of us do. I'm sorry, but Ter—"

Eerlen felt the relief wash over him. No etiquette and hierarchy breach to punish. A load off his mind. "I don't like routing around Ter," he said. "But I confess I've also been doing it. He acts so put upon when I schedule him for the wounded wards, and he acts as though I have no right and... I've started not scheduling him. I don't like it, though. Bad for discipline." He paused, feeling suddenly very tired. "And I don't like leaving the palace. It will look like we kidnapped Brundar."

"Rotten ice, Troz. I don't like it, either, and the child will give us grief over it, but I can't see him die, Troz. I can't."

Eerlen laughed without mirth. "Nor can I. He's my only descendant."

"I know," Almar said, with a very serious look. "And my sire's only body child. Only surviving body child. The Mahar of Mahar. The last of Amissar's line."

"And can you stand what might turn into months in ice caves with me?"

Almar's mouth quirked, but his eyes were serious. "It will be difficult."

The seriousness caught Eerlen by surprise. He felt as though he'd been slapped, and hesitated to speak. He heard his voice a little shaky as he said, "So you do hate— This— This last year, I assumed I'd been wrong, and that you didn't hate me after all."

Almar's eyes widened. "Hate you? I never hated you," he said. He hesitated. "Oh, I might have acted it when I was very young because I was jealous."

"Of Myrrir's attention?" Almar had been what? Fourteen? When Eerlen had come into Myrrir's life. He had seemed quite young to Eerlen, but he supposed there were only three years' difference, and Almar might resent having his sire pay a lot of attention to someone almost as young. Ter, who was two years older than Eerlen, and had been heir presumptive till Myrrir birthed his older, doomed child, hated Eerlen passionately on sight.

The eyebrows went up and a genuinely amused grin erupted. "I thought we'd established I'm not that Erradian. You're worrying me for the nomad lifestyle, Troz, if you think that's normal." And then rapidly, "Go wash and dress, Archmagician. Eat something, so Nikre won't badger us both, and pack your bedroll. I'll stay with Brund and guard him. Then you stay with him, and I'll go." He turned and went to kneel by the bed.

SCHRODINGER PATH

SKIP

It is not true that the engraved plaque you see when you come into the IDS buildings devoted to the training of future diplomats of Britannia says, Abandon all hope ye who enter here.

I do understand why that has become widely believed, and to be fair, given how strict the testing of incoming students, it could be that. But my guess is that it would be too much blunt truth-telling for the IDS.

What the plaque, a fine sheet of silver, or perhaps a glassteel imitation of silver says, in raised golden letters—it is also not true that the IDS has ever had any aesthetics—is: You Can Never Know Enough.

This was certainly true for me. Through the year of my initial training, I was often grateful that the initial problems, first contacts and negotiations were virtual, done in mersi chamber, and with species, worlds and issues created from whole cloth by instructors. This is good, because no matter how much I studied on the upcoming situation, learned all the trigger words I should never use, the relationships I shouldn't mention, implied we'd consider their just cause—even if their just cause was wanting to eat their neighbors raw—or whatever I did, it ended with food thrown at me, elaborate insults offered to me, or me running out of the mersi room with a virtual lynch mob at my heels. Fortunately, they evaporated on the threshold. Unfortunately, after a year of this, I started thinking whatever I was suited for, it was not being a diplomat.

I might have said that failing wasn't an option. Not for my mother, at least. But at almost nineteen, I was starting to get a feeling Mother's view of reality might be unrealistic.

So I read the card she sent me to congratulate me on finishing my first year of training with flying colors—what kind of bilge were the instructors selling her? Oh, yeah, under no circumstances is the IDS truthful—and tell me she was proud of me.

I set it on the table, looked at myself in the blue uniform of a diplomat trainee—why did I always end up in blue uniforms?—and thought, Well, it was time to find something else to do with my life. Which was a pity, because the small room with its single bed, its reader and its music system, had been a refuge of sorts. Since I didn't use my title here and went by Skip Hayden, no one seemed to know me. Because the IDS frowned on lack of self-control, I'd been celibate as a monk, which I found oddly restful. Out there, or on the estate, I'd have to become the viscount Webson, and yes, the prodigy war hero. And I'd probably have to hide in someone's bed again.

But one thing my father had told me is that many people spent their lives in pursuit of careers they weren't suited for and that it was a waste. He was speaking of a particularly thick-headed student at the Academy, but considering my performance here, I was sure he would say it applied to me and diplomacy.

I walked out of my room, stepping crisply. That was one of those things they'd told me to change—among the other hundred things. My walk was apparently too crisp and "military." Which, since I'd lived in a military academy for most of my life, should be no surprise for anyone. But one of the many mottos that the IDS threw around was: A Diplomat Always Looks Relaxed.

Well, I wasn't going to be a diplomat, and I didn't feel particularly diplomatic. I didn't try to correct my walk—which attempt, at any rate, meant that instructors told me I was walking like a sick duck—and just left the dormitory floor, in search of the first instructor whose face I knew. I was going to ask for a resignation form and then I was—

Well, probably going to go back to the estate and figure out what to do with the next 100 or 150 years. The impulse to become a diplomat had probably been stupid, anyway.

Of course the instructor I ran into was Matt Crowe, who was walking out of the mersi room with his own crisp step, probably just having set up hell for the next patsy to walk in for a simulated diplomatic interaction.

Crowe, or Mr. Crowe—though none of the instructors had less than a doctorate, mind—as he preferred to be called, was one of the youngest instructors. He was about forty, had dark hair, grey-blue-green eyes which could assume a laser-point intensity if he thought I was being particularly stupid, always kept close-shaved and looked like a military academy graduate, as I should very well know. Which meant I was always tempted to salute and call him "sir."

I controlled with an effort of will, as I came to a stop in front of him, and of course, predictably, what came out of my mouth was a weak and wandering, "Er... Mr. Crowe?"

"Hayden?" he said. As though it were a big surprise to find a student wandering the halls of the instruction wing.

"Yes, sir," I said, and there must have been something to my voice, because he didn't correct me. "I wonder if I could have a few minutes of your time, sir? Or do I need to make an appointment?"

He frowned at me. "Is it vital that you see me right now?" he asked.

"Yes, sir. We could wait, but it would be a waste of both our times."

His frown got more thunderous, and I swear he'd had someone install laser light behind his eyes. That kind of look with a glow should hurt. Him, I mean. It did hurt me. Or at least made me sound like an idiot.

He nodded once, pivoted on his heels and said, "Come."

I followed. We walked past the mersi room, past the study rooms where we had to read over the records that we weren't trusted to take to our private rooms, and past a rowdy group of just-enrolled trainees making jokes about their last mersi experience.

We stopped by a row of doors at the back, in front of the one that read "Matt Crowe." Like most things at the Academy, they were low-tech wood doors—I guess they didn't want to get us used to unnecessary gadgets—and he pushed the door open and gestured for me to go in.

Inside, it had the look-feel of an interrogation chamber, with a battered wooden desk, and two chairs, one on each side. I took the one in front of the desk, and looked around to make sure there was no glaring interrogation light to point at my eyes. Crowe took his seat behind the desk, looked at me, as if that would tell him anything, and then leaned back—I guess a diplomat must strive to look relaxed, or something—and said, "What is wrong, Hayden? How may I help you?"

All my instincts from my Academy days reared up. When an instructor asked how he could help you, you inevitably found out he wished to help you improve your attention to detail by making you handsew a whole new uniform between night and the morning, or perhaps clean all the restrooms in the building in two hours, given only a small sponge and a bottle of breath freshener.

But I took a deep breath, told myself I was being an idiot, and said, "I would like to resign, sir."

He looked... I wasn't sure how he looked. It wasn't exactly surprised. But it was... Okay, I was a failing diplomat, but I'd lived with humans before. If I weren't talking to an instructor, I'd think he was angry.

I cleared my throat. "I signed up for instruction voluntarily, and it is my right to—"

He nodded, once. And then he did the most bizarre thing.

He took something out of his pocket, got on a chair and, reaching to what looked like a completely featureless piece of ceiling, stuck the something on it. From my perspective, it looked like a round, colored paper dot. Green dot.

Then he stepped down from the chair, walked to the door, and locked it. He took his chair back behind the desk, and sat on it. Then he leaned across the desk. "Please don't."

I blinked, looked up at the dot, back at the door, and then at Crowe, wondering which of us had taken leave of his senses.

He smiled, but it was a weird, restrained smile. "I suspected that's what you wanted to do. Which is why I brought you to my office, instead of to one of the learning rooms, which is more common for this sort of interview. You see, for whatever reason, video pickups just don't work in my office, and the audio becomes oddly random and choppy, even when I'm not here. They're used to this, so I doubt it will be noticed."

"Sir? Is this an exercise?"

The smile became rueful. "In a way. Something you'll learn, Hayden, is that at the IDS, nothing is ever simple. Or at least that's what I'm learning. Look, I looked at your file. There are weird whispers about you... Someone tipped us you'd been visiting houses of ill repute in certain quarters."

"Sir, I haven't—"

He waved it away. "I know. I checked. I've crawled over your records and everything you've done the last year. You're Viscount Webson, right? And your mom is a countess who is sixth cousin to the queen or something?"

I blinked again. "Something like that." It was actually third cousin, but who was counting?

"Then what I suggest is that you tell your mother someone is trying to make you wash out of the training. And tell her to have the Queen send word she would like you to graduate as soon as possible."

I was about to say that my mother wasn't in that kind of relationship with the Queen. And it was true. Although there was a blood relation, Queen Eleanor might be a cousin—a lot closer than sixth and probably on three sides, because Father, despite being a mere commoner, had some royal bastard blood and relatives who'd married into the nobility or bought into it—but I didn't think Mother had the sort of friendship where she could ask a favor of the queen. Mother didn't have that sort of friendship with anyone. Mother commanded—she did not plead.

On the other hand, it occurred to me that I might. Well, not that sort of friendship, but that sort of reach. After all, I was a war hero. Things being done against a war hero would be bad news for the monarchy's image. I had a feeling—though I'd never paid much attention to politics—that the Queen wouldn't like this.

I sat up straight. "Tell me exactly what's been happening, besides my rather unspectacular performance."

He made a face. "They have been ordering you to be put through third-year mersis. The ones given to the trainees who have done both three-month rotations in the field."

I blinked.

"Frankly, the fact you have lasted almost the full simulations is a sign of enormous talent. Which is why I'd prefer you don't resign. Queen Harmonia left us in a hell of a mess. To clean it up, we need real talent. Which is why I was brought in, from the Space Force, having finished a doctorate in diplomacy while deployed. And why I am an instructor despite my having no title, amid all you noblemen, instructors and students alike."

I narrowed my eyes as the picture formed. Crowe had been given a sponge and a bottle of breath freshener. "You're on cleanup duty?"

"Of sorts."

"But why would anyone put me on third year—" I stopped. "Did they misjudge my ability?"

He snorted. "Oh, no. I can't find the details, on account of not being a director."

Really, a small sponge and a tiny bottle of breath freshener. "But?"

"But it bothered me. Both the completely unsubstantiated rumors and that they were ordering this course of action, and I poked around enough and spied at doors enough—"

"Sometimes good diplomats listen at doors," I said, piously, another plaque in another room of the complex.

He made a face, which exactly reflected how I felt about the plaques, too.

"Anyway, I get the impression that one or more of the directors were... We won't say bribed, but something very like. 'There would be a donation coming' sort of thing if you were made to wash out." He opened his hands on the desk. "Nothing I can prove, or take to her Majesty. Not with the directors all being noblemen and women at the highest levels. And I very much suspect the bribe was less tangible than money changing hands."

I sat back. Well. That could have come from anyone, though my main suspect would be Mother, complete with the card complimenting me on finishing out the year. It was just the sort of thing she would do, since she would much prefer I go back to the estate, and learn to do estate things, not to mention marry and set about producing a long line of heirs. Though the marrying might be optional. I had no idea if she knew my proclivities, but even without, I suspected she'd be absolutely happy with my having a lab contracted for children which would be wholly hers to raise, while I managed the estate, or perhaps went back to the Space Force.

For the first time, I wondered if Father had stayed so long in the Force for a reason.

But if Mother was behind this, I obviously couldn't go to her. And if Mother was behind this, I definitely didn't want to expose her. Our relationship was fraught enough.

Well.

I looked up. Crowe was looking at me, eyebrows slightly raised, as though trying to divine my calculations.

"Look," I said. "It's a very long gambit, but I can send a note to Queen Eleanor through some contacts." From what I understood, my great-uncle, the Judge, took tea with Her Majesty fairly regularly. "I need a half-day pass. But I warn you, it might not work."

He made another face. "Very well. I will, at the same time, pass a message through my contacts. It is all a very long shot, but I'd prefer the diplomatic service of the Star Empire did not lose you, Viscount Webson."

"Just...Skip Hayden," I said, and offered him my hand. Yes, I knew this might all be some complex lie, but somehow, it didn't feel like one.

He shook my hand and did his best to break it, the bastard, then nodded and got a disposit pad from his drawer. He set it on an away pass, and signed it with his gen-print, then handed it over. It was a little thing, smaller than my palm. I slipped it into a pocket.

Yes, that did mean I had to endure tea with Great-Uncle Zymon. And yes, the tea in his ornate office, with a footman behind each of us—making sure we didn't drop crumbs or throw the cups on the floor, I guess?—felt unaccustomed and oppressive, though I'd done this once a month when I'd been in the Academy.

Great-Uncle Zymon had a completely different idea of who and what was causing my issues at the Academy. He was fairly sure it was that the directors themselves were jealous of me, and afraid the Queen would appoint me to the board. Which would make perfect sense, of course, if I had a doctorate, which I didn't. Or have any intention of getting one.

But my paternal uncle thought the Haydens were the most illustrious and brilliant family in all the Star Empire, and all the other families conspired to bring it down. Pretty much constantly. It was a pet paranoia which I suspected he kept in his bedside table, fed on chocolate, and only admitted to other Haydens—that is, to me—otherwise, someone would have locked him up long since.

But the end result is that he took my note to the Queen and I returned to training at the IDS, not expecting much of anything to result from that afternoon. I'd planned that if nothing changed, I'd resign in a week.

However, things changed.

The first thing that changed was that I found I did indeed receive stellar grades for my first year, each of the exercises being graded on a curve, for being far above my ability, and therefore the portion completed counted as more than enough.

The other change is that the mersi experiences became more...related to how much I had studied and how much I concentrated.

This is not to say they became easy.

GATHER AND GOSSIP

EERLEN

Eerlen didn't hear Lendir approach, in the confusion of the Nomad Festival outside Var Leed, in Brinar. He was jumpy, like a chicken at a tiger get-together. It was always a risk taking Brundar out of the ice-nomad circuit.

Makers balls, if he had told someone he'd be here!

And the worst part of it was getting everything done that needed to be done, and keeping Brundar from feeling like he wasn't doing anything.

If not for the occasional, unscheduled battle front healing duty, Brundar would already be climbing the walls.

He'd let Brundar organize—on his own—a magician's spy corps in Draksall. Brundar, in the way of an eighteen-year-old, had thought it was a bad idea that he got woken in the middle of the night when there was a breakthrough and he thought they could use the loose network of people who rescued those taken as slaves into Draksall to get warning. Then he'd recruited people for the impossibly dangerous job of posing as slaves in Draksall to...spy on Draksalls' plans.

Like Myrrir, Brundar could convince people to do the impossible. But— But their situation was also impossible. And Brundar had said he needed to come here, to this Festival in Brinar to coordinate with his spies. But— But this wasn't the battle front, where they went in and out, and Brundar was watched by Lendir, and this was not a brotherhood meeting, with Eerlen in full power and full control of all magicians. This was a gathering of complete strangers, and— And Eerlen felt like his heart was going to jump out of his mouth.

He'd been standing, his back against a tree, when Lendir's warm, outsized hand came to rest on his shoulder. He felt extremely proud of himself for not jumping or screaming. And not reaching for his ankle daggers.

Instead, he just turned around to see Lendir standing just behind and to the side of him and offering him a vast leaf containing... Yes, as the spicy warm scent hit his nostrils, Eerlen identified the food as bits of spicy meat on little sticks. Called for reasons known only to the locals, Stag's Horns. One of the many things sold by the locals in the Brinarian village hosting the Spring Festival of Brinarian nomads.

The Festival was called something complicated like "The day of thanks for boats," although whom they were thanking and why for boats, Eerlen didn't know and doubted anyone did anymore. It took place at the edge of Var Leed, capital of Brinar. And Eerlen didn't think it was sane at all being here. He'd also imagined from a distance that they'd stick out like sore thumbs, since most of the inhabitants of Brinar came to about his shoulder, varied in color only among shades of gold to chestnut, and were dark-haired and dark-eyed. But it turned out he was wrong in that. There were enough tall blonds interspersed with the giggling, singing, running crowds that they passed fairly unnoticed. Besides, who looked closely at Erradians when Brinarians and Lirridarians were present?

Still, Eerlen kept a close eye on Brundar, who at the moment was standing in the shadow of one of the boat-shelters on the beach, talking to Selbur Deharn, who was lithe and surprisingly tall for a Brinarian. And who was also an eighth circle, a weaver of illusions. And a member of Brundar's daring, ill-advised spy corps.

Eerlen was still not sure how Brundar had managed to convince magicians of Elly that it was a bright or even a sane idea to go to Draksah and impersonate slaves to get intelligence.

Sure, there were enough Ellyan slaves in Draksah. They had been captured in the various Draksall incursions, wars and breakthroughs. And some were descended from those captured in the first invasions and who'd not followed Amissar back to Elly. But going there and passing as a slave was—

Distasteful didn't begin to cover it. Draksalls simply didn't consider the inhabitants of Elly human. Neither rape nor cannibalism were out of the question. And if discovered as spies and magicians— Draksalls had their own magicians. It was not possible to hide magical power very well, and—

Suddenly, Eerlen blinked, and Brundar talking to Selbur Deharn fell in a different light. They looked like... Well, Deharn looked smitten.

Eerlen sighed, and smiled at Lendir and took one of the bits of meat on a stick, bit into it and, before he could let out a yelp, found Lendir offering him his canteen. He took a drink from it, which cooled the burn in his tongue, but burned a different way. "Alcohol?"

"From corn. A distillate. New thing. I thought we'd try it."

"I'd best not try a lot. A drunk archmagician is dangerous. And besides, you might have to carry me back." For purposes of not being noticed, he'd tucked the ruby under his light linen tunic, next to the skin. But a lot of magicians sensed it, gave a double take and nodded to him.

Lendir laughed. "With pleasure," he said. "You're light enough."

Had Lendir already been drinking? Eerlen took another bit of meat and nibbled at it, absently, while staring at the body language between Brundar and Selbur. "I think I know how Brundar managed to create his deranged idea of a spy corps."

"Oh?"

"He put Selbur Deharn in charge. Watch them a moment. Pay attention to Deharn's body language."

Lendir watched silently. He passed the canteen to Eerlen twice more, seeming to have a sense when it was needed. Then he said, "Oh." And then, "Well, it wouldn't be a bad thing, you know? I mean, the throne needs heirs, and it would at least stop some of the danger he's in. If there's a lot more of them... It excludes Myrrir's sirelings."

Eerlen sighed. "I've told him that. He's not interested. Look at him. He's completely oblivious."

Someone nearby had started singing a bawdy song. Couples walked by, all but doing it in public. But yeah, Brund was talking rapidly with Selbur, and utterly oblivious to anything but his grand plans.

"He's a lot like my sire," Lendir said.

"Your— Myrrir? Who seduced me into his bed the day we met? Who had more sirelings by more different people than—"

"No, hear me out. Myrrir... As far as I understand, I'm the result of an accident." He grinned sheepishly at Eerlen's snort. "No. Both my parents told the story the same way, so it must be true. My sire was wounded and my parent—also a third circle…it's a mystery how I ended up fourth—was sharing his bed to keep track of him, and in delirium, Myrrir—"

Eerlen laughed. "Well, if he said it, it must be true. Delirium as an excuse wouldn't suit him. He never shied away from admitting past peccadillos."

"Yeah. So I'm the child of fevered dream. My parents were friends, but not lovers. Which I think was good. There was never resentment on either side when it wasn't repeated, and I had the assurance both of them loved me while respecting the other. My parent hadn't the slightest bit of jealousy over you, which helped, too. The others? Well, Ter was the child of Myrrir's first love, his first sworn when both were far too young, and Sarda the child of a young governor starstruck with Myrrir. Since Sarda's parent died birthing him, who knows what would have happened? They might very well have sworn. Myrrir hadn't sworn easily after the first. But the not-recognized sirelings were mostly had for the purpose of controlling someone, or perhaps distracting them." He paused. "You know there are others, right?"

"Oh, yes, he admitted to others. Five or six, at least. Though I don't think any others in the palace. Almost for sure in the brotherhood, though. Too much magic in Mahar blood for his sirelings to be born without power. He never told me who, though. And the children would have joined before I was archmagician, as did Ter, of course. I understand what you mean. For Myrrir… Except perhaps with me, sex was a means to something, even if the something might be strengthening a friendship, making sure someone was loyal to him, or some related purpose. Not that he didn't care about people as people, but he—" Eerlen shrugged. "But he was always working on some other purpose. And I'm not sure about me. Perhaps—"

Lendir gave him an odd, sideways look. "You were different. He wouldn't have sworn otherwise, and he certainly wouldn't have been faithful."

"Maybe. He secured a pretty strong work relationship with the archmagician."

A quick laugh from Lendir. "No. We all knew it. Everyone in the palace. From the first day. It was different." A long pause. "And I was eaten up with rank jealousy."

"Oh, yes," Eerlen said, recognizing the tease and parrying it.

"Because nothing was more desirable than an awkward ice nomad."

Lendir muttered something about mirrors and said, "Definitely more corn liquor." And wandered off.

Which was when Brundar turned and came running towards Eerlen.

"Eerlen!"

He looked, Eerlen thought, for all the world like when he'd been eight and had just managed to hit the target with his bow, under Lendir's patient tutelage.

But he was in command of himself enough that, as he came to skid near Eerlen, he dropped a silence veil around them.

"There is an emissary from the star worlds in Draksall," he said, and grinned, as though he'd made a particularly amazing discovery.

"Star worlds?"

"You remember." Brundar's face displayed impatience. "The people from the stars with weapons beyond anything—"

"Who are Draksall," Eerlen said. "Yes, I remember."

Brundar grinned. "Well, I don't think they're quite Draksall. Just male and female, like the Draksall, and they are intending to murder the ambassador," he said. "The whole thing is a setup to murder him, somehow, and then the star people will give them weapons."

"Brund, all these theys are a bit overwhelming. If I follow you, the people from the stars intend to murder their own ambassador."

"Yes. But they arranged for the Draksalls to do it. So it looks like an accident."

Eerlen's eyebrows shot up. He could feel it, before the words even hit. "Uh."

"Right. So we're going to interfere with their plan and bring the ambassador here. Deharn and I have a plan."

"Bring the ambassador here?" Eerlen was aware his voice had squeaked embarrassingly.

But before Brundar could answer, Lendir was back. He had another leaf filled with pieces of meat, which was greeted by Brundar with glad cries of, "Oh, good, I was starving."

And Lendir must have acquired some sanity along the way—a feat for one of Myrrir's whelps—since he handed Brundar one of those orange peels that the Brinarians filled with fruit juice and sugar, but mostly sugar, while passing his canteen of corn alcohol to Eerlen.

Eerlen took a deep pull. If he knew his sireling, and he knew his sireling, it wasn't going to be possible to talk Brundar out of the insanity, anyway.

"Brund," he said. "Brund, under no circumstances are you to bring the ambassador here. You can have him killed, if you think he's a danger, but you're not going to bring him here and you are not going to get more involved in this than you already are. You are not to take any risks. You are not to get near this ambassador." He waved his hands in what he was aware was an embarrassing way. "Or any Draksall. Any."

Brundar shrugged, in a way that Eerlen knew was dangerous, and Almar gave Eerlen a long look. As the liquor burned a path down Eerlen's throat and he looked at Brundar, elaborating on his information to Lendir, Eerlen wondered precisely how impossible the task of keeping the rightful heir to the throne alive was. And why he had to be the one trying to do it.

Sure, he'd allowed himself to be seduced by the king... But he'd been only seventeen and an ice nomad. It's not like he knew any better.

Ah, well. Fate was fate. And he'd keep trying, even if it was all doomed.

ICE CAVES AND BED ROLLS

EERLEN

Eerlen woke up with a sense of doom, and his heart pounding so hard, it felt as though it might come out through his mouth.

A moment to sense his surroundings, before he opened his eyes. No one nearby and the undisturbed state of the ruby on its pendant told him no one had mind-touched him.

Opening his eyes, he looked above him at smooth, polished golden stone. About four feet above him. He was warm. He could hear the crackle of fire somewhere to his right. The sound of running water to his left.

He was in the Yanda shelter, the oldest of his line. So old, in fact, that probably no one who hadn't been born and raised a Troz knew it existed. Partly because it was so old and so weird and, as far as ice caves went, it wasn't one at all, except for being beneath the ice and snow of Erradi. It wasn't cave, long covered by ice, like the others, but something else. Parts looked like they had been willfully excavated, part of a buried structure of unknown materials.

It was also a dead spot, where no mind touch could find them, a risky place for an archmagician to hide. If he had less confidence in his second-in-command, he wouldn't do it. And Nikre Lyto could reach him. But only through the ruby.

On the other hand, it was also a place to sleep in peace, knowing whoever the enemy was wouldn't be able to find Brundar. The entrance to Yanda was long, circuitous and tight, and equipped with a lock that would only allow those of the main line blood, their sworns, direct descendants within two generations, or those specifically allowed in by those of the main line blood. And given Eerlen was the only Troz remaining in the world—and no collaterals, either, as both his parent and grandparent had been only children—that meant he and Brundar, his own sireling, could come in alone, and Lendir with them. So the three of them were the only ones allowed in. The others would meet with a power barrier as impassable as granite.

So there was no reason to be afraid, and yet the sense that something was wrong persisted.

He reached to the bottom of the bed for his cloak. Not his magician cloak, but the thick, fur-lined one he wore during the day and when out hunting.

Wrapped in it, he stepped out of his chamber. His chamber was on one side of the main entrance and isolated, normally—if this had been a normal shelter where relatives flitted in and out—given to parents with small children, while the older children slept in the smaller and close-together chambers on the other side of the entrance tunnel.

The chambers which were almost certainly made, though no one knew precisely what the material was, led to a vast room that was not: a room twice the size of the big front hall in the palace at Elly. At the far end, a river ran, surprisingly warm for the latitude, though that made it cold, anyway, even if it came from deep under the Earth. Around the river, there was an edge of vegetation thriving in sunlight reflected through a system of mirrored tunnels above. Over the centuries, Troz had planted it with fragrant herbs and built a bathing pool by the side of the river. Past the river, a narrow tunnel. Eerlen had been told by both his parents that it led deeper for miles and miles, but he'd never actually followed it. He and his older sibling—long dead—had played at the very entrance. But his parents both said it became more and more of a dead zone, where magic could not operate, as you went further. They also said it became almost tropical. The relative warmth in this cavern was probably due to sitting atop volcanic activity. Eerlen's parent said further on there were warm rivers, and strange plants and animals, all illuminated by an eerie light. It wasn't so much that Eerlen had never had enough curiosity to find out, but that by the time he might have gone exploring, he was thirteen and training as archmagician.

He gave the dark entrance of the tunnel a glaring look. If Brundar had gone—

But before he could call, he heard Lendir's voice: "Brund." And looked ahead to see Lendir emerge from his chamber, also wrapped in his fur cloak, and probably naked underneath, with his hair lose down his back and his feet bare. He looked magnificently barbaric, powerful, unleashed, a nomad on the hunt. He stopped short on seeing Eerlen. "You—do you know where he—?"

And at that moment, a scraping sound from the tunnel entrance made them both turn, just in time to see Brundar emerge into the cavern. He emerged head first, saw them, pretended not to see them, pulled himself out and to his feet.

At eighteen, he'd grown probably almost to his full height and to a full, powerful third circle with a little extra power from his siring. He had studied and was a full healer, specializing in births. The best birth-healer in the brotherhood, in fact.

Right then, though, perhaps Brundar was consumed by lack of duty. Already taller than Eerlen, he was now also broader of shoulder, but so svelte he managed to look fragile, like a hastily made sketch of an adult.

And he was wearing a short linen tunic and sandals. Eerlen spared a glare and let his eyes do the parental rebuking. "You were not out hunting, I presume."

The brat gave him a glowering look, as though he were not the one caught at fault. "Portal. Temporary. Just outside the entrance." Pause. "I went to Brinar."

"Why? Trying to get tracked?" That was Lendir, and Eerlen wondered if it was perhaps unfair that the child should have two parents, neither of whom was his real parent, which was what these confrontations usually devolved into.

The brow came down over the impish green eyes. The eyes looked...wounded. Turbulent. Eerlen couldn't quite imagine what was going through Brundar's mind. It would have been easier before Myrrir died. But even after that, when they'd been at the palace, it had been easy. Not in the last few months or so. Brundar seemed to be spinning on himself, in ever tighter circles, eaten by something he would not share.

Eerlen had tried to tell himself the child had some romantic interest, but it didn't seem right. It wasn't that kind of brooding at all.

"Brundar!" Lendir said, while Eerlen hesitated. Normally a yell from his older sibling brought confused excuses from Brundar. This time, it didn't. Brundar turned and crossed his arms on his chest. He was still a head shorter than Lendir, but the gesture, the posture made it seem like he was standing on the throne.

"Brundar Mahar to you, or Your Majesty, Lendir Almar, Commander of my guard. And may I ask when you intended to tell me there have been incursions on the palace? That my people have been killed?"

Almar turned white, but answered, "Your people were my people. My guards, who held the palace, Your Majesty." The last two words managed to be perfectly respectful in appearance, while dripping with sarcasm. "Malin, my half-sibling, was wounded, Lord Mahar."

And Eerlen recognized the mood of both siblings. Both of them had inherited Myrrir's temper, which, once stoked, would spin and spin and spin, gathering energy as from a high wind, till it unleashed a storm that tore everything in its path. Myrrir had never been physically violent. Not to Eerlen. Not to any blood relations of the Mahars and certainly not to his servants and dependents. But he had a wicked tongue that could cut and freeze, like a blade of ice. He'd never turned it on Eerlen but once, but that once had left a wound that took years to heal.

"This is not the way—" Eerlen started, trying to step in between the two, his hands up, in the ancient gesture denoting peace and the lack of armament. "I don't think anything can be won by—" he said.

Brundar rounded on him, eyes blazing, "And you, Archmagician, would you care to tell me who has been making the decisions of my government? Who has been governing for me, in all but name?"

"I—" Eerlen started, his hand still open and now extended. "Look, it is all routine decisions, of troop provisioning, the solving of minor disputes. Myrrir used to delegate those decisions to me, and I am used—"

"Oh, you are used to governing behind the throne, are you? Perhaps the governors of my lands were right to suspect it?"

Eerlen opened his mouth, but no sound came out. Of course he'd been doing what he could to keep the world working, the battle front provisioned, while they were on the run, because he didn't want Brundar to die. But at the same time, perhaps he'd taken liberties, which he didn't know how to justify. He put his hand around the ruby, a habit when he felt threatened.

"Brundar, that is unacceptable. Eerlen has given up everything for you, to keep you safe and alive. You do not have the right—" Almar yelled.

"Oh, do I not? I am the king. I supposedly have the power of life and death over both of you. Under what right do you reproach me? Is it an older sibling, or do you intend to claim the throne on your siring right?"

"If you weren't my king, I'd already have taken you over my knee, which is the treatment your insolence to your sire merits."

Internally, Eerlen knew that Almar had gone too far. He could feel it, like pushing on a stuck door that suddenly falls completely. This time, he extended only one hand, towards Almar, almost touching his wrist, but staying. Staying because he realized he would be trespassing, and courting a duel would do no one any good.

Brundar was very quiet. Scarily so, staring at Almar with green-ice eyes. His eyes had seemed to get greener, his hair redder, as he grew into himself. "What? You hope he'll notice you if you defend him? I'd think you were in this together, but you're not, are you? No, you're trailing him and hoping he'll realize you're mesmerized by him, while he ignores you. Why don't you single-swear to him? At least it would be out in the open. It's not like he'll ever return your crush. He was the same way with Myrrir, as though everyone didn't know that Myrrir was sleeping with half the world and—"

Eerlen didn't realize he'd made a sound, as if he'd been struck, until Almar glanced at him, quickly, the type of look one gives a comrade at arms that falls in battle.

And then Almar turned, very quickly, and, in a controlled way, that gave the impression he was executing a maneuver that he'd practiced for several years, grabbed Brundar by the arms, and lifted him. It wasn't much, less than a palm off the ground, but being lifted made Brundar's eyes widen in shock while he froze.

"If you were a normal young fool," Almar said, his voice level and controlled, but somehow giving the impression that he was making a great effort to keep it that way. "I'd already have slapped you hard enough to get some sense into you. And afterwards, we'd talk, and perhaps you'd learn something. But you are, by the Maker's withered tits, the king of Elly. If I slap you, I might as well kill you. And if I kill you, I might as well slit my own throat afterwards, because Eerlen Troz, your long-suffering archmagician and sire, will be honorbound to kill me for it. So I suggest you stop that vicious tongue of yours and listen, Your Majesty."

Brundar drew breath and opened his mouth, and Eerlen, half-aware that disaster would follow, prepared to somehow step between them and take the fatal blow. If they weren't in a magical dead zone, he could immobilize them both, but as it was, he had not a hope. Maybe one of them, but never both. He had a brief, ridiculous idea of hitting both their heads together, but it wouldn't do. For one, Brundar was the king. Almar was right.

But by a miracle, Brundar didn't speak.

"Not that it matters what your parent and sire did, if the other didn't object," Lendir said, his voice low. "But I suspect you know as well as I do that Myrrir was faithful to Troz. Again, not that it matters to you. And as for my feelings for Troz, I suspect everyone at the palace knows. But note no one has ever said a word to me. That is because anyone else who dared say what you did just now would have had his tongue removed and fed to them. Because it is private and none of anyone's business. Do you understand me, you majestical brat?"

Brundar nodded.

"Now, I'm going to let you go," Almar said. "And when I do, we're going to speak like adults, all of us, about what is really eating you, and what we can do about it, shall we? And you will keep your viper tongue off Troz's affairs, understood?"

For a second miracle, Brundar nodded, slowly.

Lendir released him, letting him fall. Brundar instinctively widened his stance, catching himself, then rubbed his forearms where Almar had held him.

"Can you speak rationally?" Almar said.

Brundar took a deep breath. "I am the king and a magician. I have responsibilities. I am supposed to be making decisions. I am supposed to be at the battle front, holding the shield, rescuing wounded, healing. I'm supposed to be on regular rotation. I am supposed to hear pleas, administer my family holds, oversee the Lords of the Land, keep the nomad clans peaceful—" He made an odd gesture, both hands wide, as though trying to catch at the air. "I am failing my people."

"You don't need to be at the front. Not as a king," Eerlen said. "As a third circle magician, perhaps, but we do give people passes for circumstances. Yes, we've had you there once or twice every few months, in extreme need, but...you don't need to. I do understand Myrrir was a battle king, but Brundar, it's not safe till the line is secure."

Brundar frowned. "I'm still supposed to be king. And people say that I'm dead. And people tried to take the palace. No one knows whose troops for sure, but they had strange weapons. And you didn't tell me. Either of you."

"Granted," Eerlen said. He still felt wounded, not so much by the implication that Myrrir was sleeping around. He knew Myrrir wasn't, simply because it would have shown in their bond-pattern, and Myrrir didn't have sufficient power to hide it from Eerlen. Rather, he was wounded because Brundar would go that low, reach that far to wound him. "We did not wish to worry you, because there was nothing you could do."

Brundar advanced his lower lip, managing to look several years younger and far more petulant than Eerlen had ever seen him. "And you should not make decisions for me, even if you made them for Myrrir. I didn't delegate my power to you. You know very well it's usurpation."

"I do," Eerlen said, not fighting it. "But the times I've managed to get word out I do it via the ruby, and it was easier—" He stopped. He'd been in the wrong. "You're right. It's absolutely unjustified. I'll present the decisions to you, and you can make them. I'll transmit them."

Brundar's eyes widened, as if he'd never expected that and probably, Eerlen thought, more than a little panicked, as he realized he knew nothing of the matters at stake.

"I'll advise, of course, but I'll present all sides of the decision to you," Eerlen said.

For a moment, Brundar said nothing, then inclined his head with immense gravity. He might as well have been on the throne, in full regalia. "But you mistake me. I'll make those decisions, or at least know what they are before I delegate them. But neither you nor Lend— Almar see the crux of my anger, or why I feel betrayed by both of you."

Spare us adolescent storms, Eerlen thought, but aloud, he said, "Enlighten us."

"The palace was stormed by people using alien weapons, Troz. Regardless of what you think of what you two set up to keep me safe, consider the alien weapons. I told you that the Draksalls had set up to ensnare people from the stars into helping them.

"Now I hear of alien weapons that throw targeted fire. And you don't see the connection? And you denied me the chance to get the ambassador, to find out if we, too, can get the weapons."

Eerlen knew when he was defeated. Yes, it was immensely dangerous to have the spies in Draksall kidnap the Star Ambassador. But if they were willing, they were willing. And they could hide the ambassador in Erradi. They were already hiding Brund.

Yes, he risked losing some magicians. And nothing might come of this. On the other hand... On the other hand, Brundar was correct. Eerlen had read the report of that incursion on the palace—he wondered where Brundar had got it, but he'd have to ask when things were calmer—and the weapons were almost too much to be held at bay by the magical shield. A few more weapons and they'd not be able to re-form the shield. It had collapsed twice. Guards had died, and Malin, Lendir's sibling, had been wounded.

"Granted, then. You can tell your spies to bring the ambassador to you. But we will be with you and any meetings, and messages will be sent through the ruby. No more courting danger."

Brundar stood, looking suddenly very young and very embarrassed. He nodded. He opened his mouth, then closed it, as though he'd thought to say something, then thought better of it.

Suddenly, he squared his shoulders, with the effect of gathering himself up. "I am going to make plans," he said. And left, down the hallway and to his room at the far end.

Eerlen took a long exhale, feeling as though strength and stress both drained from him with that breath.

He heard Lendir Almar laugh.

WHAT THE MIRROR REVEALS

EERLEN

He turned on his heel, offended, to glare at Almar. But Almar was staring down the hallway, shaking his head.

He turned around, and his expression turned from amused to hesitant. "He's making no plans," he said. "He's hiding, because you met his bluff."

Eerlen sighed. "I don't think it was a bluff. I think he's right about my taking liberties with his role." He said it almost automatically. The truth was that he wasn't thinking about Brundar or governance.

As important as those things were, his mind was full of Lendir's expressions and reactions, things he felt he'd misjudged and misinterpreted and—

He felt as though things were tumbling in his head, falling into place in strange ways. He felt like a fool. A blind fool. He'd thought—

But beneath it all, there was excitement building. His heart was faster. His ears were buzzing faintly. What Brund had said about Almar. And Almar hadn't denied it. He hadn't. But I thought he hated me, Eerlen thought.

Looks and feelings, not all of them Almar's, built up into a picture. How jealous Eerlen himself had felt of poor Ad Leed, as though— There was a sense of building pressure in his mind. His breath accelerated, and there was a feeling like before a thunderstorm, when power crackled and fizzed in the air, making paths for the lightning. He looked up at Almar, and for the first time didn't see him as Myrrir's sireling. He looked like Myrrir. Somewhat. The same as all of Myrrir's sirelings bore the mark of their siring, but he was different. His own person. He was, what?

Thirty-five?

Close to Eerlen's age. Closer to Eerlen's age than Myrrir had been.

And then Eerlen heard the strangest question coming out of his mouth. "Do you have a line child?"

Almar's eyes widened. He stared. A dark red suffused his face. "What?"

"I'm sorry," Eerlen started. It was a question he had no right to ask. An intrusion. Not duel-worthy, but offense-worthy, surely. "I don't know what came over me."

Lendir grinned. "Emotion letting go. And..." He paused. Took a deep breath. Looked at Eerlen out the corner of his eye. Looked at his feet. "I am sorry. He only went after..." He took a loud breath. "Brundar only mentioned my feelings to hurt me. It had nothing to do with you." Another pause. "And no, I don't have a line child. I don't have any children. Or sirelings."

Eerlen felt more embarrassed at being answered than he was at having asked. He wanted to say something, but his mind was a turmoil of feelings from which words emerged only occasionally, in a disjointed way, like leaves carried in a high wind.

He managed a deep breath. "Almar." His voice shook on the one word.

Lendir looked up from his feet. He was bright red, which some-how didn't make him look bad, just mortally embarrassed. His lips quirked, as though he were trying to force a smile.

"Don't," Eerlen said. "Don't pretend it's nothing. Is it true?"

"What? That I've been flying the flag for you since you came into that confirmation audience twenty some years ago?" The words came out almost angry. "I told you. It was like— I'd never thought or felt much about anyone. I was solely focused on training; on the fact I would one day inherit command of the guard. I ate, lived and breathed exercise and weapon training. And then—" He shrugged. "And then you walked into that audience room, looking so much like an Erradian nomad, I expected you to have a sword at your belt. And you walked about a palm from me. I spent the entire evening trying to come up with words to speak to you, to...to try to start a conversation. And then my sire walked away with you, to his room. And two years later swore with you and you...lived in the palace." He bit the corner of his lower lip, then let out a bark of laugh without joy. "Over the next...until two years ago, standing guard outside the royal room at night became a form of hell." And then, as though realizing what he'd said, hurriedly, "I didn't kill him, Troz. I wouldn't. The hell of it was I loved my sire. Worshipped him, in a way. He wasn't a great parent, but he was a great sire. Just the right amount of attention. And I loved you. And you loved him. I didn't want to hurt you, even if I'd wanted to hurt—"

"Stop. I know you didn't kill Myrrir. You'd never have called a quorum of fourths if you had. And I know you wouldn't hurt the child—Brundar. I guess he's no longer a child—" He was now very close to Almar, and he had no idea how he'd got there. He extended a hand to touch Almar's shoulder, under the fur cloak, which had come open to reveal he wore a short linen tunic beneath. "Almar, I'm half-Draksall, I don't know—"

Lendir shrugged. "Yeah. When you— There was a lot of jealousy in the palace. You didn't just capture the king's eye. You made him faithful to you. And you sired his first and second child to survive birth. The half-Draksall was the nicest thing they called you."

"No, you don't understand. I don't care what people said in the palace. Actually, I think the nicest thing they called me was 'the ice nomad,' but there was far worse than half-Draksall, I know that. What I mean is, I know what I am and what I look like. I never had any idea why Myrrir was interested. I thought it was a matter of my being the archmagician. But I know your mind doesn't work that way, and it wouldn't have that far back. That's why it never occurred to me you would... I'm just Eerlen Troz— Why?"

Lendir made a sound. It wasn't quite a sigh, but it was somewhere between that and exasperation. "Oh, Eerlen," he said. And if he hadn't whispered it, Eerlen was almost sure there would have been a laugh behind it.

And then things happened very quickly, and Eerlen would never be able to fully explain it, except that he found himself in Lendir's arms and being ruthlessly kissed, before a pause, when he could very well have said something in protest, but instead he stood on tiptoes to return the kiss.

Which was when his cloak fell open, revealing he'd been sleeping naked before throwing it on. Well, almost naked.

Lendir chuckled. As he pulled away, he said, "You're wearing ankle daggers."

"I'm always wearing ankle daggers."

"Always?"

"Well...perhaps not. But—" Eerlen looked down the hallway. "Perhaps we should adjourn before Brundar comes out to do something..."

Lendir lifted him off his feet, which he supposed was a benefit of his being outsized.

They ended up in Eerlen's chamber without discussing it. But it made sense, since it was the furthest from Brundar's. Eerlen didn't know if they'd keep this secret or want to. He wasn't even sure what this was. But being caught in the middle would put the cap on this evening.

Hours later, he felt strangely relaxed. He felt as though he'd been running, running, since Myrrir had died. Which, in a way, was true. But he felt as though he'd been running utterly alone through a snowstorm, and had opened a door and found a warm room, a lit fire.

There was a lit fire. He woke from a light nap, put on his cloak, grabbed a towel, and headed for the bathing pool. Before he left his chamber, Lendir called, "Eerlen?"

"You were sleeping. I was going to bathe."

And Lendir put on his cloak, grabbed a towel from the pile in the corner.

They bathed together, speaking only what had to be said and in whispers, both conscious of not wanting Brundar to join them.

Later, they sat in front of the fire, naked. Brundar would not come into Eerlen's chamber unless there was an emergency.

"My sire was a Draksall deserter. Or at least, he was a very young, wounded Draksall," Eerlen said. "My parent found him collapsed in front of one of our shelters. Not this one. He should have killed him. He knew he should have killed him. Instead, he disarmed him, brought him in and nursed him. Somehow, in all that, they ended up sworn to each other. Which caused interesting ripples in the brotherhood and got my parent banned from shield holding and healing and cut off from the brotherhood power and communication. They didn't trust his sympathies. And then—" He shrugged. "I was the second child, but the one of the name. My sibling had some illness... I don't know. He died when I was two, so I don't remember. Then it was just the three of us. But my parent had my power linked to the brotherhood when I was a baby. At thirteen, I was called to be apprenticed to the archmagician." He shrugged. "My parents disappeared midroute shortly after. No one ever found out where or why. I tried to trace them for years. My clan only accepted me when I was sixteen. After they disappeared. It took them time to accept the half-Draksall, much less obey him." He looked up. "I told Myrrir. That night. When he— He laughed at me and asked why it mattered."

Lendir slid off the stool by the fire, and knelt at Eerlen's feet, looking up at his eyes. "I won't laugh at you. But I'll tell you it doesn't matter. You are Eerlen Troz. And I've been in love with you more than half my life. I'm just worried that tomorrow you'll realize I'm not Myrrir, and wonder what possessed you."

Eerlen reached out, running his fingers through Lendir's wavy, bronze-tinged hair, spreading it to dry by the light of the fire. "I know you're not Myrrir. I've always known it. I was afraid you'd think that was why— I think that held me back, more than anything."

Lendir sighed. "You're lonely. It's probably being alone with me and Brundar as only company for a year."

"Oh, no. It was before we embarked on this madness. When... The night we left the palace. I was so jealous of Ad Leed, I could have murdered him. And I had no idea why I even felt that way."

Lendir looked bewildered. "But Kalal is my crossibling."

"Yes, but I had no idea. I supposed he was one of the palace children. Other than Nikre and Kahre Sarda, Myrrir's sireling, I paid no attention to them. I was only aware of Ad Leed when he became a healer. Never occurred to me to connect him to you," Eerlen said, laughing. "He's tall for a Brinarian, but—" He laughed again.

After a while, Lendir joined him. "Poor Kalal. He told me he thought you were furious at him. And he didn't know why. He'd saved Brundar, after all."

"Remind me to be particularly nice to him next time we see him."

There was another long interlude before they were fully awake. Lendir was baking flat bread over the cooking stone when Brundar woke.

Brundar acted reserved and quiet, though if Eerlen read him properly, it was more embarrassment at the argument the evening before.

Eerlen was so busy observing his sireling, he forgot himself, and when he'd eaten, he offered, "Lendir, do you want me to finish cooking so you can eat?"

It took three breaths, and the fact that Brundar had stopped, staring poleaxed, as though he'd been struck mute on the spot, before Eerlen realized what he'd said.

Brundar's mouth closed with a snap. "Well, I thought so!"

Valhalla is for Heroes

Skip

I was on the third week of my mission in Valhalla when I realized I was going to die.

And it was only partly because I'd been sent on a mission half-briefed. Though to be fair, my superiors had tried to talk me out of it.

In Valhalla, men are tall and blond and muscular, and women are tall and blond and buxom. The last one was, to my purpose, nothing, of course, but the first was enough to keep me having to calm down the caveman at the back of my brain because I was not, certainly, going to try to read the body language and whatever the social hints were in this society. Partly because an ambassador didn't get horizontal with natives. If he did, the IDS would stuff and mount his privates and display them in Justice Square. Or at least that's what I'd gathered. I'd been pure and lonely for almost three years. And I was sent to a world of stunning, strong and just a little insane men. I could manage it.

Partly because, alas, Valhalla as a world and as a society was completely, screamingly insane. Also, vital to the Star Empire and to humanity at large.

You see, the issue is that the universe in which the Star Empire subsisted was a very complex one. Okay, I might be understating things a little.

Father was—as my name should testify—enamored of Roman History. I could almost understand that. All those far-flung lands the Romans conquered, all those strange cultures. All I had to do is make them planets, star systems and alliances of worlds, and it all made sense. Almost. I mean, there were limited models of humanity and social organization back then, while we'd opened up the Pandora's box of biological experimentation and planet transformation and—

To start at the beginning, what made no sense whatsoever was the history of the late twenty-first century, with a lot of different nations, packed cheek to jowl in a planet where transportation had shrunk the distances between different cultures, at the same time that technology and wealth made the dysfunction of royal families throughout the ages available for every citizen, at least in the more wealthy countries. Truly, some of the ideas that animated the age were truly bizarre.

One of my instructors at the Academy said the twenty-first was a struggle between globalism and localism, communalism and individualism. And then he had to explain one of the ideas on Earth at that time was world government.

Some of the boneheads in the class had thought that was a good idea, but I ask you! I mean, this was some six or seven billion people—billion with a b. The fact they didn't and couldn't know precisely how many is a complex issue tied in to other dysfunctions—belonging to hundreds of cultures with different languages and histories going back thousands of years on a particular place. Who can govern all of that that closely? Or even understand it?

Sure, the Star Empire has many worlds that are under a single government. My mother's domain, for instance. But that world was a single colony, started less than twelve hundred years ago—by the colony's timing—and if we topped five hundred million people, I'd be very surprised. Not that I'd looked at stats recently, or indeed at all. That was Mother's lookout.

And in fact, though, yeah, the Star Empire is an empire on paper, commanding over many different worlds, it's more of a commonwealth with some hard and fast rules considered absolutely necessary to civilization, and the rest held very loosely indeed.

For one, "nobility" would be more properly described as "those whose ancestors set down the investment money to colonize a world...and who get to administer it and other investments." Though that was just the beginning, you could buy into the nobility later on, by, well...settling a world. Or rescuing a settled world whose stakeholders had totally messed up. Second, other than basic rules for how the worlds were governed, and the interaction between those worlds, Britannia left her constituent parts alone.

Trying to govern a world—or an empire—with a hundred different cultures and make them all follow the same rules, and— Well, it's kind of like the Nivirims and it all ends in slavery, repression and shit, while you have to take over more and more worlds into your dysfunctional tyranny just so you can plunder them and minimally feed the worlds you already have.

This wasn't available to the Earth at the time, because that they knew—they were obviously wrong—there were no polities outside Earth they could plunder to feed their one-Earth-polity, should they ever achieve that. Which they fortunately didn't. The people who wanted it just turned the entire world into "a sack stuffed full of rabid rats" instead, meaning the areas of calm and sanity were rare and far between.

So you take the Earth of the twenty-first century, and we probably shouldn't be surprised that people packed into the colony ships as soon as they became available.

...Even though the ships quickly became nicknamed "Schrodingers" because half of them just disappeared mid-translation.

Men and women by the hundreds of thousands packed into ships that had a reputation for reaching their intended destination about fifty percent of the time.

My instructors said it was because the entire period was psychotic.

I thought it was because sometimes you just have to get away. Or perhaps you want to try your really whacky idea.

My ancestors' whacky idea was perhaps not insane. They had collected a population that wanted to live in an anglophonic world, ruled—to some extent and loosely—by a constitutional monarchy which harked back to some idealized version of the culture of Great Britain—a nation on Earth, for those outside the Star Empire—somewhere between what my father judged as the Tudor age and the Victorian age.

They had then colonized ten worlds within easy translation of each other—one of which was Aeris, Mother's domain. Those who had paid for the ship and materials and the initial colonization were "noblemen," but at this point, our role was more of a pain. We were administrators who got one percent of all the profits of farming and industry.

And the royal family? Brother, multiply our headache by ten. I didn't want their job.

To these worlds, fifty newcomers had been aggregated since,

and more were protectorates.

We had a constitutional monarchy, a strong common law that protected individual freedoms—at least on paper—and a culture of exploration and alliance-making. Or at least that's what the instructors said.

Anyway, it took almost a hundred years—Earth timekeeping, because this is where things become complicated—for people to realize all those colonies that had gone to Earth orbit and entered the Bardell-Vicari-Broz gate were not only affecting a translation in space—virtually instantaneous, as a highly sophisticated AI simply relocated the mass from one point to the other—but also in time. And don't ask me how, on any of it. I never understood the physics, but they have something to do with a holographic theory of the universe, though my cousin Charysea, who is a Time engineer, said it doesn't mean it's a holograph, and also that I'm stupid because some things can only be described in math. And also shut up. So now you know everything I do about the process.

Anyway, the AI was sometimes also translating the ship in time for what appeared to be a random number of years. Or hundreds of years. Or thousands of years. Or possibly even millions, though we never found one of those, even if some ruins we found seem suggestive. It probably wasn't random, and if you want, I'll try to catch Charysea between kids and when her husband is otherwise occupied and get her to explain it to you. If you're like me, you still will think random is the best description.

I don't want to give the impression all these time-transitions were to the past. It wasn't common, but it is not unheard of, to discover a newly arrived colony, aghast and upset at the idea that they'd jumped—Earth Time—fifteen hundred years into the future. Or confused at the profusion of humanity all over the inhabitable worlds.

What might not be readily understood, at least if you didn't study history, is that for the free worlds, of which the Empire was one of the main alliances—the other being Earth's Commonwealth—the most important resource were people. Oh, habitable worlds, too. But particularly people.

You see, a lot of the strange ideas that had gone to space and been lost for thousands of years had evolved into totalitarian horrors, reaching ever outward to subjugate more and more worlds. The Quan Empire, for instance, was rumored to not even be composed of people anymore, having replaced all their wretched subjects with cyborgs: brains inhabiting specially designed machines. And the Nivirims started out with the idea that they'd all be closely bonded and equal together and—

Father said the estimated number of people in mass graves there were around a million per hundred years, and that was not counting chronic starvation and death from overwork.

So to anyone ethical or anyone who wants human freedom to survive, finding the smaller lost colonies and bringing them into the sphere of the Empire is absolutely necessary. As fast as possible. And also, they might help us out, because—

When I said our greatest resource was people... It wasn't precisely a metaphor. What we'd found is that many colonies had developed...special abilities, like that place in Proxima where they had taken gen-geniering to the next level. Or where the people themselves had evolved and changed.

What it had done to the natives of Valhalla was make them the only ones capable—granted, with the use of a powerful drug—of mind-linking the Schrodinger machines and forcing them to recognize time as a variable. Apparently, it takes a human brain to "see" time. And unlike the Qan, we don't take the brains out of the humans before attaching them to the machine.

It has made Valhalla—started as a lost and accidental colony, and therefore very inbred, besides being in a world with scarce resources—the most disputed world humans ever colonized. Both the Star Empire and the Earth Alliance have tried to lock them into exclusive contracts, which would make the rest of us subject to the other forever. Even for free humans, that's bad. But then consider what would happen if the Qan Empire captured Valhalla... Millions of cloned brains serving in machines

So we desperately want others with the same capacities, or others who can find a way around the problem with the Schrodingers. Bonus if they don't need the drug that allows the interface, but which kills most Valhallan men who do this in their midthirties.

The problem is that many colonies started out strange, and evolved weirder.

So that motto of You Can Never Know Enough is actually true. But you can know close to enough. Particularly with the help of various technologies.

It starts with linguistic nano translators. Don't ask me how

it works—I have no idea. As far as I'm concerned, they're
virus-sized computers that contain within them the entirety of
human linguistic knowledge from the time humans recorded languages—and some shrewd guesses before that—which colonize
your brain and allow you to understand and speak everything after
being exposed to it for a few minutes. But I am science-illiterate,
and when I explained it this way to an acquaintance of Father's
who was a scientist, he'd looked at me with wide open eyes, and
then laughed so hard he turned purple, and Mother pounded his
back and wanted to call the medtechs.

Whatever they are and whatever they do, it's like having a
linguistic computer between your ears that scans everything you
hear, and can assemble a linguistic model within a few minutes,
and start feeding it to your lips without your even being aware of
it, so that you answer in the language you're spoken to.

I imagine what it was like to be a diplomat in old Earth.
Or rather, I don't. A lot of them—from the rare bio that survived—seemed to go from country to country. How did they
learn all those languages so well? Or did they make egregious
mistakes? None of this was revealed in our lessons, and a lot of
things we know from the twentieth and twenty-first centuries are
fragmentary.

After the language, there are tomes and recordings, and virtual
training sessions, so you know the history and cultural touch-
points, and be trained so your body language doesn't present
weird.

You can learn enough to prevent having to run out of rooms
with people on your heels.

My first assignment was to Novo Mundo, an amazing place
which had been rediscovered after being lost for what, for them,
was about five hundred years. But honestly, they hadn't made
much of an effort to be found, and hadn't cared much about it.
They came from a place called Brazil in old Earth and had devoted
those five hundred years to developing newer and stranger foods,
and much much more interesting dances than I'd ever seen. Other
than an incident where I'd drunk some liquor distilled from algae,
which they assured me was non-alcoholic and—

The mission went well. I was only junior observer, anyway, and
I got top marks—partly because my supervisor had extricated me
very fast after the liquor incident.

The second one, and the graduating determinant was more serious. I was sent to Valhalla to persuade them not to sign onto an exclusive treaty with Earth, which would require them to send those sons possessed of the ability to communicate with the Schrodingers to Earth only.

I wondered at the time what they were doing, sending a barely minted diplomat on a provisional license—since I had to accomplish the objective to graduate—to Valhalla to secure a vital treaty.

Failure had such strong implications for the Star Empire's ability to travel at all.

And it was hard. Really hard. It took me two weeks of listening to and responding cogently to official speeches and objections; being polite when I wanted to tell them to take a hike; and eating a lot of feigleire.

I understand the translation of this from the weird native language means "mud chicken." It was neither chicken nor... Well, I guess it is a mammal of some sort, which borrows into the muds of swamps in a world where most of the solid land was either swamps or deserts, since they had a single continent, and a vast one, at that. I'm told there should not be anything particularly objectionable about the feigleire, except for looking like a hairless six-legged rabbit. In fact, there was a lot objectionable about the feigleire. As in, the Valhallians processed the meat in a manner which worlds of more civilized Scandinavian ancestry reserve for fish and which produces lutefisk.

Let's say I never want to see or smell anything similar to feigleire or lutefisk again, if I live to be a thousand. And I cursed whatever accident of parallel evolution made every alien creature so far discovered have the same DNA structure as Earth life and be compatible enough to be eaten.

So while in Valhalla, I was in danger of starving through being served feigleire until the mere smell of it made me want to vomit. I was also in danger of starving because, well, before letting us eat at all, the family that was hosting me made us sit through a recital of all their dead in Hel who were invited to partake the...ah, spirit of the feigleire we were about to eat. One of the names of that list, by the way, for the family hosting me was Rhyatt Nyheizor. Yes, the lost prince of Denarcia. Which led me to wonder whether the natives were a lot more cosmopolite and clued in than they appeared to be.

Which, to be fair, Mr. Crowe had warned me about before I went to Valhalla.

He'd met me outside the training facilities, at a little café in a backroad of New London, where mostly working people and locals ate. Over sandwiches and coffee, he said, "Look, Skip, the training videos won't tell you this, because our intelligence sucks, and we tend to take cultures at face value of what they tell us they are, but the first thing you need to be aware of is Valhalla is not barbaric."

I raised my eyebrows at him. Any culture was barbaric who was willing to sell their superfluous sons—for some reason, only men, and not all of them, had the ability to connect to the machines—to a richer culture because during the brief life they'd have after that, they would make enough money to make the mother world rich.

"Yes, I know. You think that they're sending their sons to brief if glorious indenture on other worlds is barbaric. But you're missing the culture. And that's what I have to explain to you. Valhalla is also not like other Scandinavian colonies, which were planned before they went out and many of which—including the Nivirims, by the way—were experiments in egalitarianism."

I arched my eyebrows again. I'd come to know Mr. Crowe. Liked him, even. But the thing about him is that when he was in lecture mode, and particularly if he thought training had left me without much clue, he could go on with very little interaction on my part.

He sighed. "The name of the planet should be a clue. We don't actually know how it ended up that way. We have names of the crew of the ship that got sent not just backward in time, but somehow sideways in coordinates to Valhalla. They were a mixed crew. Not even all Scandinavian in origin. The ship, by the way, was a scientific expedition, not a colonizing ship. They were lucky it was a massive scientific expedition, designed to study several worlds in a row. But you know, they were mostly eggheads from all over Europe and a bit of North America. And they seemed to be normal for twenty-first century Earth."

"Which is to say, completely insane."

"Well, yes. But part of it, or perhaps the whole of it, is that one of the crew—one of the scientists, a physicist—on the crew was obsessed with...ah... Not Vikings, but the idea of Vikings. What Vikings had become in the literature and culture of twenty-first century Earth. And not by reputable historians, more by the myth-makers. This gentleman, David Burkhead, was a neo-pagan and interested in Norse gods. But possibly what he actually did to shape the culture was bring aboard this role-playing game—"

He stopped abruptly and gave me weather eye. I knew he was sometimes wary of my background, which, no doubt, he knew as well as I did or perhaps better, since they did intelligence work on every prospective diplomat before allowing us to graduate. "Not that kind of role-playing game."

I laughed, though aware of blushing. "No. RPG. I know. Dice and rulebooks, and a lot of imagination. I had a group in the Academy."

"Ah. Weird, how that particular form of socialization has survived from the twenty-first."

I agreed it was, and he went on. "Anyway, this David Burkhead had a rulebook, which no longer exists but was still there when Valhalla was recovered. It was for a game called The Way of the One Eye, and it was, I suppose, self-conscious, campy fun for the time, because Vikings were not the historical Vikings, but the creatures of myth and legend. Horned helmets and capes, honor in combat, a short, glorious life downing flagons of liquor. And being created in the twenty-first century, it was equal opportunity for the sexes. I think some historian is attempting to recreate it, by the way, and our time would probably enjoy it as much."

He shrugged. "The thing is, crashed on the world, once their entertainment systems and mersis stopped working and power was best used for things like making sure they survived and got crops in, while they could have power, The Way of The One Eye became their main form of entertainment, and you know what they say. Literature—"

"Literature when done properly becomes culture and sometimes even religion," I said. Another of the little aphorisms we were taught. "Yes, sir."

"So Valhalla is...RPG Vikings. Or at least that's its underlying culture developed over the five thousand years they were lost. But they were discovered in the twenty-third century. And they have had intensive trade—lucrative trade, mind—with the rest of the human worlds for two hundred years. They're not primitives. Still, things remain. That thing with indenturing their sons? Well, the culture of honor and familial obligation means they'd have trouble keeping the sons from indenturing themselves. For the glory and prosperity of Valhalla and all that."

I gave him a dubious eye. He gave me a collection of syllables that sounded like, "Ogshi boshgi babalet!" and grinned. "That's their drinking oath. It means Valhalla is for heroes."

"So you're telling me the culture is very masculine and full of derring-do and sacrifice for the tribe, and that's not...barbaric."

He laughed. "No more than we are, but—" He paused. "Skip, the thing is, they present their oddity up front. They would wear horned helmets if they thought you'd buy it for one second. What they'll present to you is not exactly what they are—remember that. And I don't think there's any chance they'll sign an exclusive with Earth, by the way. By playing Earth and the Star Empire against each other, they get to make the best bargain for the sons they do send away. And, by the way, they're not nearly as poor as they seem to be. Most space benders send most of their earnings to Valhalla. Over two hundred years, that adds up. Don't go in thinking you're dealing with hicks. They know they're sending their children to early death, and they want as much honor and glory as well as wealth for their sacrifice as they can possibly get."

Which I really tried to remember.

But things were made worse by the fact that the Earth representative was there at the same time, and that we were each being hosted by one of the Twelve Houses.

I know that sounds more lunatic than it should, but remember the society was based off an RPG, okay? They didn't have a king or a parliament, but were ruled by The Twelve Houses.

The houses were noblemen—noblemen being defined as "owns a lot of land and has sufficient industry on it," so you know "rich" would also apply—who were elected to their position in ten-year chunks.

I could get into the rest of their organization and society, but honestly, it would just give you a headache. It gave me one.

The house hosting me was House Braxladen. They had twin sons, and the firstborn—a blond giant named Alexander—was the heir. I never could quite get a read on him, either, and ignoring what seemed sometimes to be clear signals kept me on edge.

His younger-by-some-minutes brother was serving as a space bender on Earth.

You'd think this inclined things towards the Earth representative, right? Well, so did he. And the house hosting him, House Askrian, also had a son on Earth. This led to a certain smug certainty for the Earth representative, while I was being kept on my toes.

But all I had to do to have the mission be considered successful was to get a contract with the Twelve Houses. It didn't have to be an exclusive contract, just one that ensured that we also would get Valhalla's sons to serve in our spaceships and Earth would not have an exclusive contract.

My attempts at discussing this with Alexander, who was my designated—well, auditor would be a translation, though I always got the feeling what it meant was "poor sap who has to put up with insane foreigner"—was diverted into pursuits that had nothing to do with it.

We rode horses to the shore, which was a feat, given the spongy ground. We watched some kind of violent wrestling, where— Never mind.

We went sailing in a ship filled with 200 people who needed instruction and help.

I helped build a wall to divert a flood that threatened their land. I was asked for opinions on how better to build a factory producing glassteel on Braxladen lands. We discussed how best to fairly compensate workers and keep them happy and productive.

We went hunting the Kalispen Boar. And if you don't know what the Kalispen Boar is, you are really, really, really fortunate and should give thanks fasting, because the creature isn't even mammal. It is an arachnid. I'm told it tastes nice, but it fights like the devil incarnate, and has the cunning of your average Earth coyote, which I hunted once, with Dad. They say the Kalispen tastes like Earth lobster. By the time they roasted the three we'd brought in, I didn't want to eat or do much of anything except go to bed, where I lay groaning and bleeding while my bruises turned interesting colors.

And all of this, by the way, made me really grateful for the training I'd had at Dad's instigation. Because otherwise, I'd have died two days in. But still, by the third week, I was sure I was going to die, and accomplish nothing.

If it hadn't been for Mr. Crowe's reassurance that Valhalla didn't want an exclusive with Earth, I'd have been sure all was lost.

And then there was a banquet and Alexander told me to attend and what to wear, which was weird because he'd never done that before, and because what to wear was "something formal and yet functional and practical to move around in."

I'd defaulted to my uniform as a diplomat, which looked kind of retro, with dark blue tight pants, boots, a white shirt and a dark blue Elizabethan doublet, but was made of fabrics that kept the body temperature right, and allowed you to move freely.

The Earth Ambassador, about thirty or a little older, smaller than I and starting to bald, which took effort in our day and age, wore something more ornate in black and gold, but I suspected with the same properties.

It soon became obvious the entirety of the Twelve Houses, male and female, was in attendance. Reading the list of invited dead took forever, but at least the food ran to large roast indeterminate beast, and I didn't care what it was so long as I didn't have to hunt it. Tasted like beef, and cannibalism was not a Valhalla custom.

And then, after the meal, while we were all full and sleepy, the Earth representative and I were handed swords. A space was cleared in front of the fireplace, and we were told to fight for it.

To my surprise, my counterpart from Earth knew swordfighting, but he hadn't been trained by dad. And he seemed to be playing by some rules I didn't even know.

I was angry, tired of Valhalla. I wanted to graduate and get back to New London. I fought like a demon.

Fortunately, they didn't require I kill him. Which is a good thing, because the diplomatic repercussions would have been amazing. I disarmed him twice, got first blood once, and the treaty was signed.

It will give a flavor of Valhalla that in the aftermath I was offered my choice of any of the daughters of the Twelve Houses for the night. I had no idea if they were for real, or if—having figured my predilections—they were winding me up.

I had no idea until I met Alexander's highly amused eyes as I made a careful speech refusing it.

So he knew. What he thought he was doing was none of my business. I'd had enough of Valhalla and Vallahallans to last me a lifetime.

I went home in triumph and ready to graduate.

I got the very strange impression that no one expected me to succeed. It was little things, like the fact that my name wasn't on the graduation list. And no one had taken care to make sure I was given the formal robes for graduation.

Which caused a bit of a scramble in the final weeks, but which I considered a mere slip-up until much, much later.

For a surprise, Mother came and cried over me at graduation, and told me she was "so proud."

And then it was off to my first assignment.

IT'S JUST A JUMP TO THE LEFT

SKIP

I knew the mission to Draksah had gone seriously wrong when I saw the slave.

One of those things written in unerasable letters on the walls of IDS buildings was Slave societies cannot join Free Humanity.

Now there was a ton of argument—as about everything else—about what "slave societies" meant, ranging from very subtle shadings on the power of a central state, to people who insisted ours was a slave society since we had a queen and nobility of birth. It probably will surprise no one that this later didn't gain much acceptance in Britannia or in the Star Empire itself.

Me? All those shadings were too subtle for me. Surely, I could see how a society with hereditary noblemen and a quiescent and obedient population would become a tyranny. Everyone could see. It had happened several times in the history of mankind. But it was not that clear-cut. At our level, where the queen and the nobility mostly existed to perform unenviable diplomatic and administrative tasks and sometimes to lead war, should it be needed, or have the power of ultimate decision in complex cases, I was fairly sure that royalty worked for freedom. On the other hand, there was the Quan empire, where eventually their sovereign and nobility would decide they no longer needed citizens of any kind.

Edge cases? Ask me. Show me the documentation. I'll know it when I see it.

What wasn't an edge case was a society with the existence of actual, for-real chattel slaves. As in, people who had no right of self-determination at any level, and could be used and abused at will, and bought and sold as things.

The Star Empire would accept no slave societies.

Not because slavery was uniquely evil, but because slavery corrupted. Once the habit of thinking of some people as things set in, coming out the other side with a free society was difficult.

And yes, I'm aware every human society was a slave society at the onset. It was often a necessity in pre-industrial societies, simply because there are jobs so difficult and so stupidly bad for you that no free human would do them willingly. And I know that almost of all those societies eventually redeemed themselves, and came out as non slave societies. But on the way there lay the terrific wars of the nineteenth and twentieth centuries, and some in the twenty-first, too, and a couple of utterly destroyed cultures, and socio-psychologists see them as related.

Note that slavery reappeared in space for the same reason it first appeared on Earth: human workers were hard to find, and sometimes had to be forced to tasks that no one wanted to do but which were required. Also, it reappeared as an extreme form of integrating two warring societies, arguably towards the more viable. As in, the loser was forced into the culture of the winner.

But that didn't make it justifiable, nor did it make the infection benign.

The Star Empire—Britannia on High—would not accept societies where some portion of the population was kept as chattel. That was the beginning and the end of it. And though some cases might need to be brought to the attention of the socio-psychologists, the case in Draksah wasn't one of those.

One entire section of our training—three months of it—was in identifying slaves when we saw them.

So, to recap for those not following along at home: my first assignment after graduation was to Draksah.

I was to be sent out alone. While it was unusual to be sent out alone on your first mission, it wasn't unheard of. The team there before me—whose names I was never given—had prepared everything to admit Draksah, a level-two monarchy, barely industrialized, in the early stages of individual rights assertion, attempting to liberalize with mixed success, into the Star Empire.

The day after my graduation, I was sent a dossier detailing several years of investigation and visits by envoys, depicting a monarchic society, fairly wealthy, which could be made modern with the use of our technology.

Look, from where I stand now? There were holes in that case

history that could have hidden entire herds of elephants. Which, at one time, I thought was why they sent a newby, fresh off training. Of course, now—

Anyway, from where I stood, the mission was a lot like Valhalla, only not as fun. Sure, Draksah didn't have feigleire, but I went almost entirely vegetarian while there, because all the meat dishes were strange. Look, I didn't think they were cannibals, but I still didn't want to eat pork in a society I wasn't sure of. And it was all pork.

However, I didn't go hungry. I was always dressing up in some very specific costume to go to banquets, or to watch some dance extravaganza.

I was told the culture was so old—ten thousand years or so since the lost ship—that there were no traces of Earth customs or culture. Because lost colonies often lose tech and therefore culture. And some deliberately set out to forget Earth.

But the entire thing felt like a down-and-dirty 1,001 Arabian Nights to me. Fewer flying carpets and bejeweled robes, more big men with dark eyes who would as easily pull a knife on you as poison your drink, and women who were covered up all but the eyes or sometimes the face and who scurried out of sight when barely glimpsed, unless they were whores or dancers. I wasn't sure there was a difference between whores and dancers, either.

Work got done around me, from food being served, to my room being cleaned, to clothing washed, refreshed and put away, but I never saw servants. Even the banquets had all the food laid out by the time we arrived. That should have tipped me off to something being off, also, and the only excuse I have for not realizing earlier is that I was green as grass and twice as stupid.

I stumbled from banquet to party, and party to another banquet, and eventually stumbled into my bed. I had early on refused the girl in my bed, and then the boy in my bed. This was per protocol, but also because when I say the boy in my bed, I'm not using it in a colloquial sense, and I never had any interest in children. Also, even had he been older, I couldn't tell to what extent being in my bed was compelled, and I never had any interest in rape by any other name. And again, even had they been adults and willing, you don't get horizontal with the natives. There were rules about getting horizontal with natives. They were complex, detailed and amounted to a big flashing sign saying, Don't.

And when the official signing ceremony was supposed to happen that would bring Draksah into the Star Empire as a probationary member and let me go home, I forgot the documents for signing. It was a special paper, not only non-decaying, but impregnated with something or other, likely nanites, same as the translator thingies that worked with my brain to make me understand any language. These were essential, because they recorded the DNA of any person who touched the papers. Which was important for the obvious legal reasons.

So I forgot them in my room.

I know, that is a freshman blunder of the type not even I as a freshman should have been able to commit. Except, of course, I did.

It's entirely possible that my father was right when he said sometimes we know things we don't know, and that our subconscious causes accidents or forgetfulness in ways that are needed to save us, while our rational brain refuses to catch the signals.

Maybe it was that, or maybe I was sick and tired of Draksah, and of feeling like I was always watched, and always in peril and that there was stuff going on just beyond my sight, even though, rationally, that made no sense.

So, I forgot the documents, and I went to my room for them.

Honestly, I don't know why they let me go unescorted, except that I turned around unexpectedly, then I got lost, and wandered off into something that might have been the women's bathing room, and it's probable whoever was watching me had some cultural taboo about entering that space.

I swore—in Valhallian, because it seemed appropriate—with "Thor's rusty hammer" and turned and got out, by another door, though I didn't realize that until I noticed the corridor was not the overly ornate space I'd come to know, but a lot simpler: stucco over stone with some patches all but bare, and just worn stone underfoot. But I knew I was on the third floor, and my room was on the fourth, and I headed for the stairs.

And stopped.

Because I saw the slave. He was young, and for a moment, I thought he was a she, given the angelic, beardless face. But the body was all he, at least as much as was visible, between the slave collar and the linen kilt. And the legs below were male, too, and the bare feet sure looked it, though both looked larger than I'd expect from a beardless youth.

I looked up from the feet to the face, the averted gaze, the lowered eyelids, the shaven head. I really didn't need the tattoo on the chest, which my implants helpfully translated as "Property of the royal house of Draksah" to know I was looking at a slave.

And I lost my mind. I mean, I was outraged on so many levels, I could barely think.

I was outraged at the massive deception of myself and presumably the previous ambassadors. I was furious at the very idea they kept slaves. I was livid at the dehumanizing quality of the getup they forced the slaves to wear.

It was quite the most appalling thing I'd ever seen, and yes, I'm aware that I'd been shown films of the Daycean massacres and forced to play through some diplomatic disasters in which I and all my friends were virtually massacred. But this was different. I was not on a simulator. And also, this wasn't—

They had lied. To the Star Empire. To envoys of the queen.

I started to march down the hallway, and then it occurred to me I was here alone, and while I had weapons, they weren't the kind that could take out an entire rogue planet. Not that I would know how to take out a whole planet.

I mean, if it came to that, I would try. I'd been trained by Dad. Diplomatically speaking, it was less than advisable. Who can you diplomat at if they're all dead?

I stood in that back staircase, breathing in through my nose and out through my mouth. I wanted to grab the slave by the arm and drag him back to the banquet room, and denounce the entire travesty of a joke of an insult, of a—

I went so far as to grab the slave's arm. He looked up, and for a moment there was something in his eyes, something deep and dark, a hint of rebellion, perhaps a warning. But my translator nanos didn't translate eyes.

I started to pull him towards the dining hall. And then—

Look, there is a reason diplomatic delegations, at their most stripped down, are at least two people. At worst, while one of them is discovering the slaves, the other can go and beam a signal to the Star Empire. A mayday. A sign that things have gone seriously sideways.

Because something was going seriously sideways. This was the sort of situation in which things went...violent and destructive.

The type of situation where I might get sent back to my people in a box. A small box. Filled with ashes. Or maybe with a single ear in it, the rest being unfortunately lost in the fracas.

I backtracked. Still dragging the slave, mostly because, do you know how hard it is to let go of someone's arm once you've grabbed it, and they're letting you drag them? Okay, I don't know, maybe the slave had become a sort of security blanket, in that I wasn't in this thing all alone because there was another human being in here with me.

Though what I expected him to do was beyond me, except serve as a meat shield. Which would make me as complicit in slavery as anyone ever.

I dragged him all the way to my room. Because in my room was the last resort of a diplomat in need: the ripcord.

Okay, it was neither rip nor cord. What it actually was was a panic button. You pushed that button when your mission had gone so horribly wrong that the next step was the ear in a box, or the box of ashes, or whatever.

Yes, I should have had it with me. Same as the contract.

When you pull the ripcord, everything stops. Whatever process was underway, whether to admit the world to the empire or simply to negotiate a truce, it stops the moment the panic button is pressed. At the same time, the ships nearest the world start heading for it to extract the ambassador, or more often, the ambassadorial team. Note that when things are that bad, they usually only retrieve the corpses. But all the same, the process must be followed.

So I marched into my room...

Where there were three other slaves. Same shaved heads, same ridiculous getups, same words on the chest, same beardless, too-pretty faces. One of them looked like a Scandinavian blond, and the other two vaguely Mediterranean.

They were doing something near my bed, and looked up in shock. I got the impression I'd interrupted them.

It didn't matter. More slaves was just more evidence.

I let go of the arm of the one slave, who, strangely, got surrounded by the others, wordlessly.

And went for the button in my wardrobe.

I'd grabbed the box that contained it, and used my thumb to open it—it was coded to my genetics—when I caught movement by the corner of my eye and turned...

Three men stood in the doorway. I registered they were Drak-salls, wearing Draksall clothing, but they had—

Blasters. They had blasters. They had Imperial armament. And they were pointing them at me. When had they gotten blasters? And how in hell had this gone so bizarrely wrong?

I did what came naturally. What had been trained into me in the Academy, what had been part of me for so many years, it might as well have been born with me.

I had forgotten the treaty. I'd forgotten the panic button. I'd forgotten just about everything, but would be more likely to go out stark naked in a place where nudity wasn't accepted, than go out unarmed. And when I saw the eyes of the men pointing the weapons at me, I knew they meant to kill me. I got my burners from their hidden holsters and fired. I cut the first and the second, the third fired, and there was a cry of alarm, and a fourth fired, too.

This is when everything got too confusing.

First, because my brain, having decided I was going to die, directed my finger to press that panic button and thereby invalidated the mission and called for help.

Second, because two of the slaves grabbed me, one per arm. They were stronger than they seemed, or perhaps they simply caught me off balance as they rushed me to the window.

And out.

The window was on the fourth floor of the palace. As they jumped with me out the window—I registered a moment of surprise: I hadn't been simply defenestrated, but they were apparently committed to this as a suicide mission—I caught a glimpse of an ornamental brick patio underneath.

I remember thinking, Third floor, so far so good. And then the stone yard beneath my window became verdant. Something Father used to say, probably from some stuffy old document, and which he used when things changed drastically and unexpectedly, ran through my mind: It's just a jump to the left and then a step to the right.

And then I hit. But not the brick, and not as hard as I should for the distance I fell. Oh, no. From the distance I should have fallen, I actually only fell about...six to eight feet.

I hit springy grass, at a moderate velocity. I remember thinking, Son of a bitch, there's grass after death.

And then I think I passed out.

THE GREEN HILLS
DEFINITELY NOT OF EARTH

SKIP

I think I passed out, because I don't remember losing consciousness, as such. It's more as though my brain decided things were too silly and turned off momentarily, only to come back on as I rolled to a sitting position on the green grass.

I became aware of myself while sitting on the grass, with four people surrounding me. They were— They didn't look— No, one of them looked like one of the slaves, but his hair was long, and he was wearing something that covered his chest, so I couldn't check for the slave tattoo. He was one of the shorter, darker ones.

He was not behaving like a slave at all, though, as he was arguing, in voluble gestures and a language composed of gutturals with two other people: a huge blond man—he also had a too-pretty face, couldn't tell if he had facial hair, nothing approaching seven feet tall, with shoulders that gave you the impression half of him could do the work of a draft horse and could be anything but male—in some kind of knee-length tunic with what looked like tights under it. The other was a shorter, paler blond of more normal proportions, on whose sex I wasn't going to pronounce, except that the not-endowed-with-breasts chest was muscular and looked masculine—look, I was confused—and who wore some kind of short tunic, pants and a blue cloak.

They were all screaming at each other like... Well, like my father's family at the only family reunion I'd attended. And what a shock that had been for the little boy raised mostly in his mother's bloodless domain.

My translator nanos were going berserk, probably because the volume and raspy tone of the language was confusing them. At least—I thought with alarm—if this language came from Earth. I mean, they looked human. But the language sounded like they were alternately growling and clearing their throats with some hard dentals in between for the fun of it.

You'd think, I thought, they were discussing whose cook was better than the other cook and— No. That was what my grandmother and aunt had argued about. I felt weirdly muzzy, like I had missed sleep? Or perhaps falling from a height had scrambled my brain? Or perhaps dying just wasn't good for you.

The words that came at me were disjointed, and sounds were spit at me randomly. The nanos were catching occasional fragments they translated—and none of them seemed to make sense.

"Bring him back."

"Danger."

"Are you?"

"Brotherhood."

A soft touch on my arm and I turned and—

So, when I was fourteen, Father came and took me from the Academy at Christmas.

Oh, my parents weren't the most horrible parents in the world. They allowed me holidays. The problem was me. I had decided to stay in the Academy for Christmas. I didn't allow myself holidays, because I wanted to finish and be commissioned. Mostly because I hated the Academy, but I didn't dare tell Father that.

And then Father had come and cajoled me out for a couple of days, during which he took me on a trip of discovery of cultural institutions in New London, which for the season were putting on magnificent displays of the historical glories of old Earth.

We traipsed through a recreation of the Tuscany of the quattrocento and stopped to admire Leonardo DaVinci's work, then Father took me to dinner, and after dinner he took me to—

Midsummer Night's Dream. I'd read Shakespeare and watched him in recording and experienced him in mersi, but I'd never watched it performed by live actors.

Whoever staged that performance had made all the elves—except Queen Titania, of course, though I suppose it would be play-period-accurate—boys on the edge of manhood. Well. About my age, then.

And whoever did the makeup gave them a sort of unearthly beauty: eyes a little too large, features a little too soft, and hair in whatever color, styled in such a way that you imagined it just grew like that, and yet accented their faces perfectly.

I believe watching that play was when I figured out I had a problem, or at least that I wasn't standard-issue, and wouldn't fall in love with some insipid Earl's daughter and breed a passel of brats.

And at that moment, sitting on that postmortem grass, confused and feeling slightly nauseated, I felt a touch on my arm, turned and—

It was one of those elves. I'd swear to it. Peaseblossom, with the green eyes and the wavy butt-long red hair, unruly, some strands falling in front of his face, the rest in a sort of bramble-arrangement around his features. And though he looked concerned, he also still looked... Well...not quite standard human. And breathtakingly beautiful.

He knelt, but in a way that made it look easy, and like it was a perfectly natural way to lower his height to mine. Like—like you see among people whose culture doesn't include chairs.

And he was looking at my arm as though there were something profoundly wrong.

I looked at my arm. And I passed out again, that time for real.

It couldn't have been the sight of blood that covered what was left of it. In case it's not obvious, I wasn't in the habit of passing out at the sight of blood. It wasn't even the realization that I was going to lose everything from slightly below the elbow down: there was nothing else to do when all that was holding half of my arm to the other half was a bit of charred bone.

I came to almost immediately, thinking that honestly, that wasn't even the problem. The problem is that I was on a primitive planet that probably couldn't get me home, and if too much time passed before regen, regen wouldn't work.

"Fuck," I said as I woke up. And realized, with perfect timing, that it had been said as a guttural two-syllable sound, which meant the nanos had found the way. And from the gasp from my right, I'd just committed a possibly unforgivable social solecism.

But on my left, I felt a touch on my wrist. I looked. My arm and hand looked perfectly intact if perhaps a little pink. Had I dreamed my arm being burned? Peaseblossom's green eyes looked full of concern, and he spoke, very slowly. He had a low voice, a well-modulated bass that sounded out of place with his soft features. I had no idea what he was saying, but he sounded as though he was gentling a scared child.

I could practically feel the nanites running like crazy in my brain, trying to make sense of the words. I can't quite explain, but my brain seemed to be trying on linguistic matrixes for size. Finnish? Bantu? The Neu Deutshe of South Elburg? The weird amalgamation of languages of Hesperius en Haute?

No. No. Something synthetic and—

It clicked suddenly. It clicked, with that weird feeling that I should have understood what I'd just heard. I knew from the simulator that this meant it had found the pattern.

"I'm sorry?" I said. "Come again?"

Peaseblossom made a sound somewhere between laugh and delight. "I said," he said. "That your arm might still get an infection, but the healing should hold. Unless the infection is bad, you should be fine."

I blinked. "Healing?"

The nano translation glitched. I swore he'd said, "Magic."

But I was sure he was crazy. Or I was crazy. Heck, I probably was crazy. "Ma-gi-c?" I said.

He smiled and nodded. "I am"—garbled—"brother of magicians, my power is third circle bend high power, so I can perform healing."

I blinked again. "Peaseblossom?" I said. "I mean...elves and fairies? Magic? Where am I?"

He looked decidedly worried. He touched the side of my head with the tip of his fingers, and there was a strange sensation, like a static shock. He frowned.

"I think it's a linguistic difficulty," the short, dark one who had been—playing?—a slave said. "The star people have—"garbled"—in their heads, and it takes time to catch up with the language they're hearing."

"But—" Peaseblossom cut his eyes at me, sideways, like I was the strange one here, then back at his companion. "What can it have to do with blooming peas?"

The other shook his head. "The—" my translator scrambled. Spell? Setting? Program? "In their heads takes time to get the right words."

I was both shocked and impressed that someone in what looked like a barbarian culture, at least from their attire, and the weapons I glimpsed—I'd caught sight of ankle-daggers on the shorter blond, the giant wore a sword and had a quiver of arrows and a bow slung over his shoulder, and I suspected the others had something along those lines—understood the process well enough.

I cleared my throat and said, "I beg your pardon. Your...friend has the right of it. I don't quite have the right words, and some of the translations seem impossible. Also, I might have a concussion from the fall." Peaseblossom shook his head almost imperceptibly, as if to deny it. I ignored it. Not getting in arguments with people who have full control of you, while you're not quite yourself, is a good idea. Or at least diplomatic training said so. "But I have no idea where I am. I don't think this is Draksah, and you are not speaking a language related to Draksall."

Peaseblossom shook his head a little, then gave a feral grin. "Oh, there's a lot of borrow words, including given names. A lot of the names. Though they have different meanings. Because the cultures have been at war so long, but no. We're not Draksall. This is the world of Elly." He looked at me, chin tilted up a little defiantly, as though he'd said something shocking and must spy my reaction to see if I would run screaming into the night.

Which I would, if I had any clue what that was supposed to mean. Elly. The word seemed familiar. There was some mention of it in literature about Draksah. Something about it being a mythical world, similar to the lost continent of Atlantis on Earth. A place that couldn't exist, which existed, nonetheless, in legend and myth, and which kept rearing its fanciful head in the culture. There were references to it being a wild land inhabited by creatures not quite human. Wild creatures. I had caught a laughing reference to there being no men on Elly, too, in a conversation during one of the interminable banquets, before it was shut down.

But while my saviors—or captors, I wasn't sure right then—were barbarians, they didn't look particularly wild. And they certainly weren't women.

Of course, this was the moment at which my translator decided to take a cue from my thoughts and start glitching on the gender.

"I am—" Peaseblossom hesitated, then shrugged. "Brundar Mahar, third circle of the brotherhood of magicians." I got the impression his introduction of himself had startled his companions. The giant made a sound like a groan, which combined annoyance and surprise. "And these are my—" Parent/father/sire scrambled through my brain. "...Eerlen Troz, and my—" Cousin/stepsister/stepbrother/half-sister all scrambled in turn. "Lendir Almar. And this is Selbur Deharn, whom I believe you met in Draksah."

"The slave!" I said. My brain was having real trouble, okay? And my mouth had mostly taken over. If this were a simulation, someone would have thrown something at me by now. "One of them."

The slave-like being's lips twisted in amusement. "Mahar? I think it's time we just tell him everything."

A HEADACHE SHAPED COLONY

SKIP

One of those sayings in the IDS that used to strike me as funny was, Expect the unexpected. Like most of the sayings they drilled into us, it was wrong. It should be, Expect the insane and unbelievable.

So Peaseblossom—Brundar Mahar—had talked, with interjections from everyone. And when I looked completely lost, he explained again. First, they explained that they were a different world from Draksah. Not even in the same solar system. They actually couldn't tell me where they were in relation to Draksah in space, because their way to get to Draksah and back was the way they'd used to bring me here. However that was. Falling out of a world and into another seemed like a very silly way of traveling. Should only work in fever dreams.

Draksah was the easiest world for them to get to through... Whatever it was they'd done. The "closest" world to theirs, that way. I didn't understand, but I could accept.

Then there had been real slaves and two operatives from Elly, passing as slaves. The other spy? Operative? Informant? Had taken the real slaves who had somehow jumped with us elsewhere to get them help. They were generational slaves and freedom would be hard. Selbur, the dark-haired one, had stayed behind to help these three explain

And again. Around the third iteration, I understood why my translator was gagging. "Both?" I said. "You are both? Male and female? Hermaphrodites?"

There was a round of resolute nods, though later I would realize they hadn't got the last word. But they'd understood enough.

I thought it made perfect sense, of the too-pretty features that

translated in the back of my mind as "very young," because beardless and...other things.

But then they started interjecting details that they thought
completely described their society and its strange arrangements.
Look, I didn't understand anything, okay? I was like someone who
dips a toe at the ocean's edge and declares he knows the ocean.
But I'd understood enough to baffle me.

"So your lineage is through your parent? Your womb-parent?"

The giant nodded. "How else?"

"Right, then. And your sire, is just...your sire. It's not the same
relationship."

He shrugged. "There are exceptions, but yes."

"And cross siblings are children of the same parents, but reverse
womb-parent and sire. And you and Brundar Mahar are cross
siblings?"

For some reason, the giant looked at the other one, not the slave
and not Peaseblossom, and blushed a florid red, complete with
an embarrassed laugh. "Thank the Maker, no. Half-siblings. His
parent was my sire. That is all."

The shorter blond, Eerlen Troz, laughed and blushed, too.
Peaseblossom rolled his eyes.

By then, I was rubbing the center of my forehead with two
fingers, like when I was trying to solve a difficult math problem
back in the Academy.

Look, it's not that many of the crazy people who set out into
the unknown in spaceships they weren't exactly sure of being
able to aim properly—which was good, because they really didn't
know how to aim them—hadn't had themselves or their children
modified. There were people who tried to make themselves and
their children telepathic, and achieved limited success; there
were those who made their children strong; those who made
themselves and their descendants agile, or cold-resistant, and
let's hold a moment of silence for those who tried to make their
children unselfish and communal-minded.

There were two rules, however, that always held: whatever the
ancestors thought the modification would do, it was inevitably
wrong, and the wildest attempts didn't survive.

So, hermaphroditic human, breeding true who knew how long...
The tips of my fingers rubbed a circle in the middle of my forehead. It shouldn't be possible. "How long? How long have you

been stranded here?"

They were baffled. They looked at each other like I personally had lost my mind. They exchanged a couple of words, too fast and low for me to get. Then Peaseblossom, who, though he wasn't the oldest, or certainly the largest, seemed to have some sort of authority, looked back at me. "We have always been here. All other humans, the Draksalls, even the star people, are descended from us. They're sports, where things went wrong and they reverted to male and female like animals."

I groaned deep in my throat, and then realized that I was actually having a nightmare. I'd probably got really cut up while hunting the Kalispen boar in Valhalla, and was lying in bed, delirious, dreaming all of this. Or perhaps I had never actually come out of the regen after my father's death. I was floating in the tank, at seventeen, and everything else was a dream. A wild one.

Because I ask you: is this sense? The world I was sent to turned out to be playing a double-cross. And now, now, I'd run into the oldest chestnut of a newly rediscovered population: the People Of The Land fallacy.

If I had been here in the normal way, with a support group for the first contact, and support personnel and, well, the normal expedition to make a first contact—not that they'd have sent someone with so little experience—we'd have produced proof that Earth came first, and explained about the Schrodingers, and—

And that wasn't going to happen. And the People of the Land was not something that I was going to dispel all by myself, little Skip Hayden, with nothing to back it up. So I asked the next logical question. "How long do you have history, recorded or...or legends?"

This time, the argument was longer. Apparently there was the Mahar dynasty, the Ad Leed Dynasty, the time before settling and the occupation and before that, the great unknown, but palaces had been built and...

"Recorded," said Eerlen, who was Mahar's paren— No, sire. "Recorded history goes back four thousand years. At least—" His hand clutched in what seemed like a reflexive gesture. "At least in the ruby and the other instruments, we have at least four thousand years of records. Since Amissar Mahar. And the time of the occupation before that was five hundred years. And before that, the time of the ten lines. We don't know how long that was, though. We know the palaces, and some structures in some of the line shelters, date from that time or before, and they're... We have nothing like it, so it must be longer."

So the poor bastards had been lost for at least five thousand years. Not the longest. The longest recovered colony had been in the world fifty thousand years, and it had become very strange indeed. But having acquired a form of science, they could be convinced of what had happened, and had, in fact, integrated completely as allies of Earth. But five thousand years was long enough for any real memory of Earth to be lost.

My nanos—now that the relationships had fallen in place—let me know their language was definitely synthetic and weird. How weird? Well, humans had no gender. There was no way to refer to a male or female human. Those pronouns existed only for animals.

They'd been dropped in a world, with no contact with civilization. Their language itself was something that held no continuity to the past, and if I was—and I was—familiar with the other variants of "new start" colonies where they had nothing to do with the past, on purpose, they probably were given no history, not even literature.

A colony this modified spoke of extensively educated founders with strong willpower. If they'd been well-provisioned, they might have been able to hold onto and create a parallel human civilization. In theory. Few colonies do, even well-provisioned ones, unless they never go beyond contact with the main trunk of humanity.

What we'd found is that, for the lost ones, in the shock of a new world, even non-modified colonies returned to barbarism in a few hundred years. For these people, under the impact of completely new ways of relating, and no history or tradition or narrative to guide them, it would be the equivalent of hitting the culture with a hammer for the sheer pleasure of watching it splinter.

My guess would be they'd gone back to barbarism in...probably two or three generations.

I self-consciously forced myself to draw my fingers away from the middle of my forehead, before they poked through and massaged my brain.

Which was good, because these lost souls were giving me their history and present predicament.

They had been free and wild, living off the land as nomads. The only recognized bond was between a parent and his minor children, and the bond ended when the children reached menarche. After which, the parent only usually cared about the eldest, the line-bearer, and even then, it struck me as a loose relationship.

So, revise. Their social structure had probably lasted a generation. I would have to figure out how this extreme individualism set in. Humans were, after all, social apes. Even these poor, lost children of humanity.

That time of happy wanderings, also known as the time of the ten lines, as ten central lines had held the knowledge and the magic—the magic thing was driving me insane, because it made no sense—had lasted for an indefinite length before their great enemies, the Draksalls, had opened a portal—

My brain rebelled, and I told it to shut up. I'd seen a portal open, after all. I'd tumbled from a tower in Draksah onto green verdant prairie. It wasn't possible, but it had happened, which meant it was possible. Right. Like magic, I'd file it for now, till I had time to investigate.

Their great enemy the Draksalls had opened portals into Erradi, where the shielding—protection?—was weak, and from there they had conquered the land, enslaved the inhabitants of Elly, and kept them in durance vile for five hundred years.

So stipulated, although barbarian cultures weren't all that good at the counting thing, so it might be five hundred or, you know, five thousand. Or twenty thousand. Probably not fifty, because there would be living memory of the conquest. On the other hand, with sufficient killing and trauma, who knows?

And then Missa Mahar—

"Uh?"

Amissar Mahar—familiarly called Missa, "My line ancestor," said Peaseblossom with no small amount of pride—born a Draksall slave, blah blah, insert culture hero, led slaves from Draksah back to Elly, fortified the shields in Erradi and the shields all over the world, so they held for a hundred years—see caveat about counting—organized the defense, and created the brotherhood of magicians.

Okay, so they didn't think he'd created the world from a mudball, invented language, domesticated horses or discovered how to fish, so overall, he was a moderately amazing culture hero. And, I guessed, an amalgamation of at least ten people.

Because if one single person, on his own, over a short life—dead by his own hand at forty-eight, according to Peaseblossom—had turned a culture of fractured and detached nomads, with no concept of social links, into at least a semi-functional society that could be organized for defense, he was the culture hero of humanity itself, a demi-god capable of wonders.

Then I thought of the magic and the portals, and thought maybe he was.

Anyway, since then, they'd had kings, and done a lot of things that had brought them close to human pattern. They had families, including marriages of sorts, though if I understood correctly, groups of three weren't uncommon. Not normal, but not uncommon. Also, you could marry someone who didn't marry you back. And some nomads still thought marrying—swearing to—anyone and being faithful was shameful. Oh, they mostly did it, they just didn't talk about it. But they had couples or trios of people who raised children. And while there were still nomads—most of them were in clans, which was an improvement, because the head of clan was an arbiter which was better than endless feuds, and because the clan cared for the children, if there was no one else—there were cities, and villages, and farmers, crafters and normal occupations.

They had kings, which made a certain sense, since they had patterned themselves on Draksah, I thought. Then I paused over the frequent mentions of the Mahar dynasty. If Peaseblossom was a king—prince?—he was the most casual I'd ever seen. Perhaps the concept should be chieftain.

All of which brought us to the present moment, with Peaseblossom's parent dead, someone trying to kill Peaseblossom—

"Please? What do I have to do with flowering peas?"

Which is when I realized I'd called him that and blushed. "It's a cultural reference."

He widened his eyes. "To peas? Do I look like a vegetable?"

Well, no. He looked like an angel in a renaissance painting on old Earth. "I... It's the name of someone in a work... In a play..." I had a feeling the word I'd said was illusion, which was odd. "You remind me of him."

He squeezed his eyebrows together and nodded hesitantly.

He continued, telling me they were running around the world, kind of hiding, though not disappearing completely so they couldn't be replaced, which they couldn't be, anyway, since Pe—Mahar's sire was the archmagician, whatever that meant.

My fingers were massaging my forehead again.

"And so you kidnapped me?" I asked.

The not-slave, Selbur Deharn, shook his head violently. "Rescued."

Apparently, the plan hadn't been to bring me. They knew there was some form of double-cross happening, and the Draksall were trying to kill me, but the people from Elly thought they could warn me. And then—

And then all hell had broken lose.

"Only tell me," I said. "Do they really have slaves?" Because if I had pulled the ripcord over nothing—

But no. They had shot at me, so something was going on.

"Oh, yes. Mostly Ellyan slaves. Though people from other conquered worlds, too. They just prefer us as slavers. I am not one, though. I just...play one, having established an identity as one, so I can—"

"Spy," I said. "Intelligence. And I'm grateful. You saved my life."

"Oh. It is nothing. Brundar organized it."

For some reason, this caused raised eyebrows between the giant and Brundar's sire. I filed it away.

"My question is," I said. "What do you want from me?"

Struck by Lightning

Eerlen

The mission had either gone amazingly well or disastrously wrong. There really was no way to tell.

Or at least there was no way that Eerlen could tell.

He sat at the outskirts of the group, watching the children—he must be getting old, all of them read like children, even occasionally Lendir—tumble over each other to explain the situation to the man from the stars.

Though Lendir wasn't that voluble. He looked a little dubious, casting looks at Eerlen as though hoping for his support and not sure of this venture.

The man himself had been a surprise. While he was definitely male, or at least had facial hair, and felt male, like male Draksalls, he was far better-looking. On a scale of terrible to the most beautiful Lirridarian, he looked like a reasonably attractive Erradian. At least if he weren't wearing a strange haircut and in outlandish clothes and if he lost the facial hair. And he was young. How young was he?

But they hadn't meant to bring him to Elly. And now he was here—

"Do you mean you're completely powerless and unable to contact your people?" Eerlen asked.

The poor creature looked harassed. He rubbed the middle of his forehead, where he was fast developing a bruised-looking circle. "Not precisely. I pulled the ripcord; that is, I gave the alarm. It should have sent word to my people. They should come looking for me. And the deal with the Draksalls is definitely off."

Eerlen felt as if a big weight had been lifted off his chest. At least that part was good. Of course, now they had a person from another world with them. And they would have to keep him safe.

As though their lives weren't complex enough.

Speaking of complex enough, had Brundar allowed Deharn to call him by his first name? And did that mean they were now lovers? Well, Brundar was not underage, Selbur himself seemed— Well, he himself was a decent eighth circle, but his parent— Not that he'd hold the child to blame for his parent. Still the whole thing was a complication that Eerlen would happily forego.

"Deharn," he said, politely, keeping in mind this person might very well succeed him as sworn of the king of Elly. "We need to go. I think he's in some danger, and needs to disappear, same as ourselves. Not be easily found."

Deharn stood and bowed, in acknowledgement of the arch-magician's orders, then went on tiptoes to whisper something in Brundar's ear that made Brundar smile.

"I will pass word to the second circles," Eerlen said, pretending not to see. "That they must watch for strangers in the world, as they might be looking for our guest."

Brundar smiled. "Good idea." And turned to the stranger. "Can you walk? I think you'll be safer with us."

The person from the stars stood on unsteady legs, and shook himself, as though to wake up. "I'll be fine," he said.

"You lost some blood," Brundar explained, his professional third circle magician voice in place. "And you might develop an infection."

"No infection. The nanos see to that."

Nanos was an alien word, even though the stranger had started talking perfect Ellyan with an overlay of cultured accent much like Brundar's after a few minutes with them. Deharn had explained and Eerlen had no idea what it meant, but he'd assume it was some kind of spell or magic.

"Very well," he said, trying to act the powerful, assured archmagician, and setting forward while Brundar helped the stranger.

It lasted to the portal, and across a snow-blowing expanse into the Troz shelter he'd selected for the night and perhaps the next few days. Selected it, because, though it was a dead zone, it was a relatively small and safe shelter, where even a stranger couldn't get in trouble.

When they got in, the stranger was shivering, because his clothes were inadequate for snow, and he was wearing sandals.

Eerlen found him a tunic, home-pants and slippers, and Brundar showed him to the bathing pool, which was fortunately heated in this shelter.

When Eerlen returned to the vast main room, from which rooms and bathing room turned as in a spoke, Lendir was laying logs in the fireplace with force, as though they'd personally offended him.

"Brund can't be serious about Selbur."

Eerlen raised his eyebrow at Almar. "Dir, love, he's of age."

There was a hiss, which amused Eerlen, since Lendir had never acted so much the older sibling. "Selbur's line is a new line. And Selbur means Lightening. Which kind of parent would—"

"We know what kind of parent," Eerlen said. "His parent is Sryt Deharn, but only because he changed his line name from Vornit, after he ran away from his parent's farm."

Lendir stared At Eerlen. "Vornit? Nomad Vornit? The one we warn the young magicians about?"

"The very same. Because his favorite trick is to have a child and then keep the sire paying him to avoid abuse of the child."

"And Selbur?"

"Sireling of his first victim, Tyrim Calenir, who I understand did a good amount of raising Selbur, who..." Eerlen forced himself to speak dispassionately. What he felt about the child was irrational and he knew that. He'd be fair. "Who, as far as I know, is unexceptionable and... I've never heard ill of him, not even the normal trouble that eight circles get into."

Lendir pursed his lips. He finally said in a waspish tone, "Well, nomad is already a problem, and it certainly isn't one of the ten lines. Or even a prominent clan. Or any clan."

Eerlen never knew quite how he found himself leaning against the wall of the cave, nearest the fire, laughing so hard he had trouble breathing. And he only realized it was at all abnormal when he found Almar's hands on his shoulders, and Lendir's very concerned face looming over him. "Len? Len! Are you well?"

"Yes," Eerlen managed to gasp out. Followed by, "No." Followed by, "I don't know." He looked up and saw Lendir's very puzzled gaze, and a hint of panic to the tautness of Lendir's features, and wanted to laugh even harder, but managed to rein it in, gasping, "And that's a truly revolting nickname. You're younger than I!"

"I'm not calling you child! I'm calling you Len."

"Which means the same in naming language," Eerlen said, and

laughed till he choked. There were tears down his face and he
wiped at them. It came to him that it was the first time he'd
laughed like this since Myrrir had died, and that he'd laughed like
this when Myrrir was being... Stoically absurd, such as when he
insisted that something completely bizarre like the arrangement
of his game pieces in a drawer must be done before he could
rest; or that he must design the plantings in the gardens after a
full day of healing the wounded at the front and fighting back
through a breakthrough. Or of course when he, the king of the
settled people of Elly, heir to twenty generations of kings, became
as snobbish as the wildest nomad about nomad pedigrees, as Dir
had just done.

Eerlen hiccupped, and drew shaky breath, and heard, "Here,
drink."

He realized Lendir offering him a cup of water. He took it more
to have something to do with his hands than because he was
thirsty, but sipped at it as another hiccup escaped.

He looked up at Lendir, who looked weirdly tentative. Something Dir's size shouldn't be tentative. "Now," Lendir said gently.
His hand pulled Eerlen's disarranged hair back. Lendir, giant that
he was, had proven the gentlest, sweetest of lovers. "Do you care
to explain to me what's so funny?"

"You."

Lendir's eyes flinched. He looked as though he'd been slapped.

Eerlen advanced a hand, blindly, and laid it on his lover's cheek.
"Not like that. Please. No insult meant. You reminded me of Myrrir
when he became more nomad than the nomads. Next, you'll tell
me only a descendant of the ten lines is suitable for Brundar."

"Oh," Almar said. "Well, it would be—" He crossed his arms and
sighed. "I suppose it is none of my business."

"It is your business, at that," Eerlen said, sipping again from the
cold water. Ice melt spring in the cave. "You want Brundar to be
happy and well. So do I. But it doesn't give us the right to choose
how he's happy. That's his lookout, and his decision."

Lendir inclined his head. He went back to the fireplace, this one
a huge thing of well-laid stones, beneath a massive chimney in the
middle of the room. One of the reasons Eerlen had chosen this
shelter is that he knew the smoke was channeled, through a series
of natural tunnels, to end up some miles from here, because the
cave was a "distress cave" used when enemies—either Draksalls

or feuding Ellyans—might be looking for Troz blood.

Lendir looked in the long-term storage at the edge of the fire/and/eating area, which was delineated by a series of low benches. The storage was a large compartment on the ground, with a wood lid, and it contained food that someone else using the shelter—probably Eerlen himself, on one of his occasional visits, but possibly one of the distant cousins to whom he'd given rights of usage long ago – had in excess and left behind. The storage had a stasis-spell on it, so nothing actually went bad, since technically time didn't pass inside the compartment. It was one of those spells credited to Missa Mahar. Might even be true. The Draksalls had nothing like.

"There is some strange stuff in here," Lendir said.

He pulled his hands out and sat down. He looked up at Eerlen, his eyes very wide, his cheeks flushed. Like a child daring the unwise. "Eerlen, love? Would you swear to me?"

Eerlen's breath caught. They'd been lovers now for three months. He blinked, as he suddenly realized he couldn't imagine life without Dir. He wasn't Myrrir, but he was... Eerlen loved him as dearly. Lendir had become...half of him. It seemed...odd. To love like that twice.

Eerlen came to kneel beside him. "Depends. Is this a one-way swearing?"

Lendir shook his head. "No. You'd have to accept mine."

"Well..." Eerlen sighed. "You know I'm half-Draksall."

He got a darkling look. "What the rotten ice does that have to do with anything? If we can bed each other, we can swear. If I objected to who you are, I'd not have bedded you." He sighed. "I wouldn't love you."

"I only gave Myrrir two children. And he gave me seventeen that died before or shortly after birth."

"Oh, that. I have half of my sire's share of Draksall and none from my parent. Though there is some Lirridarian, and rumors of a Brinarian or three."

Eerlen put his hand on his chest. "Brinarian? Heavens. How defiling for the Troz line, one of the ten lines."

Lendir laughed aloud. "Idiot. You'll swear, if I swear?"

"Yes." It occurred to Eerlen his proposals were the strangest. Myrrir had suggested swearing when Eerlen was just recovering from his first stillbirth and almost dead from the ensuing infection. Myrrir had said he realized Eerlen had become essential to Myrrir's happiness when he came close to losing Eerlen to death.

Now he was being wooed in the cooking space of an ice cave. But in a way, he and Lendir were intensely practical, people who cooked and hunted. People who did the needful, whatever that was. So why not? "Witnesses?"

"Do we need them? We're both magicians. The binding will hold and show."

"True. Belts? I mean, I have one…"

Lendir shrugged. "I've heard of people swearing with blades of grass, or bits of ribbon."

Eerlen laughed. "Well, at least I have a belt. I suppose you do, too. Something. A belt of some kind. Doesn't have to be fancy. I'm a nomad. I believe my parents' swearing belts were strips of hide. Tonight?"

Lendir nodded. "After our guest and Brund retire." He turned seamlessly to look in the stasis compartment. "What on the Maker's Tits is this? Sausages?"

Eerlen came and looked over Lendir's shoulder. He remembered. "I laid it in on a visit about a month before Myrrir's death. He was shield-holding, and I came— I like to check on shelters and make sure—" He wasn't about to admit he and Myrrir had had one of their rare but titanic arguments. Eerlen had birthed a child born dead not a month before, and Myrrir thought Eerlen should take a contraceptive shield because he was going to kill himself and still not give his line a descendant. And why not let Eerlen's adopted child, Myrrir's adopted sireling, Nikre, take the Troz name and make Nikre Eerlen's line child?

And Eerlen said that it wasn't Myrrir's line. And Myrrir had said it cursed well might be, as they'd been sworn for decades and he was king and should have some say in whether his sworn killed himself.

The insult, claiming power over the Troz line, would be enough for Eerlen to challenge anyone else to a duel, to cover the offense in blood. But Eerlen loved Myrrir. He didn't want to kill Myrrir. He'd go a long way to protect Myrrir from that. And it wasn't soppy cowardice, dishonorable to Eerlen's line. Myrrir was king. Killing Myrrir would throw the world into turmoil.

So Eerlen didn't reach for his knives, bit his tongue and then answered back that if Myrrir didn't want to get Eerlen with child, he was welcome to stop putting in Eerlen. After that, they'd both descended to gutter language and ripped at each other like mad people, using their love and their intimate knowledge of the other to forge lances of ice to carve the other's heart.

Myrrir had gone to his shield holding duty—though Eerlen very much hoped he wouldn't need to do healing. Not in that frame of mind, and Eerlen would be boiled in oil if he waited meekly in the royal bed for the king's return. So he'd come here. In retrospect, it seemed idiotic.

When Eerlen had woken, he'd gone back to find Myrrir awake in Eerlen's bed, in the small room, his face marked with tears, his eyes haunted. Words of contrition poured from the king's lips, interrupted by Eerlen's own.

They'd made up and been themselves again, but if Eerlen had known Myrrir would die so soon, he'd never have given up those hours to anger, bitterness and being alone.

So many days and nights wasted. And now it seemed like a long-ago life, with another Eerlen. He missed Myrrir, sometimes. Thought of something he wanted to tell him. Or imagined him laughing at something.

But it no longer hurt every wakening hour, every night before sleep. He'd always mourn Myrrir, but he didn't live in sorrow. Accounting for the mad flight, the exile on the ice, he was...happy. His life with Lendir was one of quite understanding and quiet contentment. They belonged.

From the calculated look that Lendir gave him, Eerlen thought he'd caught something of the hesitation, but Lendir smiled back over his shoulder, kissed the tip of Eerlen's nose playfully and said, "Any idea if this is something to serve a distinguished ambassador of the Star People?"

Eerlen chuckled. "Likely not. Maker only knows what distinguished ambassadors eat. I think the sausages are venison. I bought them in Verkrat, and meant to have them for dinner, but wasn't hungry. They won't hurt us." He knelt besides the compartment, next to Lendir, and dipped his hands into the storage. It felt very odd and strangely soft, as if the entire area were filled with down, as stasis always felt. "Ah, and there are onions," he said, pulling them out. "And potatoes."

Lendir gave him a feral grin. " And probably flour, because I've yet to see a Troz shelter without flour."

"We do like bread."

"I've noticed. It will be a feast fit for kings. Or at least one king, and he's not picky."

"Come, Lendir. Brundar did a healing. Major healing. And I think he's growing again, is what I think."

"Hopefully not. Seeing eye to eye with Brund would be disturbing."

"Why would it be disturbing?" Brundar's voice, curious, coming from the edge of the cave.

"Because my height is the only thing that makes you respect me," Lendir answered.

Brundar raised his eyebrows and waggled his hand back and forth, indicating the respect was dubious. He dropped onto a bench. "Oof. I got him taken care of. I gave him clothes to put on, and he's in the pool. I gave him his privacy."

Eerlen wanted to make a comment about how Brundar talked as if that took effort, possibly because he was curious about the stranger, but he didn't. He also swore the name Selbur Deharn would not cross his lips. Not unless it was legitimate brotherhood business. Instead, he took the onions and potatoes and started chopping them over a smooth board he kept for the purpose. Lendir was heating up a pan on the fire, presumably for the sausages.

"Is there anything to eat right now?" Brundar asked. "I'm starving." The last word had a tragic and unavailing tone, as though he were confessing to a fatal condition.

Lendir said something that might be "greedy gut." Reaching into the stasis chamber for the sausages, he grabbed a small cloth bag from his belt pouch with his other hand and threw it at Brund, who plucked it out of the air.

"Ooh. Walnut-honey balls."

"And if you eat too many of them and don't want supper, you leave more sausage for us," Lendir said.

Brund made scoffing sounds. Lendir leaned over to Eerlen and whispered, "Some swearing feast. He'll eat everything and we'll starve."

Eerlen shook his head, then whispered back a line from Missa's Confession. "I'd starve on ice rather than lose you."

"Poetic," Lendir said appreciatively.

"Can you two stop whispering together?" Brundar ask. "It's embarrassing." And then, without stopping, "Do you think he's that different?" Brundar asked. "The Ambassador, I mean? Or just like male Draksalls? And what do you think his world is like? I hear they have weapons that can destroy entire worlds."

"They do," the stranger's voice came, emerging from the bathing chamber. "But it's rarely done. It's generally considered bad manners."

Eerlen startled and straightened. The stranger had changed into what they'd given him: a suit of pants and tunic made of thick wool, and clutched a fur cloak about himself. He'd probably finger-combed his blond hair—Eerlen realized with a pang they'd not given him a comb—and since facial hair wasn't visible, he looked startlingly Erradian. Not bad-looking, for an Erradian, at that. If they could make his hair grow faster, a normal healer spell, and another minor spell—used by those with too much Erradian blood—to stop his facial hair growing, he'd look wholly Erradian. Might be useful for hiding him.

"Welcome," Eerlen said, and making a shrewd guess as to status. "Milord. We never asked your name."

FIRESIDE

SKIP

I must have been in shock, having been caught out in horrible, blowing cold, suddenly and, to my body, inexplicably, though I assumed it was through the same sort of portal that I'd experienced before.

I must have been in shock, because what I remember is a disconnected series of images, as though they happened to someone else.

Peaseblossom hurrying me into a cave, then through the cave to a side chamber which was markedly both moister and warmer. He'd disappeared for moments, then there was the image of his coming back with towels and clothes.

He'd more or less thrown me onto a built-in bench and removed my sandals. I think I stopped him just short of removing my pants, by putting my hands over his and saying, "I can manage" amid a musical noise of my teeth, beating like castanets.

"Good," he'd said. "The water in the pool is warm, almost hot." And then he'd left. But he must have been somewhere, listening, because as I managed to divest myself of my shirt, pants and underwear, and splash into the pool, he looked around the side of the door. "Oh, good. You made it. Do you want me to stay so you don't fall asleep?"

I must have given him the bleary eye, because he gave me the most faux innocent "shucks, I didn't mean nothing" look I've ever seen. Not that I thought he was interested in me per se, just curious about the stranger in their midst. Which I supposed was normal. I couldn't judge ages at all, but he was a teen, I thought. Or maybe a little older. Maybe as much as my age, but it was still normal if you weren't as cosmopolite as people raised in New London. "I will manage," I said, my voice much firmer and closer to normal.

I did manage. There was a bench built into the pool, which allowed me to sit, with water to my shoulders, and eventually I got warm enough to look around. There was a series of clay jars on the edge of the pool. Feeling the contents, I decided they were soap and probably shampoo, because the second was more liquid, and since I was wet—and probably sweaty from earlier adventures—I used them. I had a moment of panic, because after all, the stuff in the second jar might have been hair remover. But my hair stayed in place. Among the things they'd given me was a blade in a sheath. It was sharp but cheap. I suspected it was as close to disposable as the world had. I could take a hint. I'd learned to shave with a dagger. Believe it or not, it was part of the training for diplomatic personnel. But I'd learned to do it while hunting with Father on Earth. Doing it without a mirror made it harder, so even I was surprised when I didn't cut myself.

Eventually, I stepped out of the pool, dried myself, dressed in clothes that strangely fit me just right—though I had some trouble negotiating the full ankle-length linen underwear, something like trousers, which tied around the waist. I'd much later find out they were specific to Erradi, the region we were now in—and ventured out onto the cave.

To find Peaseblossom contemplating a bit of genocide. Or perhaps not, since when I joked about it, he looked over his shoulder with a grin. "I just don't want it used on us."

I inclined my head. I found I didn't want it used on them, either. These refugees from sanity were growing on me, like fungus, I suppose, and I didn't want them dead. They were...people. And this was obviously an informal family group.

I didn't know what exactly my arrival had interrupted between the two older ones, but I had a feeling I'd definitely interrupted something. They were still polite, polite enough to give some of my colleagues lessons, but there was a tension and looks between them. As though they wished they were alone. Sometimes by the edge of my eye, I caught between them a straying of fingers, hands that touched too long. This made me curious, because surely they knew each other, and if there was a relationship...

Eerlen, the shorter blond with the air of authority, asked my name, and I bowed lightly before announcing, "My name is Publius Cornelius Scipio Africanus Kayel Hayden, and I am Viscount

Webson, and a first-year ambassador from Britannia on High. At your service."

I didn't know what the translation had made of Viscount, but Eerlen Troz wrinkled his nose, in thought. "Viscount. Is that like...governor? Do you govern a territory?"

"Of sorts," I said. "It's actually a world, but sparsely settled. Though my mother...er...parent rules right now."

"I see," Troz said. "But you are the heir?"

"Only child."

"Like Brundar," he said. He nodded. "I was right to call you Lord, then."

"Honorific of those who govern?"

He shrugged. "Yes. And elders of clans. Leaders of merchant lines. And of course, all magicians."

Of course, I thought. I was going to have to track down this magicians thing.

"You, however," Troz said with a heartfelt sigh. "Are probably Lord of the Land."

I laughed. It was impossible not to. He sounded so despondent. "Yes," I said. "I apologize."

He looked up with a little smile, all polite, and said, "Apology accepted," but his eyes danced. "As offensive as it is to a nomad such as I, I know Lords of the Land exist."

I thought it was interesting. He was dignified and gave an air of being in charge, but there was humor there. "If it mitigates the offense, I often find it a great burden."

Peaseblossom had gone solemn. "Like being king," he said mournfully.

"Possibly not as great," I corrected, though still sure that king here meant "chieftain." He looked...young and impish. Part of it would be the hairlessness, but the other part was that there was something playful and wild about him, as though he'd rather be running for the pleasure of it, or perhaps playing some sport. He gave me a dubious look in reply, as though he suspected me of sarcasm. I hastened. "I mean it. I'm an ambassador. We never joke."

This startled a chuckle out of the smaller blond, but he smoothed his features almost instantly and said quickly, "We have no idea if you eat what we have? Venison sausages, potatoes and onions?"

"And hasty bread," the giant said. He was stirring something in a bowl while minding the sausages.

"Sounds wonderful," I said.

Brundar raised his eyebrows at me, as though confused.

"As long as it's not something you've buried in lime and dried in the sun, I'll be glad to eat it," I said.

Brundar made a face, then shook his head. "You eat meat? My people...the spies in Draksall said—"

"Oh. There... I don't eat pork in strange environments." To Brundar's puzzled look, I gave him a sickly smile. "Look, I know it sounds stupid. The Draksalls aren't primitive, but I sensed something wrong, and pork and human are indistinguishable when cooked."

I immediately felt bad for mentioning cannibalism before a meal. Brundar flinched. The giant made a strange sound. But his companion sighed, looking up from chopping what looked like an endless amount of potatoes and onions. "Your instincts are good," he said, calmly. "They aren't precisely cannibals. They don't consider us human."

I think I turned green, because Brundar put his hand on my arm. "It's all right... It's not everything they eat. It's a rare and expensive delicacy. They do eat a lot of pork, too."

"No. I'm just very glad I stuck to vegetables and fruit." I gave him another sickly smile.

"What do we call you?" he asked. "Hayden, or?"

"Friends call me Skip."

They all looked horrified. I'd obviously blundered full feet into something. "No?"

"Well..." Eerlen looked confused. "We're not...related or...or intimate."

Ah. A formal society. I didn't know what "intimate" was, but I wouldn't use first names till I knew it. "Very well. My call title is Webson. And what should I call you?" Which, of course, I should have asked upfront, instead of getting used to thinking of them by their first names, which would mean I'd slip up and likely end up giving mortal offense sooner than later.

Eerlen touched his chest. "I am Troz." He pointed at the giant. "He is Almar." He looked at Peaseblossom and sighed. "Technically, he should be Highest Majesty or Milord, but while away from the throne and hiding, it's easier to call him Mahar."

Mahar looked at me, teasing laughter in his expression. "I don't know," he said. "Peaseblossom might be more stealthy."

"Your Majesty Peaseblossom it is," I said, wondering if I was pushing it too far, but not sure how to respond else. I really didn't want to experience the equivalent of being chased out of a virtual mission by people intent on killing me.

He grinned and blushed and shrugged. "It might be more stealthy than my line name," he said. And with a hasty look at the shorter blond. "Honestly."

Swearing Blind

Skip

The meal stays in my mind as one of the best I ever ate. The sausages were obviously venison, lightly spiced and seasoned with garlic. They beat fegliari all over. And probably Kalispen boar, too.

Almar—the giant—and Troz—the archmage—dished the food out into vast, slightly cupped red plates, which we held on our knees. The silverware was ankle knives, and when it was found I didn't have one that belonged to me personally, Troz left to return moments later with a handsome one, fine work, with an ivory handle. "My late sibling's knife. Wear it in health."

"But I—"

"We can't get another one right now, and you need it." He was matter of fact, and gave me a slight smile to go with it, but I knew barbarian societies and the importance of a personal knife, and his generosity unmanned me.

I bowed at him and said, "I am overwhelmed."

He bowed back to me, the little smile on his lips. Then grinned and said, "Eat."

I ate. Look, I had classes. Ellyan table manners and implements weren't even that terribly unusual. And the IDS taught you to eat with everything, from chopsticks to knives, to your fingers, to pincers, and do it with style.

They didn't use fingers, but were amazing with the knife, and I managed right along. The sausages were easy, speared on the tip. The potatoes and onions were harder, on the flat of the knife, non-cutting-edge-towards-lips. But as I was staring at a plate full of fragments, Almar flipped something off a flat stone near the fire. I didn't realize till a basket passed my way that he'd been making little pillowy rounds of bread. The flour was finer milled than I would have expected, and the bread was fluffy and almost sweet.

I watched Brundar clean his plate with one, eat it, then extend the plate for more.

He got a dubious look and swallowed hastily. "I did a major healing. I—"

Troz looked worried. "He did, you know?"

Almar sighed. "He already ate all the dessert before dinner." But he filled the plate another time, then looked at me. "Milord, do you need seconds?"

I took note of what they were eating, and the fact Almar hadn't helped himself. "I'll have more of the bread," I said.

"You don't feel weak?" Troz asked. "Being the recipient of a healing of that magnitude should take it out of you, too."

I shook my head. He tilted his sideways, as he sat with his plate. "Oh, well, you'll sleep well."

But I didn't. The ice cave was strange. I was led to a little room, given another loose linen shirt, which I should use as a nightshirt over the underwear, which they called home-pants. The tunic was ankle length, and soft. And I started wondering how wealthy these people were. For barbarians, they lived like kings.

Well, if one of them was really a king...

There were sheets on the bed, also linen. And they were clean. Very. I knew because I instinctively inspected bedclothes in bar-barized societies for fleas. I'd done it before the IDS, on hunts with Father.

There were no fleas or other parasites, but also the fabric was clean and smelled fresh. The bed was low to the ground and really just a deep mattress, though well-padded. There was a fur to pull over me. I thought I'd swelter, but it felt pleasant.

It was just that I couldn't sleep. I laid in the dark, staring at the ceiling. Wishing I understood where I was and how to get home.

And then...

I heard voices from the main area of the cave. I got up and walked there, thinking of company, more than anything else.

Almar and Troz were standing before the fire. Each held some-thing, which I couldn't see clearly, but it was held in the offhand away from the other, and both had their arms akimbo.

Almar wore a light green long tunic, and Troz a dark blue one. Both tunics shimmered the soft shimmer of silk, which surprised me, because silk was rare in colonies, it was expensive wherever found, and I had no idea why they'd bring something so expensive while running away to save Peaseblossom's life. More importantly, it lent credence to this being a royal escape party.

The thing that arrested me, though, is that they both faced forward, looking into nothing, and their posture seemed very serious. Slowly, very slowly, their free hands joined. They turned. They looked at each other. They smiled.

And then, either I moved too fast, or Troz accidentally saw me. "Milord," he said, looking at me. It took him a breath to compose himself, then he smiled. "You may be a witness"

I blinked at him. My voice came out hoarse. "A witness? To what? Why?"

Almar smiled and blushed, odd in someone that large. "To our swearing."

I had enough presence of mind not to tell him that I swore all the time without witness verification before I remembered the idiom "Swear to" for marrying. This was...a wedding?

Troz said, "Witnesses are not needed because we're both magicians and it will show in the pattern, but we might as well have someone who can attest we did this properly. For non-magicians."

And as they turned to each other, in what seemed a scripted movement, I heard the soft padding of bare feet behind me, and turned to see His Majesty Peaseblossom, wearing a tunic much like mine, his bramble hair braided down his back almost to the end of his spine, save for the riot of curls framing his face, his green eyes wide. He put his finger on his lips in the universal gesture of "silence," so I shut up and faced forward.

Almar cleared his throat, as though he'd been speaking for a long time, though he hadn't. "I, Lendir Almar, child of Tmart Almar by Myrrir Mahar, swear to you Eerlen Troz, faithfulness in bed and primacy in the daylight, and that my children will be your sirelings, my body your fiefdom, my care your repose and safety. And that should you die before me, I'll raise your children as though they were my own." He tied a belt around Troz's waist.

Once it was cinched, in some kind of fibula that let tips crowned with silver fall, Troz put his hand on the fibula, looked down. His voice was full of uncried tears as he said, "Lendir...what? How?"

Almar gave a small smile, but the blush threatened to acquire a life of its own and walk off his face to be more fully embarrassed. "I was fourteen. It was my first pay as assistant to my parent. You hadn't sworn. I used to dream..."

And then Troz had his palm flat against Almar's face. "It is enough. I was just surprised," he said.

Almar stepped back and stood expectantly, while Troz lifted what had been in his hand, and I realized it was a heavy belt, made of silver plaques.

Almar took a step back. "Myrr—"

"It returned to me at his death. He left a document freeing me of my swearing," Troz said, calmly. "It is mine to use. It is not part of the Mahar inheritance."

From behind me came a voice that seemed more assured and serious than I'd ever heard Brundar Mahar be. "You know the archmagician is correct. And I have no objection."

Both started, but neither said anything. Almar nodded, once, and Troz cinched the belt around his waist. It looked heavy, highly polished silver, and each plaque was inscribed with beautiful, complex sigils. They were too far to read, even if the nanos could decipher them, which they probably could, given some context.

Lendir rested his free hand on it, and looked somehow bewildered. His cheeks were on fire, which made him look younger and less intimidating.

Troz stepped back and stood still. He lifted his face. "I, Eerlen Troz, child of Irid Troz by Kerrat Strarrel, swear to you, Lendir Almar, faithfulness in bed and primacy in the daylight, and that my children will be your sirelings, my body your fiefdom, my care your repose and safety. And that should you die before me, I'll raise your children as though they were my own."

There was a snuffly sound behind me, and I turned around to see Peaseblossom wiping his face to his sleeve. He came forward, padding on bare feet. "Witnessed by myself, Brundar Mahar, third circle magician and king of Elly." He hesitated, then sighed. "Wait a moment."

He came flying back, moments later, a small cloth-wrapped packet in his hand. He laid it on the table, removed the ribbon. It fell apart to reveal what looked like a series of polished pebbles, but it must be something else, because Lendir made a sound between outrage and a laugh. "You ate all my walnut honey balls while saving your own?"

Mahar laughed. "I always have some in case I have to do a healing and I'm hungry. I try not to deplete the supply before it's an emergency. But this must be celebrated."

Troz laughed in turn while Almar shook his head.

Troz knelt to rummage in a compartment on the floor covered with a wooden cover. He pulled out a very round bottle with a narrow neck and a cherry-red cork.

"Cherry wine?" Mahar asked.

"Well, it's either that or that rye liquor Dir has taken a taste to," Troz said. "And I think it would go to your head like deav flower."

"Oh, likely," Mahar said. "Third circle. Not much head for alcohol."

Almar had got from a recessed set of shelves tiny clay cups that looked as though they'd been made for a doll or an infant. They were white and glazed, and the cherry wine poured into them looked like red paint.

It was sweet and had a strong cherry taste. It tasted like summer.

The honey walnut balls, passed around, were caramel with nuts and stuck my teeth together. I'd have to figure out what one used for tooth brushing. As fastidious as these people seemed to be, and given the look of their teeth, there was something.

But not yet. I might have been a very junior ambassador, but I knew the feel of a wedding feast. I'd not interrupt that. We drank a second round of cherry wine, and Peaseblossom excused himself to go to bed "before things start whirling around."

I mumbled something, not wanting to lie about my capacity for alcohol. There was absolutely no point in lying when they might find out it was a lie tomorrow, on this kind of trip.

For some reason, sleeping came easier and I fell into deep, dreamless sleep.

And woke up with pandemonium.

ICE AND BLOOD

SKIP

I woke up with screams, and a smell of fire.

For a moment, clutching my pillow, I wondered if it was still the wedding celebration. I mean, in this world, who knew how weddings were celebrated? But the voices coming from the common area sounded terrified, and there was a scream of pain.

I heard Troz's voice echo in panic. "I'm pulling from the ruby. I'm pulling from the ruby."

I was up before I knew I was up, my brain lagging my body by at least a few seconds. Up and lurching. Check of decency, but in a long night tunic and what amounted to long johns, I was more decent than I'd been at some diplomatic meetings.

I wanted a weapon. Any sort of weapon. I had an ankle knife. I'd solemnly strapped it on before going to bed, but let's face it, if I you're fighting at close range with a knife, things have gotten pretty bad.

I turned to run out, which is when my mind processed there was a bow and a quiver in the corner of the room. I had no idea why, but they seemed to have weapons lying around as decoration. Okay, and probably for hunting, too. Several swords and a spear in the common room. Probably also bows. I hadn't looked.

Yes, of course I would prefer a modern weapon. Even a projectile gun. Any sort of weapon. But a bow had distance. And I'd gone on a bison hunt with Dad when I was twelve, and we'd used bows. I could do this.

Outside... The room in which the swearing and the cozy little party of yesterday had taken place was a total shambles. Mahar, Almar and Troz were hiding behind an upturned table. Facing them were a group of soldiers. I tried to identify the uniform, but it wasn't the one I'd worn, and it wasn't the uniform of the Britannia infantry. It was a dun uniform, with weird glittery marks of rank I couldn't identify. Mercenaries.

But mercenaries with modern weaponry.

I smelled smoke. There were twenty of them, and they were firing. And— The cushions on the edge of the room were on fire. The cover to the place they kept food was on fire.

How were my companions not dead?

As I came into the light of the great room, five weapons trained on me, and fired.

The energy splayed and stretched over an invisible dome. Troz yelped as though hurt. There was a red flare near his chest.

I didn't understand any of this, but the bow was in my hand, the arrow was nocked.

It turned out that you didn't forget how to shoot a bow. Well, not if your dad had taught you before you were a teenager. I speared the nearest mercenary, then nailed two more before they had reacted.

Mahar—Peaseblossom—stared and made a sound, then took off running, bare feet slapping down the hallway. He came back with a bow and stood by my side. He was... He obviously had as much experience as I did at shooting. No, from the effortless way he did it, he probably had more. He was good.

I'm not going to say we hit every time, but—but Mahar gave a victory shout every time he hit, which was immensely cheering. And then somehow, Almar was behind us, and shooting over our heads.

"I can't keep the shield. The shield— I'm pulling from the ruby. It's burning me."

The shield faltered for a second, and Almar screamed. I was out of arrows.

Troz screamed. It had a gritted-teeth feel, and the shield came back up. Whatever the hell the shield was. I was going to have to figure out what this magic thing was. It existed, but it couldn't be magic. Or really psi, right? Because neither psi nor magic existed.

I grabbed an arrow from the quiver Almar had dropped. He stopped holding his arm, and grabbed an arrow. Mahar was shouting, but I couldn't understand what he said.

Troz shook. "The shield is going to drop."

There were still ten guys in dun and gold standing. There were three of us. They had energy weapons.

"I'll charge," I said. I dropped the bow. Lousy melee weapon. I grabbed a sword that was at my feet. I think it was Troz's. I had my ankle knife in my other hand.

"We'll charge," Peaseblossom said, and I think Troz said "no," but we were past it. As the shield flickered, and beams shot past us, and I knew we were going to die, there being no safe place. Hell, I'd never contemplated my death, but if I had, it would have been with a gorgeous redhead by my side. Granted, I'd have hoped to have died of tiredness, not energy weapons.

I started forward, and he jumped, shoulder to shoulder with me, and we were going to die.

The best we could do was charge in close and fast, before we died in a blaze of glory.

As we jumped forward, I heard a sound, and I thought we'd screamed, but then, somehow we were pushed aside, and the table flew past us. A heavy oak table built for eight. At least. Almar.

Well, that was a distraction in our favor. Peaseblossom charged. He somehow had his ankle knives out. Lendir Almar ran past us, and did he have a sword?

I jumped in. I actually don't remember what I did. I have a vivid memory of slitting a throat, and blood spraying me from head to toe. When I remember it, it was like the fight when my father died. There were flashes. Troz was in there with us. I didn't know what he was doing, but it had to do with the ruby burning in his hand, shining red light over everything. He had the ruby in one hand, a knife in the other. The mercenaries acted like they were half-asleep. It gave us an advantage. We needed an advantage. I grabbed hold of a fallen enemy weapon, a late-model blaster, and started shooting.

That disposed of the last three mercenaries standing. Troz collapsed to his knees. Almar wheeled around on his feet, leaned over him. "Eerlen?"

"I'm... Just tired. Yanda shelter."

"Yanda shelter? We can't do healing in Yanda."

Troz's voice sounded extremely tired, more breath than voice. "Can. Just more difficult. Emergency and then will have to risk natural healing. Deepest cover. Can you...open...portal?"

"Here?" Peaseblossom asked.

"No. Outside. They know where we are. I can...before I let go of the ruby... There are more on the way. Lendir. Open Portal!"

"Eerlen, I'm a fourth circle! Not alone. Not to deep cover."

"I can open a portal to deep cover," Peaseblossom said. "Lendir, grab our things?" He turned to me. He had blood all over his tunic. I was covered in it, and could taste it in my mouth. I couldn't ask if what he was wearing was his. I didn't know now much was mine. He yelled at me, "Milord Webson, put a cloak on. And boots. There will be a trunk in your room, and it will have necessities. Dress properly We're going to the deep ice."

"The—"

"Just do," he said, in the tone of someone used to having his orders obeyed. Which was fine and dandy, but I was going to grab weapons. I started picking up blasters from the fallen mercenaries.

"Milord Webson, we don't have time!"

"Your Majesty, we need firepower."

He opened his mouth, snapped it shut, wheeled around away from me.

I removed the belt from one of the dead and buckled it over my tunic. It didn't have enough holsters, so I just jammed the blasters on the belt, muzzle down. I don't normally carry blasters holstered on my belt, side by side. I'm not a mersi character. But there was no way I could get enough holsters, and these damn clothes had no pockets. I was still shoving blasters into my waistband when Peaseblossom returned. He had thrown some clothes on. I won't say he was dressed, but he had a fur coat thing over his cloak, and a sort of weird fur kilt, and he'd put on a cloak with a hood. Not bad if you like Barbarian with the Face of an Angel. Okay, fine. Who am I kidding? I did, even with blood smears on the angel face. I mean...who doesn't? Really?

He carried a backpack over his shoulder, a cloak on the other hand, and he threw a fur cloak over me, knelt and started, as though I were a toddler, putting fur-lined boots on me. He pulled my foot up, tried to pull a boot on. They were the sort of not particularly fitted boots, with wide openings, which he tied on me. I slapped his hands away, thinking only after that he might take offense. But I just said, "I'll do."

He turned away, stood and glanced over the surroundings. He shouted in the direction of the long hallway, "Lendir, make sure you bring all of your things and Eerlen's, and by the Maker's parted thighs, bring your cursed swearing belts and tunics, or I'll kill you both when you lament losing them."

And then Lendir Almar came trotting out of the hallway, fur cloak in hand, wearing another cloak, two backpacks on his back, one over each shoulder.

He wrapped Troz in the extra cloak and lifted him as if he were a child. The archmage protested. "Lendir! I can—"

"Like rotten ice, you can," he said. I thought he shouldn't be able to pick up Troz like that, even with their size differential, but he wasn't betraying any effort. His face was set.

So was Mahar's as he started forward.

"You help him open," Troz said.

"Shut up, Eerlen," Almar said. He gave a worried look over his shoulder at me. "Put your hood up, Milord Webson." He shouted, like I was a military recruit he was trying to break to discipline. I obeyed before I realized I was doing it.

Mahar seemed to be feeling the air for something as he stepped forward.

Troz rasped, "They're coming from the...south. Some kind of vehicle. They will be here in minutes, Brund."

Mahar shook his head, as if the sound was the buzzing of an insect.

Then he did something. It involved a glazed look, and then his hands moving in the air, as though making a vertical slice and pulling.

...Reality split. Like a torn canvas, we saw through it to blowing snow and darkness. Snow blew into this lighter, less stormy area, and the wind was like knives made of ice.

Mahar galloped in, and Almar yelled, "Milord Webson, ahead of me."

What in hell was I to do? I ran in into complete cold and snow scouring my face. My breath hurt. My eyes stung.

I would have been completely lost, but a hand reached through the blindness and dragged me.

And then things got weird. The hand that had grabbed me landed on the back of my neck and shoved down. And from the blind darkness, Mahar's voice came. "There's a tunnel. You have to go in facefirst, because you have more control than feet first. No, put your hands in first or you'll crack your head on landing." I felt the rough, maybe a little larger than me opening, and put my hands in, then the rest of me, hoping that I'd not become stuck.

I had no clue what he meant by control, and then I did. The tunnel twisted and turned, and you could sort of guide your descent with your hands and arms, so you didn't hit every bump with the rest of you.

And then I hit warmer air, and my hands met sand. I felt someone right behind me, hands touching my feet, and pulled myself out, crawling into a pitch black...cavern?

Mahar shoved me aside. I heard the sound of his dropping his burdens.

I heard sounds of wood being thrown, and the sound of Almar coming into the cave.

"Lendir," Mahar said, "I can't find the flint box. Do you have one?"

My turn to swear and make for the sound of his voice as my eyes adapted. I could see his form, and what looked like a fireplace. I pushed Mahar aside, got a blaster from my belt, pointed it at what I very well hoped was wood and shot.

There was a brief flash illuminating the pile of logs in the fireplace, and then they caught in a blaze.

Mahar looked at me and laughed, not in amusement, but in surprise. "Welcome to Yanda shelter, Milord Webson, oldest shelter of the Troz line." He turned and started lighting candles and oil lamps and setting them about.

"I think he's—I don't think he'll—" Almar said.

He didn't seem able to finish his sentence, and there was an odd wavering quality to his voice. He had lain Troz down on a long cushion on the floor and was staring at him, intently. His hand pulled Troz's hair back from his face. "Brund!"

Peaseblossom approached with an oil lamp, and set it on the low table near the cushion. He stared at Troz and let out a breath between clenched teeth.

I looked, then looked again. Troz looked dead. Marble-pale, his mouth slightly open. His eyes closed. My heart clenched within me. I flashed to my father, dead in battle. The other two ignored me. Almar pried Troz's hand open, and removed the ruby, an elongated multifaceted stone that looked like a quartz crystal but deep red, and about three inches long and half an inch in width, laying it on Troz's chest. Then he looked at Troz's palm.

I had approached and could see that Troz was breathing, and that his hand was burned as though he'd held a live coal.

'Brundar!" Almar said. "Can you heal?"

Mahar knelt down. He looked at Troz. "I can barely do an assessment, Lendir. We're in Yanda. It's possible to heal here, but...not well. I'd have to knit it to his pattern, make it personal. It takes so much more. And I'm a single magician and tired."

"Is he going to die?"

Mahar cast a look at the ruby. "The ruby is still on him. So probably not. But he is... The ruby ate at his power. He has nothing left to heal with. He might not be sane if he wakens now. And he will lose the child."

Almar's mouth dropped open. "The what?"

"Lendir, you're a magician. I refuse to believe you haven't seen the pattern."

Almar blinked. He stared at Troz's midriff. "I hadn't. Either it just showed—"

"Or he was hiding it." Mahar did something that might pass for chuckling if you ignored the total absence of joy. "He did it with the last few...my crossiblings. He didn't want to get Myrr— Anyone's hopes up."

Lendir knelt, his hands by his side. His hand went again to smooth Troz's face. "Eerlen," he said softly. "Damn it, Eerlen. Not three months for twenty-three years of waiting."

He looked up. "Brund, would you be able to help if I got you Kalal?"

"Kalal?"

"Ad Leed, my crossibling."

Peaseblossom was doing something, running his hands over Troz's unconscious form. "If you get Ad Leed and tell him he'll have to work under a shield, he might be able to. Applied spells on a body still work; they just take more power and will be slower to work." He stopped his hands hovering over Troz, cupped and inverted. "I am going to try to save the child." He looked up at Almar, who seemed about to protest. "It's an archimagician pattern, Lendir. We can't throw those away. And anyway, if you want Eerlen to fight to live and be sane..."

Lendir nodded once. He stood up, drawing his cloak around him. He ran behind us, and I heard him throwing things around. He came back carrying skis. Recognizably skis. And poles. He hugged them to himself and headed for the entrance tunnel. I blinked.

"He's taking skis," I told Peaseblossom.

He didn't look up. He frowned at his hands, but he answered me. "I should hope so. The nearest public portal is two miles away. He can't run there. Not fast enough to matter."

I wanted to know what a public portal was, but Peaseblossom was frowning like a person suffering from a serious headache, and moving his lips very fast.

He made a gesture, as though he were pulling something from outside and...wrapping it around Troz. His eyebrows descended lower over his eyes, till I couldn't see his eyes at all. It looked like he was fighting whatever it was. And then... He fell back, sitting on his heels. I realized he was covered in sweat, because some of the blood on his face was running. It seemed to me he'd got paler under the blood, too. He sighed deeply. "It should hold. I hate working under shield." He blinked at me, but I had a feeling he was blindly staring at the human nearby, not necessarily me. "I'm tired and starving." He looked at me, and seemed to be making an effort to think. "I don't have honey nut balls."

And then his eyes rolled up, and he passed out. Backward.

THE SLEEPING KING

SKIP

I stretched Mahar out. I tried to wake him. At least he was breathing. I had to feel Troz's chest to know he was still breathing.

I knelt between the two, still in my blood-soaked nightclothes, with a belt full of blasters, and tried to think. But my mind—and perhaps it was due to the shocks of the afternoon—kept telling me that I was alone with two of my rescuers, the only people I knew I could trust in this world, and they were dying.

I don't know how long I sat there. In my mind, it was hours, but it can't have been. Perhaps those horrible minutes that last hours.

Then— Well, you know, the Academy trains us in triage. They have to. Sometimes, when your comrade falls and might be saved, you're the only one nearby who can save him.

Okay, they hadn't planned for unknown biology—they were obviously modified from Earth Standard and I had no idea how. If we ever got a scientist and a lab, I'd ask the scientist—or for my being alone in a world where something like magic worked, but not here. Not in this cave. I wanted to rage about "Why the hell not?" and I might have shouted it at the cavern ceiling. But it would help nothing. If I shouted it, no one answered.

So I scooted on my knees and did a quick examination on Troz. I couldn't do anything for it ate his pattern. Whatever the pattern was. Whatever a little gem could do to it. But I could follow the line of burns. It wasn't just his hand.

He was wearing sleep-attire much like mine, under the fur cloak that had been haphazardly draped around him. Only his tunic was sleeveless. Which meant turning his arm up, I could trace the third degree burn from his hand, up his wrist, all over the under side of his arm to his armpit. It had to hurt. It would hurt as soon as he was conscious. I tore at his tunic. Literally tore, because there was no way to lift him enough to take it off.

So I tore it across his chest. It was linen, and tough to rip, but I started the rip with my knife, and then pulled it open. For the curious, his chest looked absolutely normal, standard-male human, a bit more muscular than average, but that's what you get in a barbaric world, if you survive. His nipples were large enough to ping my "that's a little odd," even in my state of shock, but not large enough that he'd be stared at in any beach of the Star Empire. At the time, I noted it, but my curiosity about their anatomy was outweighed by my fear they would both die on me. The fear didn't get better when I realized he had burns in a line from his armpit—just missing the nipple—to a massive palm-sized burn over his heart. That one was bad enough, with black charred bits and curled skin that I wondered if it went deep enough to threaten his internal organs. I had no way of knowing. All I could do for him was to...

The burns felt cool to the touch, which made no sense. Well, short of grafts, all I could do was attempt to prevent infection.

I headed to the kitchen. I'd seen the other one and its contents extensively. This one was bigger and better, I'd gathered in the glimpse when I lit the fireplace. I found the jar of honey where I'd seen it before, on a cupboard. Of course I hadn't known it contained honey, but I'd hoped it had something. And it wasn't a jar. More of a...vast ceramic container with a cork lid. I opened oil and vinegar in similar containers before I found it. Honey is unreliable, but it has antiseptic properties. I got enough in a bowl, went back to the unconscious archmage and smeared it along the line of burning, very careful on his chest not to do any more damage.

That was all I could do for him. That and pray, which I did, most earnestly. I didn't know how the Lord felt about these far-flung bits of humanity, but I hoped He felt benevolent.

Then I moved on to the sleeping king. In the legends of a thousand countries and of many lost colonies, there is a sleeping king. Check. He sleeps in a deep cave. Check. In full armor. This one was in nightclothes, long-sleeved. And a sort of weird fur quilt. The cloak was mostly under him, because he was on his back. The sleeping king is supposed to be fully armed, and as I examined him, I did note Brundar Mahar had knives at both ankles, two strapped at his waist on a belt under his nightclothes—something that would be pathological in more civilized climes—and one each on his forearms, on the inside, hidden in his underarms. At that point, I became afraid that if I shook him, he'd rain hardware in every direction.

I didn't intend to shake him. He looked to be in better shape than Troz. His skin wasn't quite as pale, and he didn't feel cool to the touch. But my gentle tap on his shoulder, and my call of "Mahar! Your Majesty, Peaseblossom" brought absolutely no response, not even a flutter of the eyelids.

And though he was breathing, his face and hands and his tunic were caked in blood. He had been actually fighting and not with magic. The chances of a wound were not trivial.

I took a deep breath. The kitchen had various containers, mostly clay. I found something that was either a large roaster or a dish pan. I found the bathing pool by sound. It was like the one I'd bathed in, the size of a small swimming pool, with continuous running water. This was warmer than the one I'd bathed in, but not uncomfortable. I filled the pan and brought it back.

There wasn't a clean bit of his tunic I could use, and I wasn't about to go rummaging through their linen stores, so I tore a bit of the archmagician's tunic, which was already ruined, and dipped it in the water.

I washed the King's face and hands, and discovered no wounds. Then I realized that his tunic was still wet, as was his groin area and his right leg, while other parts of the blood on his clothes were drying.

I removed his fur kilt, which was becoming blood-wet.

The knife went to work again, and this time I tore his tunic to pieces, removed the pants, and frantically washed as much of his body as possible. Okay, fine. If you must know: hairless chest, normal nipples, pubic patch more intense red than the hair on his scalp and what looked like normal male anatomy. I didn't investigate further, and yes, I had ideas how things would be arranged, because I know how human embryos develop and bioengineering rarely does more than tamper with that. Which is why there is no human race with functional tail or wings. And no, I didn't look. Look, my concern was: was he hiding wounds? I wasn't doing an anatomical survey.

As it was, he had two wounds. Bad ones. One, almost certainly by blaster in cutting mode, went from his belly button—normal human, innie—to under his left armpit. It was superficial, but still it had to hurt like hell, and the fact he had managed to carry things, and plan and perform healing— Never mind. My admiration was boundless.

The wound that concerned me most, though, was on his thigh. Inner thigh. Extending from halfway up from the knee to where, had it gone a centimeter further up, it would have meaningfully diminished his chances of siring children. It obviously had missed the femoral artery or he'd be dead. But it was bubbling fresh blood at a clip, anyway. And I was all out of transfusion equipment, let alone blood. So, it would have to be a tourniquet.

I tore a long strip of Troz's tunic, went back to the kitchen, found what was probably a spit, and proceeded to torniquet his thigh at the jointure with the body. The body wound was harder, but I used the pack-and-apply pressure method. For packing, I used his actual tunic. Look, yeah, it was blood-soaked, but— Then I pressed. The blood loss did slow, hopefully not because he was running out of it.

I went back and wrapped the archimagician in the cloak, as well as I could, having belatedly thought that if he was in shock, I shouldn't let him be chilled. He was still breathing. I went wandering down a hallway, found a bedroom, and dragged out a fur blanket to throw over Troz.

I didn't dare cover the king, because he might start bleeding again, at least from his torso wound.

What else could I do?

Well... He'd said he was starving and tired. Given the rate of blood loss, I'd bet he was dehydrated, too. Very. So, back to the kitchen. I wouldn't dare do this with the archmagician, but Mahar was in the sort of unconsciousness I understood. Mostly.

Most people who are normally unconscious, not in A Jewel Ate My Pattern Whatever That Is unconsciousness, will swallow liquid put in their mouths. It was used in field conditions—and in the past—to feed unconscious people and keep them hydrated. Yes, there are other ways to do it, but that would probably violate all sorts of taboos and besides, where would I find a flexible, impermeable tube of appropriate size? It's not like I had my medical field kit with me. Besides, I'd start considering that after he'd been unconscious twenty-four hours, not however many minutes.

So it was back to the kitchen. I found another source of water, before I went back to the pool. They had... Think about a faucet without mechanical parts. It was a pipe—if I didn't know better, I'd think it was glassteel—protruding from the wall and closed with a cork. From the drain hole beneath, I deduced water, and risked removing the cork. Water. Right.

I still boiled it, on an iron kettle over the fire. Then poured it into a cup, dissolved honey into it, waited for it to cool enough and found a spoon. It looked like glazed porcelain, which was interesting, as I'd not seen spoons at the previous shelter. But maybe— Never mind.

Back near the king, I lifted him by sliding my knees under his upper body, and started filling the spoon, sliding it into his mouth and letting the honey-water trickle in.

He swallowed. This was a great relief.

I was almost through the cup when I heard a gasp. I looked up and before I could react, there was... A ski pole touching my neck. Almar was staring at me in horror. Which made no sense, since he was the one trying to use a pointy pole as a lance on my neck.

I carefully put the cup down, then held up my hands, still holding the spoon, in the universal human sign of, "I don't know what I did to piss you off, but please don't kill me."

A small dark-haired person, I think one of my welcoming committee when I'd first landed in the world, dropped through the tunnel and stood, his hands covering his mouth in the universal human sign of, "Oh shit."

I cleared my throat. "I'm not going to move till you tell me I can. You may remove the point from my neck." I cleared my throat again. "I don't understand what I have done wrong."

He did not remove the point from my neck. He yelled at me, but his words came out too fast and probably too distorted by fury for my nanites to fully catch. The fact we were both panicking probably didn't help.

Enough words were caught, though, to panic me even more. Because I gathered I was being accused of defiling and raping the king.

Raping? What the holy heck? Except, of course, I realized Draksall males probably did.

It was that sort of culture.

I shouted back. For full effect, imagine the words without any pause in between. "I didn't rape him. I didn't defile him. He was bleeding. I bandaged him. I'm trying to give him water and honey."

Lendir Almar blinked. The small dark-haired person he'd brought with him walked across, picked up the cup and smelled it. He smiled at me. He had the most startling bright blue eyes. "Good thinking," he said. Then he looked at Almar. "Lendir, take that thing off his neck. He's not a Draksall, and I believe him." A cursory look at where I'd bandaged and a wince at Brundar's leg. Followed by, "Idiot child." And then in a more stern voice: "Lendir, really. He might have saved Mahar's life." He smiled at me. "Please resume giving him honey water. It will help."

Almar made a sound somewhere between a grunt and pshaw and removed the damn point from my neck. However, while Ad Leed went to kneel at the Archimagician's side, and I gingerly retrieved the cup, Almar threw the pole away as if it disgusted him, then loped away down the hallway to the bedrooms. He came back with a sheet, which he opened and put over Mahar, neck to feet.

All right, then. I mean, look. Other circumstances, I might have got curious. But I'd seen chests before, and theirs were pretty much standard male. And as for the fiddly bits down below, I'd been more concerned about the blood pouring out of his thigh.

However, some things you learn pretty quickly not to argue with, and once "defilement" and "rape" had been brought into the equation, I was not going to argue and risk getting killed.

Ad Leed removed the furs from Troz. I suspect that I got a dirty look from Almar when the archmage's torn tunic emerged, but I really didn't care. Fill the spoon, put spoon in king's mouth, tip it up slowly. Repeat.

Murmurs reached me. "Oh, dear," from Ad Leed. "Pattern burn." And other stuff. He raised his voice. "Honey is a good disinfectant. The honey won't be needed because I can set those to heal fast, but I take it you're a healer, Milord Webson?"

"No," I said. "I was a fighter, and they teach us to treat our own in an emergency."

"Um. Not a bad idea. The brotherhood should do that."

There was a long pause. "Lendir. I'm going to have to traipse all over his pattern. There will be mind contact. He... He really doesn't like me."

"He doesn't dislike you," Lendir said, in a rumble. He was kneeling by Troz, and holding Troz's uninjured hand.

Ad Leed scoffed. "I remember his looking daggers at me, even though I'd saved Mahar's life."

Lendir chuckled, with a sound of reluctance. "He thought you were my lover."

Long silence. "I'm not Erradian," in a sullen voice.

"He didn't know we were siblings."

"Oh. How— Never mind. He wears the ruby, and there was the king and his clan—" Long pause. I looked over and light was coming from Ad Leed's hand—how, even?—and playing over the archmagician's burns. "I still... I would hate for anyone to do that work on me besides close family. But I see Mahar almost killed himself saving the child." He took a deep breath. "I will need food after, but I see you have honey. It will do. At least immediately."

I had finished the cup and went back to the kitchen to refill.

Came back and started spooning it into Mahar again. He made a sound, not quite a moan, then coughed, halfway through the cup.

Ad Leed had both hands on the archmage, head and heart, and though unmoving, looked like he was pushing a rock the size of the universe. Uphill.

Almar looked like he wasn't even breathing, staring at Ad Leed.

Peaseblossom raised his hand to his mouth as he coughed, then his eyes opened. He looked up at me, green eyes filled with curiosity and confusion. I was not about to be accused of rape again.

"It's honey and water. You were unconscious."

He blinked. Tried to speak, but had to clear his throat. His voice was normally low and raspy. No, not raspy but... Like the purr of a cat. Now it was raspy, just slightly. "Good thought." He groped for the cup. "I can drink now."

I pushed my knees further under him, helping him sit up, and lifted the cup to his lips. In his defense, he made no move to take it from me. Just put his hand—warm and rough—over mine.

When the sheet started to slide, he held it up with his other hand. So, this "covered to the neck" thing must be cultural, not just Almar's insanity.

"I'm going to ease you down and get you more water and honey."

He nodded. I eased him down. I grabbed another pillow, and shoved it under his head and shoulders. He smiled at me.

When I came back with water and honey, he looked more awake. "You undressed me?" he said.

It sounded more like a question than an accusation, so I tried to keep it casual. "You were bleeding. I had to find from where and stop it."

He lifted the sheet and looked under, which almost smacked the cup from my hands. Then he reset the sheet. "You did well. Training?"

"In the space force," I said. It came out as, "In the star fighting," but never mind. "Before I became an ambassador." Then formally. "I'm sorry I had to undress you. I didn't know what else to do."

There was more purr than normal in Peaseblossom's voice. "I don't mind." He lowered his eyelids a little and I realized for the first time he had a ridiculously long fringe of eyelashes framing his green eyes.

I wondered if he was flirting, then realized I'd heard a sound like he'd been poked with something sharp from Almar, and a half-disguised-as-cough chuckle from Ad Leed. Great. Another complication I didn't need.

But I helped Mahar drink his honey water, and at the end of it, he said, "I can hold the next cup." And when I returned with it, he helped me arrange the cushions so he could sit and look at what Ad Leed was doing while he drank.

And I went into the kitchen. There was some implication seriously abused magical power needed food to recover. Made sense. Whatever it was, it was linked to their physical being.

Well, when I'd followed Father to absurd places on vacation—or more clearly, to hike and hunt—I'd become a pretty good camp cook.

I went to the kitchen in search of their food storage. And found I wouldn't be cooking in primitive conditions. Though over wood, for sure, but there was a wood oven over the fireplace. There was also a cooking pit. The storage stasis contained... My first impression was everything. My second impression was that what was here was obviously the result of worldwide trading, because there were not only some kind of steaks—allowable for hunting nomads, though honestly, they might be bear, which to me tasted like wet fur—but also some kind of cut-up fruit, in a clay container. On tasting, they proved to be peaches, and flour and butter, eggs and pecans. Pecans. Definitely Earth pecans. I tasted. So much for "we are not a lost colony." There might be some way the universe would replicate bears and even something that tasted like peaches, but...pecans?

I stood for a moment, staring at the food. Then I went in search of clothes. I wasn't about to ask them where they were, because really, I wasn't about to interrupt what was going on, even if I didn't understand it. But I'd got the idea, from the way they were laid in, including weapons, that these places were generationally stocked and there had to be clothes left behind. They'd come up with clothes for me before.

I found a room without backpacks on the bed, so I'd assume not claimed by any of them. There was a trunk. It had tunics. Nightclothes, yes, but also a long linen tunic, cut more like my impression of their daywear. Well, there were several of those, all identical except for size, but one fit me, and had a cloth belt to tie around the waist. I still found underwear, of the type worn at night, because I had no idea if there was another kind.

I took my er... Borrowed clothing to the bathing pool, stripped quickly and washed thoroughly, because I was not going to cook while covered in human blood.

Yes, I inspected myself for wounds, and there wasn't much. A few nicks from the close-in combat, but nothing worth writing home about, and the nanos would take care of it. Judging from the quantity of blood that came off my hair, though, I'd made the right decision. And my hair wasn't even that long. Lesson for the children at home: when slitting throats, face the victim away from you.

There were towels laid by in the corner. Well, lengths of linen, hemmed and folded, which in the circumstances would be towels. I dried myself, put the clean clothes on. No choice but to put boots back on. I had nothing else.

Back to the kitchen, and I stopped, and looked towards the entrance area at the sound of sobs. I wasn't sure what I expected, but I knew what I feared. Fears immediately dispelled, since Troz was sitting up. Yes, supported by Ad Leed, and Almar. But from the shaking of the shoulders, it was Lendir Almar crying. I heard Eerlen Troz's voice, whisper-thin. "Dir. Dir. I'm well. Just so tired."

Right. I went back to cooking. Steaks, seasoned. There was an herb I couldn't identify, also pepper—pepper! I tasted it!—and salt. And... Well, there are things I can resist and things I can't. Years ago on Earth, during the same bow-hunting trip in which I'd become comfortable with the weapon, I learned to make pecan cookies. Because Dad loved them.

I was sliding a—clay but smooth, and obviously used in the oven, from the look of it—pan of them into the oven, when I turned around and almost collided with Kalal, who was looking over my shoulder. "The king would like a refill," he said, proffering the empty cup that Peaseblossom had been using. "And I'd like some, please. Good idea, the honey water."

Kalal Ad Leed looked exhausted. His lids drooped. I did what came naturally. "Milord, go sit. You shouldn't be standing. I'll have food for you in a few moments. I'll bring you the water and honey."

He opened his mouth, blushed. For the first time, I wondered how old he was. He was pretty. Not handsome like Almar, or beautiful like Troz and Peaseblossom, but pretty. A triangular cat-like face, a button nose, wide blue eyes, and a skin color somewhere between dark sand and gold. He came up to my shoulder. In other places, in other circumstances, I'd be buying him drinks all night. If I thought he was of legal age, of course. And even now, I wasn't sure about that. How he and Lendir Almar could be half-siblings was something I'd not decipher anytime soon.

He gave me a little smile. His voice was a light tenor. "I just need the honey water. I need to set the king's wounds to heal themselves. And I'm going to use some honey to disinfect first. That cloth you used was not clean. Not criticizing. It was an emergency. So I'll disinfect before setting to heal."

All right. I had to figure out the difference between setting to heal and outright healing. "I'd take them back to Brinar for healing, but Lendir says Yanda is the most defensible shelter, even if they find you. He's not wrong. And they probably won't find you. Not in Yanda."

He waited awkwardly while I filled the cups and mixed water and honey, high on the honey portion. Then I handed him a small bowl of honey. "I just need to stay conscious to heal Lendir too," he said, softly.

I looked at him, startled. "Lend— Almar is wounded?"

"Yeah. Not as badly as the King, but—idiot thinks I don't know. It's like he hasn't lived with healers his whole life and his parent wasn't one."

I smiled or perhaps grimaced, and his smile had a mischievous edge. Yeah, I'd have been buying him drinks all night long a few years ago, even, though right then, perhaps because exhausted or after shocks, or very aware they were not standard-issue males, the admiration was detached and intellectual.

He went back, and handed Peaseblossom a cup, then drank the other one.

I was taking the first batch of cookies out of the oven when I heard Mahar protest.

"Very well, Your Majesty, but I need to remove the sheet to heal you, and I thought you might want to clean and dress. And cut down on the chance of infection."

Peaseblossom said something, but was cut short by Lendir. "Don't be tiresome, Brund."

While chopping onions and potatoes really small, to pan-fry with some fat—probably bear or something equally unpalatable!—on something that looked much like a frying pan over the firepit, I saw Peaseblossom clutching his sheet around himself, being led towards the back, leaning on Kalal Ad Leed.

Almar and Troz were whispering at each other.

I had finished cooking the vegetables, and got a third batch of cookies out of the oven when Peaseblossom came back, properly attired, his hair more naturally red. Ad Leed truly looked exhausted and I wasn't sure which of them was leaning on the other. Ad Leed grinned at me going by.

Seconds later, I heard him say, "Lendir. No. Really. You can let the archmage rest back on the pillows."

And Eerlen Troz's paper-thin voice. "Lendir, go."

Which made me realize the archmage probably wouldn't be able to eat. I remembered convalescing from a serious wound and being too tired to eat. Right. More honey tea. Maybe he could manage some cookies. The energy would help. I moved everything to the "next to the oven surface" where it would stay warm, except for the cookies, which were on the table I was using as work table.

Casting about, I saw other cushions. I mixed honey water, filled a small bowl with cookies, walked over, set them on the table, and squat-knelt by Troz. "Glad to see you awake," I said.

He blinked at me, as though not sure who I was, then smiled. "Thank you, Milord Webson."

"I made dinner." This elicited another slow blink. "But I don't think you'll have enough energy to eat. You see, I've been very ill before. So I'm going to bring cushions over, and lift you to sitting, and then give you some warm honey water and...well. Some things I made of flour and honey, butter and pecans." The slow blink. "If you'll allow me."

He nodded, but there was a hesitancy to it. I got the cushions over, and gently pulled him up. His hand was still wounded, and there were bandages wrapped up his arm, but when I put the cup into his left hand, and put the bowl of cookies on his lap, he used his right hand to take one to his mouth, so it must not have hurt as badly. Slow healing, they'd said.

"Do you have children, Milord?" He asked me, his eyebrow creased.

I frowned at him. "Not that I know of." And it was bloody unlikely, unless someone had engaged in test tube creation without my knowledge.

He seemed confused, looked away and bit into the cookie, and almost dropped the cup. He stared at me.

"It's not poison, I swear."

He grinned. Took another bite. Two. Put the whole cookie in his mouth and chewed. "Milord Webson, are you a baker?"

I laughed. "No, Lord Troz."

He sipped his honey water. Ate another cookie. "Well, if you wish to open a bakery, I think the king can be convinced to endorse you." His voice was a little stronger. "I've never had anything like. It's not bread..."

I was horrified. No cookies? What hellhole was this? "No pastries, milord?"

He blinked at me, and I realized my words had gotten translated as "sweet treats."

"Honey walnut balls," he said. "And somewhat sweet bread. Brund's baker makes somewhat sweet raised bread. Not as sweet as this."

So no cakes, either. Poor things. "Well, if you allow me, I might bake more for you." Plural you. "During the time I'm here."

"You might have to, once Brund tastes these. He has a sweet tooth." He ate two more cookies and looked at me, a little sideways, as though embarrassed. "I'm conscious of the debt of honor we owe you, Milord. Without you, there's a good chance we'd be dead. All of us. If you hadn't thought of the bows... And then you treated our wounds. Ad Leed told me. And now you're cooking for us." He managed to blush a little. "Our debt is beyond repaying."

"Considering you saved my life in Draksah... Well, His Majesty's plan did, I think we can consider ourselves even."

"There is never even, Milord. If we concede we saved your life, you saved all three of us. We'll be forever in your debt."

I shook my head. "That's not how it works, Lord Troz."

He opened his mouth as if to say something, and I understood, yes, the coils of honor, and a clannish nomad society. I cut him off, speaking softly so it didn't appear to be so. "Or if there is, you can repay me with your friendship. I am alone on a foreign and potentially hostile world. I need that."

He lifted his bandaged hand, looked at it, made a sound not quite a laugh, and clasped my hand with his left hand. "Forgive the wrong hand," he said. "You have my friendship and my loyalty, Milord. And that of the Troz line and allies, sparse though they are."

Lendir Almar rumbled from behind us. "And pardon me the wrong assumption, Webson. I was...startled. You have the eternal gratitude of the Almar line, for all the good it will do you. Though my cousins might give you discounts on fabric by the bolt."

I looked over my shoulder at him. "Who knows? I might need it."

He came to kneel by Eerlen, and they whispered something. Peaseblossom was in the kitchen with Kalal Ad Leed. I heard the word "starving." And then Peaseblossom yelped. I stood, scared. But he had bit into a cookie. He devoured it, I think is the right word. There was laughter in his purring voice. "Milord Webson, it goes without saying that you have the friendship of the royal house. But if you make more of these...treats, I'll give you my firstborn."

"Brund!" Eerlen said, shocked.

"No, let him," Lendir said. "I remember what he did to his dolls. Might be the only way the poor mite survives."

I tasted a family joke, and did not ask. I put food on the low table. They ended up eating sitting on cushions. Kalal Ad Leed ate his weight in food, I swear. For someone so tiny, he ate more than either of the others. I later was told this was normal after performing a major healing. Troz fell asleep on Lendir's shoulder, and was later carried to bed. Ad Leed was offered a bed for the night.

Peaseblossom helped me clear the table and clean, which surprised me but shouldn't have. In my world, kings didn't do chores, but he'd been running with his family in strained circumstances, and surely had to help.

Then he helped me wash the salvageable clothes, mostly mine, in the bathing pool, and told me the secret of Ellyan teeth cleaning: a sort of sweet natural gum you chewed. He showed me where it was kept.

We ended the night with his assigning me a room, next to Troz's and Almar's.

That is how I heard their discussion.

"I'd like to know how they traced us," Troz said, sounding suspicious.

"I'm more worried about who they were. Those were not Draksalls," Almar said. "They looked—"

"Like our guest," Troz finished.

OF KINGS AND BAKERS AND STAR EMPIRES

EERLEN

Eerlen Troz woke up hurting. For that moment, on waking, he was shocked at how much it hurt to breathe, to think, to...

And then he realized what hurt was his semi-conscious check of the ruby and his link to it.

His unlamented predecessor in the role of Archmagician, the never-sufficiently-Maker-Cursed Lahem Drahy, had said it was a good idea to check you had the ruby on waking up, because that meant you were still alive.

Apparently, of all the things that Eerlen had learned from Drahy, and of everything he'd tried to forget, he remembered that one particular piece of advice at the bone-deep level that he did it while half-asleep. And power-burned. And in Yanda.

Stopping reaching his power for the ruby stopped the overall pain, except for a line from his hand to his chest. And that didn't hurt as badly as he expected. He opened his eyes, staring at the strange ceiling of Yanda. He had the slightly blurry vision and the feel of an ache behind the eyes that were typical of power-burn. Or a hangover. And he'd had worse of each.

The ceiling held. There were no screams from anywhere in the shelter.

His hand went up and touched the ruby. It was with him, so he was alive. He felt for the child's power pattern within himself. The child was alive. For a moment, on wakening, he'd thought it was done, that this one, too, had joined the list of his dead half-siblings. But the child was alive.

Which left Lendir snoring softly by his side. And—

"Shit." He sat up. Lendir sat up at the same time, looking at him with wide, shocked eyes.

"I left two third circles alone after a major healing," Eerlen said. "You know what they're like." Third circles, after a major healing, for reasons having to do with opening their own pattern to do the healing, as well as possibly an inherent formation of pattern that allowed healing, were as likely as not to get in a to-the-death-duel or an unadvisable sexual exploit. Two of them was just asking for trouble. Particularly when the two were a King and a Lord of the Land.

Eerlen looked around for his clothes, but Lendir's hand shot out of the blankets, and grabbed at his arm. It was warm, but strong. Lendir's voice was slurred by sleep, but clear enough as he said, "'S fine. I took care of it."

"You...took care?"

"I told Brund to stay behind and help our guest clean. It's not fair to make him clean after he fed us and all. Law of hospitality."

Eerlen relaxed, but his questioning mind forced him to say, "Our guest?"

"He's an ambassador. He cannot be completely without restraint."

"We can hope," Eerlen said. But mostly said it to be contrary. From what he'd seen, the ambassador to the stars was more tempted by baking. Or at least there was no sign of impropriety when both he and Brundar had been unconscious, naked and at his mercy. Eerlen smiled, at what Lendir had told him of Lendir's irrational response to attempts at healing by a non-magician.

Lendir was stirring now, sitting up, making the very odd not-quite-a-word exclamation he made when he'd given up on sleep.

They bathed and dressed together, and in silence. Lendir had been confused at Eerlen hiding being with child. Eerlen couldn't quite tell him his pregnancies scared Myrrir. Having lost two lovers to childbirth before meeting Eerlen, and almost having lost Eerlen a few times, Myrrir would become unpleasantly scared if he knew Eerlen was expecting. And more often than not, the children miscarried before he needed to tell Myrrir

Lendir wasn't Myrrir, but Eerlen had hidden by reflex. Yet, Kalal had said the child was strong and likely to survive. Of course, healers had said that of three who'd been stillborn. So far as he understood, the problem was that sometimes his children had a mistimed gestation, and tried to take the same time as Ellyans while having the development speed of Draksalls. He sighed.

Dressed, he came into the common area. He'd heard voices, and found they'd been coming from the kitchen area. Strangely, as Eerlen emerged, he heard Ad Leed laugh, a rare enough sound that it made him wonder if he was still big-healing-punchy. For all that he was not a somber person, Ad Leed did not laugh easily.

The ambassador was at the table, and had...dough. He was rolling it out with a long, cylindrical vase, normally used to serve liquor. Eerlen paused, frowning. Webson took butter from the slightly warmer area by the stove, and spread it on the sheet of dough on the table.

"There are ways to make dough rise," he said while he worked. Ad Leed and Brundar both stood across from him, watching him. "That involve yeast. And a chemical substance from mining, that if you have here, I don't know how to find. But the simplest is this, which is why it's so weird that it's considered a gourmet form of bread in my culture. You just make dough, and you lay it out real thin and then you spread butter on it. Then you fold it." He folded the layer, over and over. "Layers and layers like...Damascus steel. No, wait, you'll have no idea what Damacus is. It's a city. Do you have folded layered steel? What do you call it?"

Ad Leed laughed again. He was leaning slightly forward, which was fascinating to Eerlen. Was Kalal Ad Leed flirting? That was something else he'd never seen. "That," Ad Leed said. "Would be Brinarian steel, Milord. My domain."

"Ah, well, then your people should be naturals for making crescents."

"Crescents?"

"Like the moon. You'll see."

He started cutting triangles of the multi-layered dough, and folding it again, then bending it, to form little crescents.

"Moon bread," Brundar said. "Fascinating."

Well, the good news was that the two third circles were not entering into the synergy of post-healing and either killing each other or very not killing each other. The bad news was that the poor ambassador would need ironclad self-control, at this rate. There were Draksalls who never had any interest in Ellyans, no matter what. They were a minority, but they existed. Maybe the ambassador would be like those.

Eerlen cleared his throat. Webson looked up and smiled. "You look better, Milord Troz."

"I should hope so. Only way to look worse would be dead."

The other two had also turned around and looked embarrassed. As they should. Or perhaps not. After all, third circles had their vulnerabilities they couldn't help. And if one of them weren't Eerlen's sireling and the king of Elly, Eerlen would find it much funnier.

"Please sit," Webson said. "All of you, really." He looked towards the sitting area near the entrance. "I will have food ready in a few moments."

"Brundar," Lendir said, coming into the room. "I thought you and Eerlen were going to prepare instructions to send to the palace and to the Lords of the Land? Your instructions? Since Kalal will be going back, he can take written instruction."

Brund looked reluctant. The image of a younger Brundar reluctantly leaving his play-friends in the courtyard when called inside to study some detail of statecraft made him smile.

But Brund nodded. "Yes. I need to do that." He gave Eerlen a doubtful look. "Are you up to advising?"

Eerlen truly felt like going back to bed and curling up, but shrugged. "I'll manage."

They sat down, side by side, on one of the massive pillows near the wall. Eerlen was grateful for the wall at his back. Brundar had questions about troop supply and also about provisioning the palace in case of siege, something that seemed frighteningly likely after the previous night. Eerlen would like to tell him there was no danger of a siege, but they'd almost been killed in one of the restricted shelters of the Troz line, which only the head of the Troz clan, their sworns and their children and sirelings and a few favored particularly allowed cousins could open. And that number should all be contained in this room, plus a handful Eerlen would swear by. If he thought too much on it, it spun upon the question of what had happened to his parents, and that was a place no one wanted to go. He was sure they were dead.

Worse, there were the Draksalls or close enough, with energy weapons. And that was a siege worth worrying about.

Together, they spun ideas and numbers, and Eerlen tried to list where and in which of the Mahar farms and possessions they could get the supplies for such a disastrous eventuality.

In the middle of it, heads together, talking, while Eerlen tried to keep figures in his head, Lendir brought out the writing desk that Eerlen normally left in his room. "I figured you would wish to write it down."

"Of course," Eerlen said, and opened the desk, thinking if they were very lucky the ink bottles wouldn't be dry. When had he used it last? Before Myrrir's death. Well, before. Six months before?

This was a travel desk, and therefore a broad shallow box, with an inclined top, inside which were kept the colored inks and the brushes, as well as the writing cloths.

Atop the fresh writing cloth, rolled as a letter would be, was a piece of writing cloth sealed with wax, and on it, written fast in a careless hand, the words Khare Sarda, Lord of Karresh.

Eerlen recognized Myrrir's hand instantly, of course. The surprise took a fraction of the second, and as questions ran through his mind—when had Myrrir written that? Why to Sarda? And why hadn't he delivered it or had it delivered? He took the letter, smoothly, he thought, and slipped it in his sleeve, before taking out a long roll of fresh writing cloth.

Just in time for Brund to grab at it. "It should be in my hand."

"You're right," Eerlen said. "Have the desk." The letter in his sleeve felt as though he'd slipped a live snake in there. But he had to concentrate. He started suggesting instructions to Brundar, who questioned some of them for explanation and suggested better ones for others.

Webson dragged a table over and started serving breakfast. There were the moon breadrolls, which were everything they'd been advertised, and were served with butter and honey. There were sausages which Eerlen couldn't even remember putting in the stasis, but which were of course, perfectly fresh, and there were scrambled eggs.

Also, he'd made tea. "I tried to find coffee," he said. "But I couldn't and Ad Leed..." He gestured to Ad Leed, who was helping him serve. "Says the only way to get it is to raid Draksah, though there have been attempts to grow it in his domain and the latest one might prove fruitful in ten years or so."

"Yes," Eerlen said, wrenching his mind from the letter in his sleeve. "My sire loved his coffee, but it cost the crown jewels, because it is obtained either by raiding Draksah or taking land from the Draksall garrison in Erradi and raiding their supplies. The seeds have been stolen, but something went wrong." He looked up at Ad Leed, who was giving Brundar an unreadable look, while Brundar glared at him. "Is your promising start from seeds?"

Ad Leed poured himself tea and made a show of sipping, though it was impossible he'd actually sipped, since the thing must be boiling hot. But the heavy blue glazed cup, the color of Ad Leed's eyes, held in both hands and partially in front of his face, would break his staring contest with Brundar. They were being very silly. And if Eerlen didn't manage it, there would be the duel portion of vulnerable third circles in close proximity.

Ad Leed lowered the cup, looking determinedly at Eerlen. "No. Plants." He blushed dark. "I—I might have obtained them in Draksah." This caused a momentary stomach flipflop, and Eerlen wanted to dig into that and ask him if he, Lord of a domain, descendent of one of the ten lines and with no descendants, had actually lost his mind and joined Brund's spy corps.

Brund must have felt that question coming, though Eerlen wasn't stupid enough to ask it, because he spoke too brightly. "Oh, those are taking?"

"Well enough. One of my farms seems to be coming along. We hope to have at least some beans worth roasting in probably five years or so. If it all works out. It's very early, of course."

The rest of the conversation was polite. Webson was curious about magic and his eyes lit up when he heard that magic formulas involved math.

"How not?" Brundar asked. "You have to calculate the energy and the time, and affect the action."

"Brundar is a brilliant mathematician, which is why he became a full third circle at sixteen," Ad Leed said, and cast Brundar a fawning look. And Eerlen's worries switched to the other type of synergy between third circles.

He had to get Ad Leed on his way. And read that letter. For something that was written years ago, it shouldn't disturb him this badly. But Myrrir didn't even write his own required letters, and normally offloaded them to Eerlen. If he didn't write down a lot of other things, including healing formulas and to-do lists, Eerlen would think he was illiterate. And why was he writing to Sarda, the youngest of his acknowledged sirelings? And why do it in Yanda?

Eerlen had thought that Myrrir had not come to Yanda with him any time in the last...two years before his death? Their escapades into Erradi were always brief, impromptu and very secret. And if they'd come here together for a night, the last thing Myrrir would be doing was writing. Also, Eerlen was sure he'd used the desk after their last escape from the palace. So—

Had Myrrir come to Yanda alone? In the Maker's Womb, why? He had the right of opening the cave and using it, but why would he?

And even as he thought that, a scenario spun in his mind. Myrrir, like all third circles, took turns in the wounded wards at Erradi, the place where those dying were stabilized before being transported elsewhere. Perhaps he was too tired to—

Use the public portal to the palace? And therefore must open one himself to Yanda?

Opening portals was not a core third circle competency. They could do it, but unless they were as overpowered as Brundar was, they didn't do it outside moments of dire necessity.

And Myrrir wasn't overpowered.

The only reason that Eerlen could think of his coming to Yanda was because it was deep shield. No magic could see into it. But why? Had he thought himself magically tracked? If so, why hadn't he spoken?

In a daze, he finished eating, finished writing instructions to send with Ad Leed, then ran to his room, and with his ankle knife, cut the ribbon holding the letter together.

THE UNKINDEST CUT

EERLEN

Eerlen dropped to sitting on the bed as he unrolled the letter. It was the least of his worries that he was opening correspondence meant for someone else, considering that the person it was addressed to was one of the two possibly attempting against Brundar's life and forcing his absence from the palace. Also, whatever Myrrir's business with Sarda might be, it could no longer be urgent.

So he opened the letter and read it. Then read it again. The words danced before his eyes and made no sense whatsoever.

"Eerlen?" Lendir asked. His voice seemed to come from very far away. There was a whistling in Eerlen's ears, and his mouth was dry. Without looking up, he said, "Close the door. And put a shield."

"Can't put a shield. We're in deep no-magic, love, but Webson and Brund are talking in the kitchen while cleaning. Are you ill? You look ill." He stepped back and closed the door.

Eerlen extended the letter to him. "Ill enough. Read it aloud. I can't seem to make sense of it. It's Myrrir's handwriting."

Lendir unrolled the cloth and read,

Kahre,

In answer to your last, yes, there have been two more attempts, and yes, upon investigation, both times, someone had seen Eerlen or a semblance of him in the vicinity of where the attack happened.

And before you mock me for a "semblance of him," Kahre, we are sworn. I can see his pattern. More importantly, I can see our link. And something like trying to poison your sworn would show in that pattern. It's a betrayal as marked as sleeping with someone else without my consent. His pattern and our link are clear.

And yes, I do realize he's the Archmagician and probably the strongest we've ever had, and that the depths of his pattern are unplumbed because no one can really determine what it is or how much power he has. Part of the Draksall mixture. Still, it would show. I'm convinced of it.

I must though say right here that if Eerlen is trying to kill me, he's gone mad. I've made him furious a hundred times in our years together, but I can't imagine his even raising a hand to me, much less trying to kill me.

Also, the concealment and compulsion spells around these attempts are—while high pattern—not our spells or compulsions at all. They're utterly alien.

No, I'll not accept he's in Draksall pay as Guinar Ter has tried to insinuate more than once. The only reason I could imagine for him to do anything for Draksah would be if someone he loved were hostage, and the only two people I could imagine his doing that for to the point of trying to kill me—but intentionally failing—would be if Kaheer—who is dead—or Brundar were held hostage. And Brundar obviously isn't.

We're left with his unexplained appearance, at times when he says he wasn't even in the palace. And with someone who has nearly come close to killing me. And with the people who know of those becoming deeply suspicious of my sworn and Archmage of Elly.

I take your meaning that Head of Fourth Circle is the person to deal with it, but this is Lendir Almar, and Lendir... He'd take off his skin and dance in his bones if Eerlen even hinted it might spare him a moment's worry. And everyone knows it. So the only finding people would believe from him would be a declaration that Eerlen is guilty. And I think Lendir would cut his own tongue off before saying such a thing. Even were it true.

So here we are. And I don't know how to solve it, except by having you and others I trust always near me.

And, much as I hate to say it, staying vigilant around Eerlen. This is making our relationship fraught, as he feels something is amiss and we had probably the worst fight of our relationship two nights ago.

I don't want to do this to him. I'm sure he doesn't deserve it. I'm sure he's innocent. But I don't know how to prove it. And I owe it to my people, and to Brund, to stay alive. You're the only one I'd discuss this with because I know you love Brund and myself and bear Eerlen no ill will.

If you have any ideas, I'll be glad to hear them, but don't, by the Maker's tits, say anything to anyone that might turn them against Eerlen or diminish his authority in the brotherhood.

Myrrir Mahar.

Lendir paused for a moment. "I'll have his power for this!"

Eerlen managed a small giggle – nerves – at the angry mutter. "Dir, Myrrir is dead. And he was third circle, not subjected to you."

"No, but Sarda is. Not subjected to me, but alive. And if he's doing fourth work, I can request his power be shut. What kind of madness were those two up to? How could Sarda suspect you? Enough to say it merited fourth investigation?"

Eerlen felt as though he'd been punched. That Myrrir had kept this from him. And from Lendir! "Obviously, there were clear signs that I'd been up to something. Or they saw someone who could cast a clear likeness of me. Or—"

"Eerlen, he didn't tell you someone was trying to kill him. You, the archmagician who should have been in charge of coordinating all actions on this, and of making sure he didn't run unnecessary risks. He didn't tell me! He thought I would corrupt my power... I'm sorry, I told you that I never wanted to hurt my sire, even as jealous of him as I was, but now I want to and he's conveniently dead, so I can't reach him."

His fury was such that Eerlen smiled through his tears, and became aware for the first time that he was crying. Which was stupid. This felt like a betrayal, which was also stupid. Myrrir was dead. All accounts were closed. And Myrrir had defended him. Even if there still seemed to be a doubt...

He wiped his cheeks with the back of his hand. "No. Turn it around. He was so reluctant to believe I was trying to kill him that he endangered himself rather than denounce me to the brotherhood." And that felt...right, and hurt less. Still, the knowledge that their last days together, Myrrir had this on his mind. That their last monumental fight— He wiped tears again. "And he died for it."

Lendir laughed without joy. "Well, he had me pretty well pegged. Except for the fact I wouldn't betray my oath to the brotherhood, he was well aware of how I felt about you. I think, love, you were the only one who didn't know what I felt for you."

Lendir sat on the bed, next to Eerlen, and put his arms around him. "You're shaking."

"You feel warm," Eerlen said. "Warmth is good."

"Love, you are in shock. You are going to need Brund. No, hear me out. He knows herbs, too, and always carries them, so he'll have something. And we need to tell him about this, anyway. He is king. We can't keep it from him."

"No," Eerlen said. "Not when he's a victim of whatever is continuing." He caught his lip between his teeth. "What if Brundar suspects me?"

"He won't. The only odd substance Brundar consumes in excess is honey nut balls. They're not hallucinogenic."

Eerlen must have been in shock, because though he remembered Lendir wrapping a fur around him, he didn't remember his leaving, much less coming back with Brundar.

But suddenly Brundar was there, kneeling at his feet, touching his forehead, and his hand.

"I don't need anything, Brund, I'm fine. It was just a shock."

"Yes, and you're not a weakling, and normally would be fine," Brundar said. "But you are healing from near-death. Take a deep breath. I'll be back soon."

"Have you read—"

"No, but I will. First, let's get you feeling better."

He came back in what was either a breath or three hours, with a cup with something that smelled pleasantly spicy. He put the warm cup in Eerlen's hands. "It won't harm the child." Then turned. "Lendir. The letter."

Eerlen sipped the herbal tea, pleasant, on the edge of burn, and felt...not calmer, but better able to concentrate. More detached.

He tried not to worry that Brundar would suspect him, but clearly Myrrir had and therefore—

Brundar made a sound somewhere between a growl and scoffing. "Whatever they tried to poison Myrrir with obviously affected his mind. Because he should have immediately told you about the attempt. He never told you any of this?"

"No."

"So he suspected you? That's beyond foolish. As for my crossibling!" He said the word like spitting. "I also never suspected him of being feebleminded. A weakling and quiet, and likely to defer to Haethlem, but not feebleminded."

"Whoever they saw must really have looked like me," Eerlen said.

But Brundar only knit his eyebrows at him. "An eighth circle. Has to be. No one else does illusions like them. But Selbur is head of eighth—"

"Yes, but I would see his pattern," Eerlen said. "An eighth couldn't hide working that kind of illusion from me."

"We'll have to go see Sarda," Brundar said. "But not you. Not while you're still so ill."

"You're in no great shape yourself," Lendir said.

"Well, not for feats of strength."

Eerlen drained the rest of his tea. "Brund, you can't endanger yourself. You can't."

"I might have to. We can't keep running. I'll take Webson."

"You can't bring him into this."

"He is in this. He's on the run with us. If I can find who is behind this and get back to the palace, we can better arrange to get in touch with his people, even if we have to do it from Draksah. It's in his best interests."

"Put like that..."

"It's the only way to put it."

"But don't go for a month, at least," this was Lendir. "Obviously, I can't command you, but you see how a month won't make any difference, and if you're going to risk yourself, I want you in condition to run or open a portal."

Brundar looked like he really wanted to protest, but couldn't. He shrugged and tilted his head, then sighed. "Fine. But you know all four of us will go stir-crazy. Also, we don't have enough food in stasis, not with the way our guest cooks. So either one of us has to go somewhere—likely Tarkross—for food, or we'll have to hunt and fish. I could take our guest fishing and tell him the whole tale. We kind of owe it to him."

"Brundar, about our guest—"

"Lendir, stop. I don't know what you're about to say, but I do not intend to seduce our guest. Both of you can stop looking concerned every time I talk to him. I'm not that desperate, and I'm not particularly interested in Draksall males. I know the complications of such unions much too well. And...oh, Maker's Balls, Eerlen, that wasn't aimed at your parents, or you as a complication."

Eerlen winced. "No, but it was a complication. Enough to get my parent cut off from the brotherhood. Might have cost him his life."

Brundar nodded. "True. But I was thinking of— I have seen Ad Leed go through a relationship with a Draksall, thank you. And I do not need it."

"Ad Leed?" Eerlen said, surprised.

"Kalal?" Lendir echoed close to.

Brundar made a sound like keening. "Right. He's going to duel me and kill me, and then he'll be guilty of regicide, and if the worst happens, Eerlen, remember I want Lendir to inherit."

Eerlen raised his eyebrows at him. "No. Brund. Seriously. What does Kalal Ad Leed, Lord of Brinar, have to do with Draksall males?"

Brund sat down heavily on the floor next to the bed, and leaned his head against Eerlen's legs. "Be aware if he kills me for it, it's on your head. It's the usual story, though how a Draksall deserter made it to ValLeed I don't know. Ad Leed didn't know he was Draksall when they got involved."

Lendir made a definitely profane comment about the Maker's womb. "He knows better than that."

"Aye, he does. And then he doesn't. He was...in love, Lendir."

"In love? Like a farmhand? He's the Lord of Brinar. His family has been the rulers of the land there for thousands of years."

Brundar shrugged.

"How old is he?" Eerlen said, more to himself than to them. He knew the names of his magicians, and he knew their patterns. He tried to know the relationships of first circles, and the ages of those he'd linked to the brotherhood himself when they were infants. That was not Kalal, of course, and obviously he'd missed Kalal's relationship to Lendir, and... Normally, he'd get it from the ruby, but right then linking to the ruby hurt. "Twenty-five?" he said, speaking more to himself.

"Twenty-five," Lendir said. "He was born three summers before I met you. Same summer my sibling was born."

Eerlen put his hand out, and touched Brundar's head, a caress, but not so obvious the child would complain. He was getting too old to enjoy parental attention. But to Eerlen, he was still a child. Maybe he'd always be. "You are friends, aren't you? I mean, besides the...whatever you have going with your spy corps.

If Lendir raised him. There was a brace of children you played with. Servants' children and traders' children from Eles. I know Lendir or his parent vetted them, but other than that, we paid no attention. We wanted you to grow up as normally as possible."

Lendir said, "They played together as children, yes. When my parent and Malin Ad Leed—his sworn—died when the shield dropped stranding them on the wrong side, I got them as mine to raise. The three of them, Nikre, and Brund, and Kalal, were thick as thieves, Malin, too, but he tended to trail behind. I didn't know they'd stayed friends."

Brundar made a sound. "We have. Particularly...well, he was the only one outside Nikre and Malin who knew why we left and— And everything. And he's Lendir's half-crossibling. He's...almost family. We stayed friends. I've—" He looked down. "Visited."

No surprise his admitting that he snuck out. Both he and Lendir knew it, to an extent.

"So this idiotic romance of my all-too-young half-crossibling?" Lendir said. "How badly did it go?"

"We don't know."

"You don't know?"

Brundar shook his head, the movement felt against Eerlen's leg. He made a little snuffle sound that mostly betrayed exasperation. "He was... Ad Leed was very happy, you know. His... Itarr was disguised as a servant in the palace, and he told Ad Leed he'd disappeared because he was... Because he was an heir to the throne, and his sibling who ascended the throne would kill him if he caught him to...to eliminate rivals, you know? And then—"

"And then?"

"Before Ad Leed could think how to tell you about this, and— He was afraid you'd sever him from the brotherhood, so he... Well, he was afraid. But before he could come up with a way to tell you, either of you, really, his lover disappeared. Just...vanished."

"How long did this fling last?" Lendir asked, and Eerlen could hear his voice tight with worry, but he didn't know if Brundar could.

"Two months."

"And how long ago was it?"

"Oh... It was shortly after we first ran. It's why—"

"It's why?"

"It's why he joined the spy corps," Brundar said, in a tone of sudden defiance. "He was hoping to find Itarr, or at least discover what had happened to him."

Lendir covered his face with his hands and shook. Eerlen suspected the tea that Brundar had given had robbed him of the capacity to be alarmed, or he'd have been very alarmed indeed.

Lendir didn't cry. "Lendir, love," Eerlen said in a worried tone.

Lendir lowered his hands. There were no tears, but his face was in a manic rictus of a smile, almost as alarming. "Eerlen," he said, and chuckled. "I have to laugh or I'm going to kick a hole in the wall of the cave, and yes, I know it's stone. Idiots. I'm related to idiots. My sire. My half-crossibling. You're excused on account of being a king, which apparently softens the brain, Brundar, but there has been no recent ascension to the throne in Draksah. And Brundar, the name for a Draksall deserter who makes it as far as Brinar is spy, and a damn good one."

"I guess that's another Lord of the Land I'll need to talk to," Eerlen said. His voice sounded hollow even to his own ears. He kept hoping he could wake up and all this mess would be a bad dream.

Lords of the Land. Brundar should have curbed this, but he was young and romantic. And obviously had seen nothing wrong with it at all. Myrrir would have quelled it with a look and a word, but Myrrir—

Myrrir had been holding deadly secrets from Eerlen.

THE MANY PERILS
OF ETHNOGRAPHIC
COLLECTION

SKIP

First, I would like to point out I am in no way qualified to do ethnographic collection. And if I were to do ethnographic collection, given my training, it would be as second-in-command to someone who'd studied anthropology, archeology, archeo-linguistics, and archeo-anthropology, predictive sociology and comparative cultural patterns, and knew how to piece together the evolution of culture and language in a long-lost colony, or even the particular adaptations to their unique circumstances and purpose.

Second, I would like to point out that no one—no one—would have sent me, even as the supernumerary in a ten-person delegation to a world where the genetic modification was quite so intrusive or the culture had evolved so weirdly. Send me as make-weight to lend luster and guard doors in a group of ten to a planet where humans had been bioed to be born with infrared sight, and where the major adaptation is that they used only sign language or something...maybe.

But magic? And hermaphrodites?

I hadn't prayed in quite some time, something that would doubtless disappoint my father, who had, in his gentle way, tried to convey his own unwavering faith. I'd always felt a little detached, a little too doubtful to do so.

And after Father died, I'd been too angry to address Him, whom the Ellyans called Maker. However, right then, if I could have figured out a way, I'd have done it.

It hadn't escaped my acute observation, honed in a lot of bars where suddenly a fight or worse could break out and it was best to be aware of such emotional currents, that Eerlen Troz had become very upset by something while he was working on figures with Peaseblossom.

I'd also noted his pocketing – or sleeving – of a roll of cloth. That they wrote on cloth was interesting, given how little of technology they had preserved, and I honestly would be making notes if only I could have had the foresight of dropping out of that window holding a recording device. Or a notepad. I'd watched them write and the alphabet looked like something invented by an artist. What kind of natural language uses five colors of ink and a brush for writing what amounted to a spreadsheet?

I'll grant you it looked very pretty when completed. And that I was going to need to learn it, just to get along in what seemed to be a literate world, but I'd have to inveigle someone—for best, Troz or Peaseblossom, though Ad Leed might do it, too, if I asked nicely—to read me some of the colored one, and then some of the no-color version like the stuff engraved on the belt Troz had given Almar. The characters were the same, but there was additional notation, possibly to mean color.

I also noted, given my sharpened powers of observation, that Troz had left the room quickly, followed by Almar, after Almar asked us if we could do the clean-up, but didn't wait around for our assent.

While we were washing dishes and drying them, and putting away the uneaten bread in the stasis box, I heard sobbing. Peaseblossom heard it, too. I could tell. It made him so nervy that he worked in silence, and stopped filching croissants, as he'd been doing when he didn't think I was looking.

I couldn't even imagine what had happened, but hoped we weren't in for some kind of marital—was it marital?—drama, because truly, I was in enough trouble already. And it hadn't escaped me that both Peaseblossom and Ad Leed had been flirting with me, nor that Troz had been half-amused and half-exasperated by their display.

As he should be, by the by. Even past the complications of my having to study a completely different anatomy, and not being sure how I felt about it, beyond curiosity, there is an unbreakable rule in the Diplomatic Corps. You don't get horizontal with your subjects. No hanky-panky with those you are diplomating at. Or even hanky without the panky or panky without the hanky. And under no circumstances are you to study xeno-human anatomy, unless they're ill and you need to do it to render assistance. And even then, only if you're sure the assistance breaks no local taboos. Probably my stripping both king and Archmage to save their lives was already enough to get me kicked out of the service.

Of course, at the moment I was spoiled for reasons to get kicked out, and almost longed to be kicked out, because it would mean I had made it back home for the out-kicking.

But one way or another, the rule still held. Getting horizontal with people in strange colonies—and they came no stranger than this—just plain wasn't diplomatic.

So when Lendir Almar came out of the corridor leading to the bedrooms looking upset, I almost hid, so I wasn't there for whatever confrontation was going to follow. If he asked me if I found Peaseblossom attractive, what could I say? Sir, my body is a dumb beast, but I have it under control. Er. Mostly. Probably.

Instead, what Almar did was nod at me and say, "If you'll excuse me, Webson." Then he turned to Peaseblossom, who was drying the cups I'd just washed. "Brund, Eerlen had a shock and he isn't feeling well. I was wondering if you'll have some herbs that might help."

Peaseblossom looked more worried, set the cup he'd just dried—the cups were clay, cylindrical, heavy, with a brilliant blue glaze—with the others on a shelf on the wall, and turned wiping his hands on the cloth. "I'll see him first." He tried to put the cloth on the table, but it would have dropped without my grabbing for it.

He asked over his shoulder if I'd put water to boil, and I did, in a heavy iron kettle over the fire. The same way I'd boiled water for our tea.

The king came back moments later, with a cup, and it must already have had herbs in it, because when he filled it from the kettle, it released a strange, spicy odor. It was no herb known to Earth or High Britannia or the surrounding worlds. Well, none of the ones I'd been in with Father, at least. I had studied herbal cures, mostly because Father knew them. Look, they weren't needed for us and people like us, because we'd been loaded with curative nanos. One of the benefits of extensive wealth. But sometimes Father took retainers and old friends who had not been so blessed on these adventures. The full nanos were quite expensive, and normally only noblemen did it, and sometimes only for the heirs.

And yes, sure, we took all the full complement of modern medicine; full range of injectors, and diagnostic tools. Things, in fact, I wish I had with me now, if this adventure was going to get any spicier. But sometimes the high-tech things didn't cover poisons or viruses peculiar to some far-flung planet. And Father didn't believe on trusting chance to bring us back alive from the hunts or hikes on strange terrain.

So I can tell that of my vast knowledge, this was a completely different set of herbs. I was starting to suspect whoever had designed this colony had gone haywire with a My Little Genetic Engineer kit. Either that or the pre-existing fauna and flora had been something to behold. Could be either-or. As long as they had no equivalent of Feglieri, we were going to get along just fine.

For something to do, I finished cleaning the dishes, and drying them and putting them away, and then sternly resisted the temptation to bake something. There were still eggs. If I whipped them, I could probably make angel food cake. I remembered some finely milled flour.

I told myself sternly they'd think I was deranged if I kept baking at them at the slightest provocation or even no provocation at all. Also, given Peaseblossom's fascination with baked goods, he'd expand to double his girth. Which would be a crying shame.

Just as I thought this, he came back from inside and told me what I'd heard were the most dreaded words in any relationship. "Viscount Webson, we need to talk."

I'd never been in a relationship where the words had been flung at me, and the longest of my relationships were casual enough, I'd not have cared. But I was dependent on these people, so I confess the phrase terrified me, even though—that I knew—we had no relationship of any kind, besides saving each other's lives a couple of times.

If he'd imagined—noticed?—untoward stares, or if he decided, belatedly, to take offense at my stripping him to doctor him, and threw me out on the ice and howling snow outdoors, the fact we had no relationship wouldn't keep me alive a second longer. And I suspected my life would be measured in seconds, in fact.

But Peaseblossom was polite, and led me to the area where we'd sat for breakfast, and sat down and then—

Okay, I think all of us know sagas, right? From the old sagas of Earth—yes, of course my father read me La Mort D'Arthur when I was an infant, and in retrospect, this was probably not normal—to the various founding myths of various worlds, each one more full of pathos and danger than the other.

But this one... Well, at least Shakespeare could have written it.

I won't give it to you in Shakespearean prose, though. It doesn't need it. The king, Peaseblossom's parent—mother, for those following at home and feeling particularly touchy about stilted language—had died of murder. And the reason Peaseblossom and two of his closest blood relatives were on the run is that the same had been attempted against Peaseblossom himself.

So something was rotten in the planet of Elly, and someone had it in for the king. Whoever the king happened to be.

But then the plot thickened. Or at least multiplied. Apparently when it came to sirelings, the old king had a wide-dispersal tip to his— Ahem. He was father to his people. We'll say that. You understand, right? And he had seeded sirelings where he pleased, at least until he met and swore to Eerlen Troz.

Three of those were known and acknowledged, one being Lendir Almar, captain of the palace guard, but also two of the Lords of the Land, what you and I would probably call provincial governors, Ter and Sarda.

Ter, I gathered, was not in good odor with Peaseblossom. This could be personality or...or something far more justifiable.

Brundar said he was the oldest child of Myrrir Mahar and his first sworn, and unpleasant with it. Sarda, on the other hand, was no worse than weak and in thrall of his best friend—cousin?—Haethlem who tended to overprotect him.

If you're following along at home, it gets worse, and man, Shakespeare would really love this plot, because he loved, ahem, comedies of errors, and people who were mistaken for other people and—

Apparently, the attempts on the old king—and I felt terrible calling him that, since from my calculations he was only in his early fifties, half a life in Britannia on High, but I had to distinguish him from the current king—had been perpetrated in circumstances where someone had seen or thought he had seen Eerlen

Troz nearby. So the Archmagician was suspected.

But they had not known of it till tonight, when they'd found a letter forgotten in the travel desk, from Myrrir Mahar to his sireling Khare Sarda. The letter had been read to me and it was pretty scurrilous, and even though I was no marital expert, it seemed wrong of him to have written it about his spouse without telling his spouse there was anything amiss.

I still didn't understand what it had to do with me. So Peaseblossom unpacked it with as much heat as light, hands gesturing, green eyes flashing. And was I glad I was not on the receiving end of that.

He explained that anyone who was trying to kill him would of course include me in the reckoning if I was nearby but further on, there was the fear that people suspected Eerlen might have taken the flight from the palace for dark reasons and be spreading rumors against him. And though he didn't give specifics, I got the feeling he'd encountered that sentiment, and also that given the culture, torches and pitchforks might be in the offing.

Being the exquisitely trained diplomat I was, I blurted the first thing that crossed my mind. "But that's mentally unhinged. To suspect Troz, I mean. He doesn't impress me as stupid enough that he'd have been seen, if he had really been guilty."

This got me a scream of glee and a sudden hug. I mean, he lunged across the sitting cushion, broaching our very proper two-foot separation, and hugged me. He felt warm and muscular and smelled of croissants.

I fortunately didn't react—very diplomatic of me, but mostly because I was taken by complete surprise—so he pulled back, a little awkwardly, in the way people do when trying to pretend they didn't do something. But his voice was still warm, as he said, "You see."

I nodded. In fact, I was completely at sea, and there were no lighthouses in sight.

"I wanted to go and confront Sarda," Mahar said. "But Eerlen says I have to wait until I'm more healed, like a month or six weeks or so, because I won't be able to either run or open a portal right now."

Having seen the wounds up close and personal the night before, I was more surprised that Peaseblossom was standing and doing things than that he should take more rest before a perilous mission.

Frankly, even with the nanos, if I had that kind of wound, I'd be lying down and moaning for a few days, if there was no regen tank available. We were taught that barbarism leads to stoicism, because not being quite well, ever, establishes that as your baseline. But I thought that they looked too healthy for that. At least these three. So perhaps it was training.

"I'm going to be climbing walls," Mahar said, glaring at his toes, which I realized for the first time were clad in embroidered slippers, dark blue with little red flowers. Uh.

"You will be patient," Lendir said. Which was the first we realized he'd come back into the common area.

He had his arm around Eerlen Troz, helping him—again, how was Troz even walking?—and they dropped on a sitting cushion across from us, on the other side of the low, round oak table on which our meal had been served.

"At any rate, Ad Leed is a more immediate problem than Sarda," Eerlen said. He didn't sound even slightly happy about it.

"Ad Leed?" I asked. And fortunately, didn't add that I really hadn't thought anything bad about him besides that I'd have bought him drinks at a certain type of bar in the New London, capital city of Britannia on High. Because it turns out despite my feelings, this was not even remotely about me.

Apparently, Ad Leed had had a romance with a Draksall male who had disappeared. This struck me as very strange, considering that Draksalls ate Ellyans, but apparently it wasn't that abnormal, and Eerlen Troz's sire himself had been a Draksall.

I should have realized before this meant Ellyans were genetically compatible with unmodified humanity. I suspect I had, but not paid it any mind. Now it struck me speechless for a full minute, after which, changing my thoughts forcefully, I started to realize the survey of Draksah couldn't have been merely incompetent—no one is that incompetent—and must have been suborned.

At any rate, Ad Leed had not got himself impregnated, but they were all very jumpy about it, because from the circumstances, they deduced the Draksall had to be a spy and therefore presumed he might have done something to Ad Leed.

What the something might have been was...confusing to say the least.

Assume magic was real, or at least that it was caused by some kind of viral stuff. I'm going to give you the high points, because I don't understand the low points. All right, I don't understand the high points, either, but it's easier to assume it was just some kind of misnamed high tech. Perhaps invented by the same kind of reverse genius who had thought it a great idea to make humans hermaphrodite, or to play alchemist with various herb species.

"The thing is, I know you don't understand," Troz said. "But Kalal Ad Leed is a third circle, which means after a healing, he's...highly susceptible to... Well, third circles become highly susceptible to emotional— They can lose control of their emotions. So there will be fights or...or flings."

Noted. I wouldn't think of Peaseblossom's hug as more than that. He'd done enough healing to pass out the day before. He was probably still in a state of emotional instability.

"It's quite likely," Troz went on, ignoring my mental calculation, because he, hopefully, didn't know about the hug. "That he was approached at that time and for that reason. And anyone sent to approach him that way would be a magician himself."

"Wait," I said. "The Draksalls have magic?"

They, all three, stared at me as though I'd taken leave of my senses.

"Yes, of course," Troz said.

"If they didn't, their opening a breach portal to Erradi and attempting an invasion every generation would be impossible," Lendir said.

"Or at least their armies of invasion would be easy to defeat, if they didn't hold shields against our magic, let alone our arrows and lances."

The impulse to say that was impossible crossed in my brain with my memory of Eerlen Troz holding an invisible force-field shield over us, strong enough to keep energy weapons at bay, and I snapped my mouth shut so hard it made a sound.

The keening noise that escaped me after had to be explained, as all of them were staring round-eyed, and Troz looked like he'd go for his ankle knives. So I explained my half-fury, half-fear exclamation. "Supposedly, Draksah was investigated by a team before I was sent. How could they have missed that?"

Peaseblossom shrugged. "They probably didn't. They were intending to lure you in so they could kill you."

"What?" And now you'll think I was simpleminded, but I truly hadn't looked at it that way. I knew they—some armed group from outside Elly—had shot at me, but it never occurred to me that this was the desired outcome. Hearing it said like that was a shock.

"From what my spies report," Peaseblossom said, and sighed, and didn't pat me on the head, which I'd have felt was earned. "The plan to kill you was from the stars. From your own people. They were just using the Draksalls to do it. They thought you knew something, and could bring the Fourth—the Law on them. That you could identify a key conspirator in their plot, from what I heard, and they must eliminate you to be safe."

Through my mind ran everyone who might have a grudge against me, but I couldn't imagine anyone who was so furious at me as to want to kill me. Slap me hard, maybe. Perhaps cause me to lose a lot of money. But kill me? I swallowed hard and nodded, so they wouldn't think I was dumber than should be allowed for a sentient being.

Troz made a sound that might have been a chuckle, but was sympathetic. "I'm sorry. I know how you feel. Because I never heard of this...problem with Ad Leed till now, and worse, he's healed all of us since. I'm supposed to mind my third circles better. Well, all my magicians, really. But the time since Myrrir's death has been so fraught and perilous, I lost track of them."

I frowned at him. "What does it matter if he— Well, if he had an affair with a Draksall? It might be considered in bad taste, and perhaps not quite the thing, but unless you suspect his loyalty..."

"Ad Leed's? No," Troz said, at the same time Almar said, "No."

"The problem," Troz explained. "Is if he caught him at a vulnerable time and somehow planted a suggestion or a...a compulsion for him to do something. Which could include planting a compulsion in one of us."

See what I mean about contagion? "Wouldn't that be visible?" I asked.

"In the pattern?" Troz asked. "Not necessarily. Depends on what it was, and if done with Draksall magic, which is different from our own, I might have missed the signs. Normally, I'd examine him, but since he healed me, I might have been corrupted to see nothing while he healed me."

"I see. So there is no cure?"

"Oh, no. If he hasn't healed Nikre Lyto, my second-in-command and apprentice, or another two or three close in first circles, they can mind-search him. It's just that I'd like to be present, because the process can be dangerous, and I'm responsible for him. And for all of them."

"But they can't do it here?" I asked.

He shook his head. "Not here. It's deeply shielded. Very difficult to do magic here, which is how Brundar almost killed himself with what he did. I could help, but the truth is, I'm not up to supervising, not for another month, at least. Maybe more"

I didn't fully understand what they meant to do to Ad Leed. My mind conjured images of the iron maiden and pulling nails, but it didn't sound like that.

"I'm going to be climbing walls," Brundar said. "We can't even have reports here very often, because someone might notice comings and goings if they haven't already. And Eerlen can't pull through the ruby, not till his power burn is healed." He sighed, then grinned for me. "Wanna go fishing?"

I stared.

"Not until we modify him," Troz said.

I jumped, finding myself in a defensive posture, just short of reaching for my ankle knife. "Modify how?" I thought—look, given the conversation about third circles, which is what I understood Mahar was—through what that could mean and, to my great pride, did not—repeat, did not—cover the essential part of my anatomy they thought might need modification. Barely.

Instead, I asked again, urbanely, I thought, "Modify?"

Eerlen Troz was looking at me clinically. "Well, we'll need to grow your hair. No one here wears their hair that short, even workmen. And we should get rid of your beard growth and some body hair and..."

"Get rid—" I put my hand up to my chin and realized I had quite a growth, even if it would be mostly colorless.

"Inhibit its growth till you leave this world. But for that, you can pass as an Erradian, and not a bad-looking one."

I didn't know whether to thank him or glare. "But I thought you couldn't do magic. I mean." I gestured. "Here."

"Oh. Not right now, at any rate, but I should be able to in a week or two. Or at least the three of us together should be able to. It's not an onerous spell."

Look, I know that many people take shots to stop their beard growth and save themselves the trouble of shaving, but for some reason, the idea bothered me. I never said I was rational.

"I don't know if they know you are here," Eerlen Troz said gravely. "So hiding you makes sense."

"I don't see why—"

"Given that they intended to kill you, and given that the attack yesterday seemed to be by your people," Brundar Mahar said. "It would seem a logical conclusion that they know where you are or at least are looking for you."

Et tu, Peaseblossom, I thought but didn't say. Heaven only knows what the translator would make of that. Aloud, I said, "You seem to have a point."

"They might or might not know that Brundar is the head of the spying ring—" Lendir Almar said.

"Unlikely," Troz said. "They'd think it too insane."

"That's because it is too insane," Almar said.

"That's the brilliance of my plan," Mahar said, and got a glare from both of the older people, though I thought the joke was pretty good. Then he turned to me. "At any rate, if they don't know I'm involved, and since none of the people sent against us returned to tell the tale, they might not know. If you fit in, you're unlikely to attract them."

My father taught me to be compulsively honest. If I ended up dying outside in the ice, it would be entirely his fault for that. "They probably have a tracker on me," I said before I could stop myself. And realized my words were a tracking spell.

"Oooh," Mahar said. "We'll have to go to the palace. Have to, Eerlen. If he has a tracking spell, Nikre can disable it. You know he can. We can sense the star magics. Well, first circles can. And me, sometimes. But not always."

"Are you out of your ever living mind, Brundar Mahar? You'd walk unprotected into the palace?"

Peaseblossom looked at his sire, and arranged his face so it looked completely innocent and sweet. "Eerlen, Maker's Thighs. I grew up in the place. I know every way in and out. No one will ever find us."

Troz just groaned and dropped his head into his hands.

A Certain Sense Of Déjà Vu

Skip

The palace of the kings of Elly was eerily familiar, only the last time I'd seen it, it had running water with actual faucets, and light and heating and—

I probably should explain, right? And, because he'll inevitably read this, I should keep in mind Mr. Crowe's instructions and Start from the beginning, damn it, Skip Hayden!

So the beginning of it is that Peaseblossom got his way. Which I was starting to suspect he was in the habit of doing. I should probably be grateful—given how dependent I was on him, just then, since he was the most important person in the party of lunatics who had saved me from assassination and continued to save me, seemingly daily—that his habit of getting his way involved relentless discussion and logic, with a certain amount of personal charm, and not royal commands.

His logic was impeccable, too. "Eerlen," he said, when the arch-magician uncovered his face. "It's only logical. I should take him to the palace as soon as possible, so that the next best thing we have to an archmagician who hasn't been healed by someone whose power might be corrupted will destroy any tracking spell on him."

Eerlen spoke intently to a spot above Mahar's head, I suspect so he wouldn't engage the look of pleading in Mahar's eyes. "Brund, we're in deep no-magic. There is no magic here. Well, very little and it needs to be channeled from the people themselves. Which means we should be eating, sleeping, and powering the healing that is draining from us, so that we heal."

"We don't know that his tracker is the same sort of magic."

"I don't think there's more than one type of magic," Eerlen said, and looked at him, and sounded exasperated. "Sure, the Draksalls pull from another source which I don't know and have different spells, but it's still the same magic."

"What if," Mahar said. "Hear me out, but what if the magic from the people of the stars isn't the same?"

Eerlen Troz looked at me with that type of look an exasperated adult gives another. "Milord, would you please tell my deluded sireling that magic is magic?"

Oh, hell. There are things you really don't want to do, but I had to. "My culture has no magic."

Troz and Almar—but, I'll note, not Peaseblossom—stared at me as though I'd taken leave of my senses for good.

"No...magic?" the archmagician asked.

"None. No magicians, no brotherhood of magicians, no spells, no suggestions, no compulsions."

His jaw dropped again. When he managed to speak, he said, "How do you do anything?"

Right, well. What the heck do you do in that situation? I stood straight, squared my shoulders. The shades of Archimedes, Pythagoras, Galileo, Blaise Pascal, Isaac Newton, both the Curies, Einstein, Robarth, Miles Tuney, Fidelia and Johannes Antal, and a hundred others whose names wouldn't come to my mind right then stood at my back, hands on my shoulders, making me strong.

"We have science," I said.

Which would have been an impressive declaration, and of course, get them falling at my feet in awe an abjuring their heretical creed, except that...

If you didn't guess it before, you should know that what the translator nanos made come out of my mouth was, We have magic.

Have you ever tried to look at your own mouth in stern disapproval? It's not easy. It might not be possible. But whatever expression I was making made Troz and Almar look like—had they been standing and not had a fluffy cushion and the back of some kind of cabinet behind them—they would have scrambled away from me.

Their eyes definitely said, "Whoa, now!"

Meanwhile, Peaseblossom coughed. Only I am not stupid, and no, he didn't. What the little traitor did was laugh. At me.

"That wasn't the right translation. Sorry, my translating nanos seem to think that's your only word for what we do. Let me explain."

I started in the age of steam and tried to give them a fast retrospective of the wonders and marvels of science. I probably should have started with the Greeks. I would have, too, if I could remember Pythagoras doing more than calculating the size of fields, or one or the other of the weirder Greeks thinking that beans were seeds for humans.

And therein was the problem. I had an extensive and exquisite education, in the military arts, the history of the military, and then languages, and how to approach very different cultures, record their approach to things and— No, not a lot about science. Not since I'd left elementary education.

When I finished my summary, Eerlen Troz looked even more confused, and said, in a tiny voice, "Your magic is powered by water boiled on coal, that makes machines move to make clothes. Lord Webson! None of that can be true."

What do you do in the face of an impossible task? Well, I have no idea what you do, friend, but personally, myself—this one behind my eyes—doubles down with enthusiasm, verve and a deep sense of desperation.

I started with the scientific method, admitted I knew nothing of science, but gave a retrospective of all its achievements, up to space travel—the Schrodingers got much frowning, and a mutter about people who open portals irresponsibly—and the nanos that affected my speech translation.

"I think what we have," Troz said, slowly, after I'd fallen silent, probably to everyone's relief, including mine. "Is a semantic disagreement."

I sighed. "Only it's not. I don't know what you do, and don't understand it, but... Okay, granted, I also don't understand what we do, but it's not dependent on individuals who can do so manipulating power flows or...whatever else you do."

At which point, Peaseblossom dry-coughed, this time just a cough, and stood up. "Allow me to explain," he said, standing between the two sitting areas, right by the table. "What we do is essentially the same thing, based on mathematical principles, formulas and experimentation, but Ellyans—and Draksalls—do it through a capability of manipulating time, space, and matter with their minds, while for some reason the people from the stars don't have this power. Which means they use matter to manipulate matter, and it all gets unholy complicated. There is a report about

this that Selbur acquired, and which we're getting translated from
the Draksall, as soon as the translator is done weaning his child.
Or at least once he gets his child past the first three months.""The
translator?" Troz frowned.

"Tarid Keres."

"Oh. Fifth circle? Another like me? Raised in both tongues? Why
not give it to me?"

"Because I thought you were a little busy with..." Peaseblossom
gestured. "Everything. Besides healing from power burn. Though
I can get it to you as soon as I can get a message to him and one
back. Say, when we go to the palace."

"Brund—"

"No, Eerlen. The Draksalls know the...magic of the stars is fun-
damentally different. Why couldn't you hold the shield in place
over us while the strange space weapons were turned on us?"

"Because they wouldn't stop. Whoever powered them didn't get
tired. And the spells didn't drain."

"That's because no one was powering them, and the spells in
this case are batteries—that's what they're called, and they store
power—"

"Like the stasis box?"

"I don't think so. But more importantly, while they run out, they
use so little of their stored power at one go, that our shielding
ability will run out long before they do."

Troz sighed. "But then how will Nikre be able to neutralize this
magic?"

"Well, because we have found we can see it, and you can, too, as
a focus of energy, but don't try it now because you're not in a state
to. We...er...stole some of the artifacts from the stars and played
with them."

"Brundar!" This was Almar.

"All right. It wasn't the brightest of ideas, and I won't say it was
Selbur's because I went along with it, but it definitely was Selbur's.
I was the one who told him we should take cover when we pushed
energy into an already fully charged energy weapon."

I think I screamed. No, really, like a little girl. I'll have you know
my screams are very manly. But visualizing lunatics overcharging
a blaster made me cover my mouth and scream.

The only person who noticed was Peaseblossom, who grinned
at me. "Yes. It was magnificent. The boulder we took cover be-

hind... Uh. Whatever your people use to make weapons actually got embedded in the rock. Three fingers deep."

I might have screamed again, but no one was paying attention. Do you know what it takes to make glassteel explode? Well, neither do I, but I know directly shooting a blaster won't achieve it. "Anyway, smaller self-powered devices such as trackers—they put them on the weapons, the goofs—and communicators, when given just the right amount of energy, just die."

"Eerlen," Almar said, in a tone of someone just passing the time of day. "We need to keep him closer, and watch him."

"In a locked box," Troz answered in the same tone. "And through a far-viewer. Until he has a dozen children."

"It's the only way to preserve the throne and his line," Almar said piously.

Peaseblossom ignored them.

"Will it also destroy all other nanos in my body?"

Peaseblossom frowned at me. "Shouldn't. We know about the speech translating spells and the...health spells, but the trackers we saw in Draksall are much larger and less subtle. If it's something smaller, we'll have to figure out some way to tell them apart. However, given that they're tracking you right now, I'd say it's a matter of some urgency."

"No one will be able to come in here," Troz protested. "Only those affiliated closely with the Troz line can enter unaccompanied."

"Which did a lot for us in the last shelter, didn't it?"

"Maybe one of the cousins—" Eerlen Troz said, and sighed. "Brundar Mahar, if you get yourself killed, I'll find a way to revive you so that I can kill you again. Over and over. I'll make it my hobby for the next ten years. At least."

Peaseblossom did not look impressed. "Heard and acknowledged. I have no intentions of dying. But if I do, I'll leave documents in the writing box naming Lendir and his descendants my heir."

Lendir yelped. "What have I ever done to you? Why not Nikre?"

"Nothing. You're my favorite crossibling. Nikre is too little and too kind. They'd kill him. And I won't die. Milord Webson will take energy weapons with us. He's skilled with them."

I didn't dispute it. I was. But I'd also take knives, swords, and if I could get away with it, bows and arrows.

Turns out we couldn't get away with bows and arrows. Oh, they made us wait almost three weeks, because Troz said we simply couldn't risk it with Brundar's power so depleted. But they finally let us go.

No bows and arrows, though. Also, we couldn't get away with swords. Apparently, it would make us conspicuous in the palace, where the only people who wore swords were the guard.

However, I was relieved to find that Peaseblossom wasn't all that bad with a blaster. He said he couldn't understand how someone could be bad at it, which I guess made sense from his perspective, since it was a lot lower effort than bows and arrows.

We each armed ourselves with a half-dozen blasters, mostly concealed in various places in our clothes.

So they couldn't make my hair grow or my beard fall out—may I confess to a fear they'd never reverse those spells?—but Mahar was sure that this Nikre Lyto who was archmagician understudy to Troz and his...crossibling—which made no sense: wouldn't he be Troz, then?—would be able to do it.

I had to shave really closely, and they put me in a tunic that had a very high collar so it hid the fact that my hair in fact stopped at about the nape of my neck. I didn't even protest it. The fact the tunic was deep blue and embroidered all over with fantastic birds and flowers was only a little disturbing "I thought we were supposed to be stealthy."

"It's the only way to blend in," Troz said. "I don't like it, either."

"Which is why he usually wore clothes that stood out by being too plain and not at all expensive," Almar put in with a laugh behind his words. "It is a sort of pride. Just a strange one. Drove my sire insane."

In addition, there were what I can only call harem pants, all puffed-out legs in blue velvet, fortunately not embroidered. But the leather shoes, what I'm told were called palace slippers, were much like Peaseblossom's, but blue and magnificently embroidered all over with tiny butterflies. Peaseblossom changed into a similar green outfit with a less exaggerated collar.

The problem, of course, was that he apparently shouldn't just open a portal from the cave mouth. I mean, not that we could. We were in deep no-magic.

But there were ways around it. I knew I was in for it when asked if I could ski.

I'm going to say right now that I don't know how we did it. There were no goggles. And outside the cave, the wind was blowing shards of ice in our faces.

Also, no, we weren't in our finery. You see, we needed to go through public portals.

Which meant we had to be non-memorable Erradian nomads. So over the finery went fur tunic and pants—I felt like a walking, well, skiing, bolster—and boots, and a fur cloak with a deep hood. We also had backpacks under the cloak, the purpose of which I figured out after we got through the public portal.

I'd never have found the public portal. Not on my own. For one, I was snow-blind, and my eyes only hadn't frozen because I'd kept them closed a good portion of the way, while following Mahar by sound. Safe? No. But I didn't like frozen eyes.

Besides that, there was nothing there that said it was a portal. No eldritch lights, no spiral of barely seen power. There were two very tall stone pillars with some writing on them.

Mahar stopped short of them, and through my lashes, I saw him remove his skis. I removed mine, and held them under my arm as he did. He pointed the portal to me, then removed his glove and offered me his hand.

I looked at him like he was nuts, but put my hand forward. He made a sound, removed my glove and held my hand. His hand was still warm. He tugged me forward.

We were...in deep green jungle, and there were birds twittering in the trees. Something large and yellow-plumed flew over our heads, screaming. He gave me my glove back. "Sorry. I had to be touching you, skin to skin, because you don't know the destination."

Instantly bathed in sweat, I looked around. "Where in hell are we?" What came out was Where in Deep Ice are we, which sounded lunatic in this warm, humid place. I suspected the nanos had imprinted on Eerlen Troz's use of language.

Peaseblossom didn't seem to register the solecism. He wrinkled his forehead, sweat pouring down from his hairline. "Brinar. I have... There's a place."

The place which didn't exist—I'd swear to that—until Mahar opened an invisible door was maybe half a mile into the jungle. A little stone house, no bigger than a bedroom in the Erradi shelter. Say, round and about fifteen feet across. He dropped skis, poles, and backpack, and started divesting himself of clothing. The clothing went into the backpacks. The skis, and poles were propped up in the corner.

"Obviously, we're going to be conspicuous on the way to the palace," he said. "But the skis and poles can stay here till we need them again. Lyto should be able to portal us to Yanda, or as close as we can go."

"Right," I said, pretending it all made sense, though it was clear as mud.

"Normally I'd just cut a portal," Brundar said. "But if I do I risk pattern burn, because of the wound and being so exhausted."

"Right," I said again, because it seemed like a good answer.

"Anyway, we'll have to be careful not to be seen on the way to the portal. And you'll have to hold my hand again."

"Right."

It was, too. I mean, I had nothing against it. On the way back to the portal—also two upright pillars of stone with writing on them—I asked, "Is that a line shelter?"

"What?"

"The place where we changed."

He blushed deeply, for some reason, and shook his head. "No. I borrowed it. I— Uh. Sometimes I needed to confer with people from the spy group."

Uh huh. I won't tell you there were tells he was lying, but there were tells he was lying. Mostly, his eyes going side to side. I wondered why he bothered since I was a stranger. He could have told me that's where he sacrificed small animals, and I'd assume it was part of the culture. For some reason, he felt the need to lie.

I didn't remember any furniture in the place, except a hammock, and if he came there to sleep on a hammock, who was I to judge? I suspected if my family dragged me through ice and caves, at some point I might have a deep hankering to sleep somewhere warm and above ground.

He held my hand as we stepped through the portal.

Okay, so when we went into it, there was no one else there. But when we came out, we were part of a throng. It was like a commuter zip station letting out at rush hour in downtown New London.

There were people of all sizes and types. Colors, too, which surprised me, because most colonies were all one color, normally a variant of Mediterranean, for some reason. Maybe because that's the color and general look you get after a few generations of blending all races and colors. But this looked much like Capitol city, having everything from tall blonds to people the color of dark wood.

Our clothes were right on point for not being recognized, but even so, I wondered at Mahar not being recognized until I looked at him and blinked, because his hair was pale blond, very straight, and his eyes soft blue. His nose had also grown.

"Minor illusion," he whispered in my ear. "It won't stand probing. The point is not to be probed."

We walked away from the portal, and a little to the side. And I was glad I did have training in looking completely at ease, while so jumpy I could barely think. Most of the throng was climbing tall marble staircases to a building, and the building...

Look, did I ever tell you that the Queen's palace incorporates the first colonizing ship?

It does. It's right up front. The very same shape that was in my decoration, glimmering in bluish glassteel. Oh, there was more to it, because behind it, the generations of Kings and Queens of Britannia on High had built onto the palace, so the building climbed and sprawled, enclosing the spaceship. Except for the front, where it was completely recognizable

They'd done it here, too, except the newer building was much shorter than in New London, made mostly of white marble, and really sprawled to the sides and back.

"We don't know what the first palace was made of," Mahar said. "We no longer know how to make the material. But it's almost impossible to keep warm in winter."

"That's because it's glassteel," I said, staring disbelievingly at the thing. "It's the ship that landed here. One of the between-the-stars ships, first generation. And it's normally heated, cooled and insulated from a fusion engine." Fusion engine came out of my mouth as "the power of the stars themselves," which I'll agree sounded cool.

And then I realized I'd just pulled the world from under my companion's feet.

He stood stock-still, looking at me, then back at the palace, and then at me again. "That?" he asked, pointing. "That is a ship from the stars?"

I sighed. "I'm sorry. I tried to tell you, but every colony thinks they're the original home of humanity. And it's very hard to argue with when I had no proof on me."

He nodded, once. "So we, too..." He nodded again. "The thing that opened the portals? Schrodkingers?"

"Schrodingers," I said. "Yes. They threw your ancestors back. I don't know how long, but...ten thousand years sounds likely. More than five, at least."

He proved more resilient than anyone I'd met because he blinked twice, then shook his head. He swallowed. He took a deep breath. The only evidence of discomposure was that his voice cracked a little as he said, "Right. Let's find Nikre Lyto."

Hunters and Hunted

Skip

The archmagician understudy didn't look it. Which is just as well, since we found him in the most unusual of ways.

Brundar Mahar took a path around the right side of the palace, which wasn't a path at all after about three steps. Instead, we were walking over loose stones, and scraping ourselves on bushes. There was a wall beyond those bushes, tall and white, and I'd guess it was shielded with some magic thing.

There was a wall on the other side, too. Or a series of them. The more surprising thing is that from the sounds, and the feel of it, it looked like the walls encircled little walled gardens. I wasn't sure what that meant. But Peaseblossom stopped at one of these walls—whitewashed, stone, eight feet tall—leaned into it and scratched the wall. I swear that was what he did.

From the other side came the sound of something scratching back.

And then...the wall opened. Not as in a gate, but with the same type of feel as a portal, like something had ripped reality.

What was revealed, in this case, was a maybe 200-square-foot garden, and a person not much older than Peaseblossom, though not nearly as decorative.

If we'd been talking Earth-types, or the worlds they colonized, I'd think him Greek. He was small, wiry, with long dark hair, deeply tanned skin, and very alert brown eyes in deepset sockets. The description falls short, because he was also...well, pretty, with large dark eyes that seemed to have a hint of laughter in them and a generous mouth that reposed in a slight smile.

And he was one of those I'd have had trouble pinning to male or female if I didn't know he was neither. He was just a little too pretty for male, a little too sturdy for female.

Also, I couldn't believe he was Brundar's crossibling, unless he was half- crossibling and Troz had born him by someone much shorter and darker than himself. That or their genetics were truly something strange to behold.

He had dirt on his hands, dirt on his white linen, knee-length tunic, and an expression somewhere between shock and outrage, despite the smiling eyes and the resting impression of a smile on his face.

He gave me a bare glance, pulled Peaseblossom in, and my guess is would have slammed the portal shut on me if Mahar hadn't pulled me in. I shudder at the idea of what being half on either side of a portal would do.

Then he waved his hand and I couldn't see anything, but I guessed he'd done something to the sound, to make it not heard, and possibly so we wouldn't be seen from the other windows above this, and then bellowed with a voice quite out of proportion to his side. "Are you out of your Maker Cursed mind, Kari? What are you doing here?"

"I came in urgent need."

Lyto looked like he wanted to dismiss it, but he sighed. "You're just in luck I happened to be here when you scratched, and that I didn't think I was imagining it. Brund, this is not an escapade where you go to the city to buy candy incognito. And take that off." He waved, and suddenly Peaseblossom was Peaseblossom again, which I appreciated because it was less disquieting.

I wondered about given name use, but there was nothing of the lover to Lyto. Then again, they were siblings, so perhaps that was permitted.

My powerful intellect also decided that Lyto had been used in the past to help Peaseblossom in juvenile escapades. I didn't sigh, but it reinforced my feeling this young king was far too used to getting his own way and skating by on being irrepressible and a force of nature. Unfortunately, I liked him. Even more unfortunately, people of his stamp eventually came up against an obstacle they couldn't move, and came apart or went sour, which could be a disaster for a king.

Lyto crossed his arms and looked up at Mahar. The sternness wasn't even spoiled by looking up, which took effort. "What is so urgent and who is—" His eyes widened. "Oh no."

He backed, blindly, and kind of leaned against the wall. I probably should say this little garden we were in had an open door to the interior, and a bit of whitewashed wall on either side, one of them with a window that had no glass but had open shutters. So it led into the palace, but, I guessed, probably into what we'd call a Grace and Favor lodging in High Britannia, meaning an apartment, separate and private, cut out of the palace proper.

Nikre ran his hand on his face, top to bottom. "He's the ambassador that the Draksalls lost, isn't he?"

"How do you know?"

"I'm keeping an eye on things for Eerlen. That includes your spy corps, when you went dark." He glowered. "I've had reports."

"Oh, good," Mahar said, which made Lyto and probably me stare at him. "It makes it much easier. Yes, he's the ambassador, and we've been attacked in a Mahar shelter, and there's reason to believe he has a tracking chip on him."

The archmage understudy groaned. "Right. But it only occurred to you now. After the damage was done. Come inside. First, we deal with the tracking spell, then you tell me of this attack."

Inside was a small space. About ten by twelve would be my guess, with only the window that faced the garden, and a little fireplace that was lit, but not blazing. I guessed it was lit for cooking and such, because the kettle was boiling on it.

I should mention the temperature felt like pleasant spring weather.

There was a set of shelves on either side, the upper ones filled with homey crockery, the lower ones at counter height and presumably with similar use, and a table in the center. It surprised me by being a normal-height kitchen table, not the low tables of the Troz shelter. It was long, and on either side of it were two long benches.

"Sit," Lyto said.

He poured water from the kettle and a jar onto a basin on one of the shelves at counter level, and washed hands and face.

"Let me take a look at you, Milord Webson," he said.

He extended his hands towards me, not touching me, and his eyes unfocused. He said, "Got you." And then there was feeling... I can't describe it. It felt like an insect sting inside my skin, at the back of my neck.

"You didn't kill his language spells?" Mahar asked.

"No," I answered. "I still understand you."

"And I didn't kill the other spells on him, too. Feel like...healing patrol? Like something vigilant against disease? I wish we could do that."

I inclined my head, surprised he'd felt the purpose of the nanos and that he could...well, reach in.

"That one felt different, like woven by a different mind," he said. He frowned at me. "Pardon me, Milord, but what is your purpose in being here? In the world?"

I explained, probably not very well, everything from what I'd come to Draksah to do, falling out the window, the odd events since, which I suspected I'd got so wrong they weren't even wrong once or twice, because he almost smiled, but not quite.

While I was talking, he got up and got us... At first, I didn't identify it, but it was fruit juice, though I wasn't sure of the fruit, and then little sweet squares of what tasted like solidified jam. I tasted one to be polite, and it was fruity and sweet, tangy and very pleasant. I didn't get a second taste because Peaseblossom vacuumed the rest, while also excitedly and without restraint adding into my story the things about his parent's letter and also Ad Leed's... Whatever it was.

Lyto's eyes sparked, alternately with amusement and horror. I must have looked embarrassed as Peaseblossom talked of Myrrir Mahar's suspicions of Eerlen, because Lyto put a hand out and touched my wrist, barely, in a gesture of reassurance. "Milord, His Majesty, though he is that now, is by way of being my sibling. His parent was my very beloved sire; his sire is my beloved and revered parent. We're family."

"But you don't look... You're not Troz."

"No. I wasn't fortunate enough to be born of them. Eerlen...went to investigate reports of a high-power child that hadn't been joined to the brotherhood in a tiny hamlet on the Brinar coast and thinks he interrupted my murder for the sake of my sire's new lover inheriting my dead parent's boat. I don't remember any of it. I was three. But I trust Eerlen, and he's legally my parent. Myrrir Mahar was legally my sire. My parents in every way that counts. And I'm three years older than Mahar, so he's my little bratty sibling, whom I aided and abetted and kept out of trouble through childhood adventures."

Brundar snorted. "And sometimes led into trouble, though no one ever believed me."

Nikre allowed his lip to curl on the right. "Sometimes. Someone had to spice up your life, Kari." Then he became serious and turned back to me. "He's telling me everything because I'm family. I'm also both surprised and not. I thought something was working at Myrrir that last year. I'm surprised he didn't— Not that... Well, they both had scars that sometimes rubbed wrong. But there was strong love there. And yet they were distant, those last days."

He sighed, then nodded to me. "I understand, Milord. I even understand your anger at having been lied to. And I agree with his Mahar Majesty, my sibling here, that preventing the Draksalls getting the power of the star people is necessary. The rest we'll deal with. By the by, bit by bit." He turned to Peaseblossom, who was drinking the juice in some enjoyment. "Brund, is Eerlen well?"

"No, not well. He has power burn, I told you," Peaseblossom said putting the empty juice cup down.

"Yes, that part I know, but.... The child?"

"How do you know about the child?"

Lyto shrugged. "Ad Leed told me. Also, that Eerlen and Lendir swore, which I suppose makes you and me very Erradian. Your parent, my sire, swore your half-crossibling, my half-sibling. I wouldn't know how to tell people. Only I don't have to, because once you emerge from hiding, everyone will know." He paused. "I'm glad he's with child." Lyto inclined his head and took a deep breath. "I'll hope. He desperately wants a line child. Maybe— If you need me...any time..."

"We do need you," Brundar Mahar said. "Because Eerlen can't use power, and we're in Yanda, anyway, and there are Ad Leed and Sarda and—"

"Yes. We'll deal with Ad Leed and Sarda. I'll put Ad Leed under an interdiction. I don't want to do anything more to or about Ad Leed until Eerlen can be present. I'll use some excuse about his power looking compromised through overuse to me. Frankly, knowing what he did and in Yanda, at that, it's only prudent. But—"

"No. Not that!" Brundar nodded to me. "He needs to look like an Erradian."

Lyto looked at me. "Oh."

It took less than five seconds. Suddenly, my hair was down the middle of my back, and I realized that it wasn't slightly wavy, as I'd always thought, as I kept it very short in the Academy, then

medium short as an Ambassador, but actually curly. My surprise
as I reached for a strand of hair and stared at it in shock made
both Lyto and Peaseblossom laugh.

And my face became smoother than it had been since I'd turned
fourteen.

Lyto grinned at me. "Tell them you have some Lirridarian blood.
You're not ugly enough for an Erradian."

"Eerlen is not ugly!" Mahar protested.

"No. He isn't. But he looks like his sire. He says—" He stopped
and suddenly looked alarmed.

And then waved his hands like someone trying to shoo chickens
or sheep. "You need to go," he said. "Now."

"Can you port us?"

Lyto put his head to the side. "Not right now. It would open
us to portal attack. There's Draksalls. His tracker disappeared. I
don't know who they are, but they're magicians. Brund, do you
still know the way to your favorite hiding place? Go there. I'll
come to you when the coast is clear, and I'll send you to Erradi
then."

We went. Don't ask how. There was a maze of hallways, lined
with tapestries I wish I had the time to study. That whole ethnographic collection thing. I had a sense the stuff here would keep
many a ten-team of properly trained people happy for a full
career.

I had to revise Mahar's status from chieftain to king. Perhaps
world-king, if what I'd gathered was true. It was just so hard to
believe that when he was leading me through the hallways, head
down, past a number of people who didn't give either of us a
second look.

But I was noticing things, and trying to correct for them. I
didn't walk right. I can't even explain it, in words. Maybe it was
a difference in the hips, but their walk was different. I tried to
imitate Peaseblossom as much as possible. I'd never noticed with
Almar and Troz, but then again, I'd not seen them walk much, not
over a long period of time.

I mustn't have been odd enough to be noticed if I wasn't specifically being looked for here. And my guess is the search was
concentrated on Lyto's place. I'd have to ask Mahar if that was
true later. And also about Lyto's place. Why would the king's full
crossibling, legally a prince, be living in what seemed like a small

and primitive place?

The door into the inside of the palace had had a guard, but the guard hadn't seen us pass, and we'd found ourselves in the fifth, I think, floor. Mahar said later it was the family floor. We took hallways and stairs, then hallways and stairs, and the only time someone stopped us was a guard as we were about to exit, and he took a look at Mahar and hugged him, then had a whispered conversation with him, from which the word Lendir emerged. Since the guard looked like Ad Leed, I assumed he was Ad Leed's crossibling and Lendir Almar's half- crossibling.

At least, it seemed logical.

Through the door he had been guarding was...a vast garden with statues. Took me a moment to realize what it was.

"It's a cemetery!" I whispered.

Peaseblossom nodded. He'd gone serious-looking. "I used to hide here all the time when I was little and wanted to be alone. Come."

He led me past a row of statues in heroic poses, with inscriptions on plaques I couldn't read, and to the back, past a broken column and a fallen wall.

We had to bend to pass under the columns and between it and the wall.

Inside, it was...surprisingly nice. There was some kind of ivy growing all over a statue of one of the most beautiful people I'd ever seen. And there was moss underneath.

It was shaded and quiet and mostly dark.

We sat side by side. And listened. It was impossible to know if anyone would hunt this far, but I didn't want to attract them by speaking. And neither did Mahar.

But after what seemed like eternity, we heard steps. Peaseblossom peeked out, and then we got out.

Lyto stood there, and smiled at us. "We're clear for now, but I'm going to send you to Brinar, and not the way you came. Because those portals might be watched."

"What— What happened?"

"I killed them. I'll get the bodies removed. Best no one know they penetrated the palace. They were disguised. I'll need to talk to the guards."

The casualness of it surprised me, but I understood they'd been at war a long time. They were all warriors, and I suspected the magicians more than most. They would be used to killing the enemy.

"I brought you clothes. You don't want to appear in the middle of Brinar near Var Leed in your palace clothes."

The clothes he'd brought us were short tunics. There were no underpants. "The Brinarians use this for underwear," Mahar said, of a kilt that went under the tunic. He only turned away to remove his tunic and replace it.

I didn't turn away, didn't see any point in it. I realized two things: first, it wasn't just my face that had lost hair. In fact, I'd lost everything but the pubic patch. And second, both of these adult people were staring at my nipples and blushing.

Okay, so different culture. Still: my nipples, really? I put the tunic on as fast as possible, surprised and amused no one blushed at my taking time to tie the underwear-kilt.

"Ready?" Lyto asked. He was very red. So was Mahar. "I'm sending you into the middle of a festival not close to where you came through. Hopefully, they don't have the forces to fan that far. Go to another public portal and then just use this." He handed Mahar what looked like a white-cloth-wrapped ball. "You know how to use it?"

"Yes. I can use your power, not mine to—"

"Right. Now go."

He opened a portal, and we stepped through into madness.

Bedlam With Food Vendors

Skip

Took a moment for my eyes to adjust and my world to stop spinning, and for me to realize that where I'd come through was not in the middle of the insanity, but to the side, behind some trees. Which made perfect sense. I mean, last thing you'd want to do is open a portal into someone. Was that even possible? I'd have to ask.

We were at the edge of what looked like a huge festival, where multitudes of people in all sorts of clothes did...from this distance, incomprehensible things. And there were tents and music and the smell of cattle and the sound of voices arguing, and the smells of cooking, and—

Peaseblossom looked at me with a disquieting smile, but what he said seemed less than disquieting. "Take your clothes from your pack. I think if we cram them in, they'll fit in mine?"

"Why? And shouldn't we be opening a portal to Yanda?"

His disquieting smile broadened. "Nah. We need to let you buy some baking supplies."

"What?"

"I want you to see what the food vendors have. Maybe you'll want to bake some new things."

"I've created a monster," I said, but I was flattered. He wanted more of my baking.

The smile became a giggle. "Probably. But also, on the serious side, we should buy some cheese and other things. I'd buy eggs if I thought we could safely transport them, but one of us will have to go to Tarkross for that. Likely Lendir. He can ask his cousins to buy them, then pay them and transport them, so there are no rumors of our presence." At my blink, he shook his head. "Eerlen.

The baby. And Lendir, too. I suspect, though I can't tell yet, because the pattern isn't showing, that he's not far behind Eerlen. Having been wounded, they'll need a lot of food to recover and grow healthy babies."

"Lendir Almar is—" My mind broke. It was like being told Hercules was broody. Keep in mind that Eerlen Troz did not look precisely effeminate, or even betwixt and between. Not like Nikre Lyto. Just like a really pretty man. But Troz was human size, not I have an appetite and I'm here to eat New London outsized. And he didn't...well, he didn't throw tables designed for ten.

Peaseblossom must have missed the reason for my question, because he shrugged. "I'm surmising. Just a feeling."

"Uh. Uh."

"So we need cheese. And some dried fruit and vegetables wouldn't hurt. Hard to come by in deep ice, you know? There will be some in the more temperate areas of Erradi, but how many times do we want to go forage?"

"Probably not often. At least not until you all are healed."

He nodded and we crammed my cloak and fur clothing into his backpack, which he tied shut. Then we put our packs back over our shoulders, and he turned towards the area of tumultuous color and people running around and shouting, and—

"Do you even have money?"

He looked back over his shoulder. "Yes. You should hold my hand."

"What?"

"Look, it's a festival. People come here from far away. Nomads, in particular, are here to look for mates. We hold hands, we're a pair of Erradian nomads sightseeing. They won't even look closely at us. Otherwise, someone is going to proposition you. And I don't think you know the polite way to turn someone down, or how to evade a belligerent and stubborn drunk. You'll end up in a duel."

"Uh."

"Just hold my hand. I don't bite. Also, easier not to lose you in the crowd."

I gave him my hand. He grasped it firmly. His hand was calloused. Why would a king have calloused hands? I knew why I did, because of various training exercises and weapons— Okay, he was probably the same.

"Won't people recognize you?" I asked, catching up with him, not to be towed behind by my hand like a recalcitrant toddler.

He looked earnestly puzzled. "From what? Even in the palace, most people haven't seen me for two years. Here? No one knows me. Oh, magicians, but they won't talk. They don't want to risk the wrath of Eerlen."

I swallowed. I'd been thinking in terms of my world, or of a tribal chief. They wouldn't have mersis or broadcasts featuring the sovereign or a likeness thereof in walk-in roles or news from the palace. The sovereign's hologram wouldn't bring his or her addresses right to your living room. And unlike a tribal chief, he wouldn't be everywhere at once, in an official capacity. He'd had to disguise in the palace, of course. Even two years later, I'd bet he was recognizable. But here? Yeah, probably just an Erradian nomad in lighter clothes appropriate to the climate.

As if to confirm it, no one looked at us twice. Children careened into my legs twice, and ran away giggling. A lost toddler clung to Peaseblossom's tunic hem, and he picked him up, one armed, looked intently at the child, looked up and to the left, and then took off at a clip, child still held in left arm. I got towed along trying to catch up—he was going so fast.

He approached a couple of people...uh, I'm trying to think of a polite term. They weren't mating, just everything-but against a tree. To my horror, he tapped the more reachable one on the shoulder.

As the person turned, I tensed, though the couple was of the dark Mediterranean type like Lyto and the tallest came to his shoulder.

"Friend," he said, his voice indicating he was anything but friendly-feeling. "You could at least pay someone to watch the child. Dangerous, but not as dangerous as just letting him wander. If your rutting is so important to you, perhaps you shouldn't have a child?"

The parent—I guess?—of the child thought he was going to take issue. He crossed his arms, and stood squarely, and looked up. "Who are you to—"

But the one he'd been – ah – rutting with touched him on the shoulder. "Nyedar, he's a magician."

A look of fear crossed the person's face. He glanced at his lover.

"Has to be. How does he know he's yours? You know what they do if you— They'll take him. And the king will back them. The king's children, they call them. Kidnappers. They just take your babies!"

"Well, the king can bite—" He stopped, perhaps because Pease-blossom was glowering. "I'm a nomad, what do I care for kings?"

"Do you care to keep your child?" his partner asked.

"Fine. Fine. Fine." The nomad took his child, took off at a trot to an area where a couple of teenagers were surrounded by children. He handed the child over, and it seemed to me paid something from a purse.

Peaseblossom nodded and we walked off, fast in another di-rection. We were pretty far away when I asked, "Do you? Take children?"

"Not unless they're being killed," Mahar said, his voice terse. "We don't condone attempted murder. But we do take the ones who are abandoned. Mostly infants."

"The king's children?"

He didn't seem to want to talk about it. He squeezed my hand hard, but his face was stony. "I had a farmhouse which I inherited from Myrrir, who inherited it from...one of his ancestors' sires, some way up the line. In Eles City, not near the palace. I used some of my money to pay for renovating it, and yes, I pay people to tend abandoned children and help them survive. Nursemaids, usually people who've lost children or who will starve feeding their own children. We feed the nurses, they feed the children. We're always short, but no babies have starved so far. We also take children of nomads, without questions, and allow the children to go back to their parents when parents come to claim them. We have too few people and I'd prefer children don't starve."

"You have money?" I asked, confused. "I mean your own mon-ey?" Did the king live from taxes or donations, or what?

"An embarrassing amount," Peaseblossom said. "My line was wealthy before it became the royal line. We have farms in Eles and Erradi and Lirridar. And properties inherited from line sires. And we're all magicians, and magicians get paid."

"They do?" I was shocked. Look, I'd never heard of fairies and elves participating in vile commerce, so why would wizards?

He laughed. "Don't you get paid as an ambassador? Yes, we get paid. We expend energy. A lot of it. If I weren't the king and embarrassingly wealthy, I'd need the money just to eat enough after I assist with a difficult birth." He shrugged. "As is, I use my stipend to try to save children who'd otherwise starve. It might be futile, but I—"

He stopped. Then sighed. "I grew up watching my parents mourn for my crossiblings they couldn't raise. For the babies Myrrir couldn't conceive. He had a contraceptive shield put on after I was born, to allow him to rest, and it became stuck. Which is why Eerlen has always refused one. But they both wanted more children. Desperately.

"I hate the idea of people who have children wantonly, ignoring them. And even more so of those who cherish their children, watching them starve to death. Beg your pardon. I'm talking too much and with too much emotion about something that is nothing to do with you." Before I could protest, he said, "I should apologize to you. That might have ended in a duel. And Eerlen would kill us both if it did."

It occurred to me he was embarrassed for all the wrong reasons, at least from my perspective. "Nothing to forgive," I said. "I'd have done the same if this were my world and I could, I think."

He sighed, then chuckled. "You know, it's just nomads. They don't see anyone but their own children sometimes for months, then come to one of these things and meet their lover, or find one, and— They get a little distracted. That...person probably isn't a bad parent most of the time."

Something I'd heard was working at me, and I finally managed to figure out what to ask. "Nomads don't like the king?"

He gave a short laugh at the back of his throat. "Nomads don't recognize the king. That's part of why they're nomads. All the kings, forever, have encouraged people to settle. Nomads couldn't care less. Some are not hostile. At any given time, we had a dozen nomad clan ambassadors in the palace, negotiating for some benefit, or to contribute something to the war effort, or—" He shrugged. "We do the best we can."

"Oh," I said. And then, "Oh. So, people would be surprised at your parents' pairing? Eerlen says he's a normad."

He gave another of those back-of-the-throat laughs. "Surprised isn't what I'd call it. They were slightly more accepting of that than of the pairing of Eerlen's parents. When Dalless the Great swore a Draksall—" He stopped because we were in a crowd.

He had taken off in a direction he seemed to know, and we emerged from the crowd of people in front of a row of vendors.

"Let me bargain," Brundar said. "You don't know the customs."

Which was kind. I also didn't know the prices, scrolled on bits of fabric pinned to barrels and piles of fabric, and baskets of fruit, and...and I didn't know the currency.

I got a lesson in all of it in the next hour or so.

First, I was surprised and probably shouldn't have been that Brundar Mahar, King of Elly, understood vegetables and fruits. Sure, he might not have two years ago, but I assumed he had been living a more normal life these last two years.

He was mostly buying dried vegetables—specifically, peppers, tomatoes and onions—because they took less space in the pack. I wasn't surprised at finding those vegetables available, now that I knew the extent of the portal network in the world. But we also bought fresh berries, in a sort of little bark basket that the vendor assured us had stasis on it. Which warranted the ridiculously high—Brundar explained afterwards—price of three rabbit skins. Only the rabbit skins were little coins that looked made of copper. "Eerlen loves berries, and it really is stasis. The vendor is a second circle. He probably did the stasis himself. And it will be useful."

But Brundar could actually examine the quality, and he fought for every rabbit skin. Which seemed to be the lowest denomination.

We also bought "Lirridar's best butter from Calenir farms," which is what Mahar said the big colorful sign over the tent said. "They really are," Mahar informed. "Better than mine." So we bought a big roll of it, wrapped in a very clean linen cloth. He also bought a quarter wheel of cheese. The person manning the tent, big, bluff and blond, looked familiar, but I couldn't place why.

I didn't have time to think about it, because Brundar was across the way, buying a sack of dried coconut.

"We should have enough flour. I swear Eerlen's line hoards flour. And honey." Then he got a lot of dried potatoes, which were fortunately very light.

I noticed rice, asked if we could get it, and Mahar looked surprised. I'd seen it in Draksah, so I assumed it was one of those imports. It was only three rabbit skins for what I estimated was two kilograms. Peaseblossom explained as we walked away, "The seller said they're just starting to grow it in Karrash. It used to be like coffee, something we got for a big treat every once in a long while."

Speaking of which, he insisted on getting me coffee. A tiny bag, maybe a quarter pound, cost us ten rabbit skins, but he didn't try to bargain it down.

My wanting a bag of sesame seeds utterly puzzled him. They were dehulled, but even so, he raised an eyebrow and whispered, "Poor food. People put them in bread to supplement, but—"

"No. There's a thing you can make with honey. It's like...somewhere between honey nut balls and cookies."

He got it for me. It was heavy, but not very expensive. I had halvah on my mind.

"I think we shouldn't overload you. Let's make our way across and to the other end, and we'll portal from there."

We walked across, away from the sellers and past animal pens with horses and cows. The horses were rangy and looked to me underfed, but I suspected it was the breed. The cows... Well, the cows were weird. They looked like they should have been stuffed toys and were small, and...needed a haircut. But they were undeniably cows.

Past the pens, we walked a path around an area of people in a circle, while two people in the center fought. Brundar made a face at it, and looked away.

After we walked away, I asked, "You don't like exhibition fighting?"

He looked at me, his eyes blank, then he made a smile of the kind one does to show something is painful. "That's not what they're doing. Those are mating fights."

"Mating what?"

"If you can't, or are too...impatient to form a relationship, you challenge someone to a fight. If they accept, you fight. The loser...risks or perhaps earns being impregnated."

"The loser?" It was baffling. "Is it...terrible?" I remembered the relationship between Troz and Almar and I thought surely, the idea of being pregnant couldn't be that horrible. Troz seemed happy.

"What? No. But it's more...work and risk. Being pregnant, I mean. Hence, the loser doing it."

"Oh." Yes, from an evolutionary perspective, it was more blessed to sire. But this seemed a horrible way to go about it. I, too, turned my head away, and that's when I saw them.

I grabbed Peaseblossom's forearm with my free hand. "Mahar."

He looked at me, followed my gaze, looked puzzled back at me, looked back, then moving very fast, grabbed me around my waist, pulled me close and bent me over backwards. This is hard to explain. We were almost the same height. The way he embraced me and bent me back meant that his hair fell on either side of his face, and mine, and effectively hid us both. From the outside, it would look like he was overcome with desire and was kissing me. We had a minute or two, I guessed.

"What?" he asked, with exaggerated lip movements and almost no sound.

"The two walking this way. Dark-haired, but...not like the people here. They don't walk right."

"What?"

"They walk like males. There's a differen—"

"Oh. Yes." He let me straighten. As he turned to look where I'd been looking, I looked ahead, so as not to be obvious. I had no idea how to look as if I had just been passionately kissed in public, so I supposed confused would have to do.

There was a young person who looked like a local. Young...well, probably my age and Mahar's, but he was also very pretty. Saucy. Something like Ad Leed, without having any features in common. He was looking at us, mouth dropped, as though shocked. I thought his eyes were suspiciously shiny. I wondered why, but of course, it could be anything. Maybe he'd just had a fight with a lover. And then I recognized him: realized he was the not-slave who'd jumped out the window with me. One of them. I opened my mouth to say hello, then stopped because I was in disguise.

Brundar Mahar didn't give me time to think about it or look at the not-slave very long. Instead, he took my hand, and dragged me towards the perimeter of the mating fights.

We stood in the circle of applauding and cheering people. The suspicious people moved closer, closer. Mahar grimaced.

He held my hand tight, tight, until they walked by us. They barely glanced in the circle, though I could tell they were looking around for someone or something. Of course, I looked nothing like myself.

Brundar put his face close to my ear. "Draksall or your people?"

I whispered back near his ear, "I think star people." I wouldn't call them my people, because they might very well be wherever the mercenaries had come from.

Suddenly, Mahar spoke, about two octaves too high for his normal speech, but no one would know who didn't know him, and sounding like the most vapid bubblehead ever, "Oh, Kaeehel, come. Take me to that inn you promised and let's make a baby!"

I almost asked him if he'd lost his mind, but the people around us laughed and a couple shouted encouragement.

He grabbed my hand, and we ran. We ran past everyone, straight into the forest, and then ran a while, past areas where couples were huddling, till we were more or less alone, and in dense foliage. He was untying his pack before he put it down.

"Quick," he said, tossing the fur pants, kilt and tunic at me, then the fur cloak. Somehow, I think by momentarily growing extra arms, he managed to get himself dressed by the time I was tying the cloak on. He got the cloth-wrapped ball that Lyto had given him. "Ready?" he asked.

I nodded. Then snow was blowing past and into my face, as he shoved me into it.

We walked maybe ten steps in the blinding snow of Erradi, and we came to an ice-covered wall. He made a gesture in front of it, then touched it and I saw the entrance to Yanda. "You go in first," he said, shouting against the howling wind. "Remember to put your hands in front of you. No, give me the backpacks. I'll drop them in between us."

I went in this time more assured than I'd been before, because I knew where I was going and there was light on the other side.

I emerged from the tunnel, and had a moment of shock. Almar was standing, lance pointed straight at me.

Neither of us moved for a moment. Two backpacks dropped in behind me. Then his eyebrows went up. He lowered the lance. "Milord Webson."

"Yeah," I said. My voice sounded raspy. Twice, he'd threatened me with pointy weapons. "Yeah?"

He grinned and set the lance against a wall. "Eerlen is asleep. I thought I should watch the entrance, in case... You know, we still don't know how they got into the last shelter."

Peaseblossom came in behind me and stood up, hands on hips. "Lendir, you must stop scaring our guest."

Almar grinned. Peaseblossom had doubtless heard the explanation. He looked at me "Let's block the tunnel, now everyone is in who is supposed to be in."

Eventually, we blocked the entrance to the tunnel with a large armoire. And by we, I mean Almar and I, but mostly Almar. Was he really with child? It seemed so dissonant, it made my head hurt.

Peaseblossom and I put the food away. And then much to my surprise, Mahar cooked rice, and from the stasis box, cutlets which he seasoned and sizzled in what looked like a vast frying pan.

"Deer," he said.

"Not bear?"

Peaseblossom made a face that exactly matched my impression of the taste of bear.

Eerlen, who had wakened and was reading a scroll while sitting on the nearby floor cushion, gave me a theatrical sour look. "What, you'll make jokes about Erradians, too?"

I blinked at him.

"Eerlen, how could he know the jokes?" Peaseblossom asked.

"Oh." He grinned. "Well, they say Erradians live with bears, eat bears, mate with bears," Eerlen said. "It's supposed to be a joke, but it's not funny."

Lendir, sitting a little away by three candles and stitching something, shook his head. "Erradians are very sensitive to jokes about them. Because there are so many. And they make them themselves," he said, in a saintly voice, and this got a laugh out of Eerlen.

Later, after eating when Eerlen was more relaxed, he smiled while leaning back on the deep cushions against the wall. "For years, I thought my sire was a bear. I only ever saw him wrapped in furs, you see. He was so cold all the time. The first time I saw him take off what I'd assumed was his skin, I was three, and I was terrified. So terrified, I still remember."

Mahar and I did the clean-up after, and he said, "You probably have a million questions. I'll explain, later."

I did have a million questions. They didn't keep me awake for even a minute after I laid down on my bed.

The Beast in the Snow

Eerlen

It took him two portals to get away from Yanda. First the public portal, and then another. Getting to the public portal was easy; the second portal took too much of his strength, but not so much that he couldn't do it. Just enough that he had to stop on the other side, leaning against one of the trees, taking deep breaths, before he could remove the skis and set them aside with the poles under bushes.

Precautions against theft seemed stupid, since it was the dead of night and there was no one out.

It would have been easier to do this near Yanda, except there was no animal life near Yanda worth the hunting and he wanted—needed—to hunt. By preference, dire wolves, if he could find them. But they were creatures that hunted in packs and needed large herbivore life, which meant he needed to go where vegetation grew and animals lived.

He was out of shape. When was the last time he'd done this? Sometime before Myrrir died. A couple of times in the last year of Myrrir's life.

He'd brought the lance, and he knew how to find dire wolves. At least, if there were any around here.

And he knew this area. It was near—but not too near—one of the smaller Troz shelters. There would be dire wolves here. There always were if it hadn't been cleaned recently.

Not too near, because he wasn't sure if the enemy—whoever it was—was watching his shelters for his appearance.

He'd hunted. He'd hunted a lot with Brund and Lendir. He'd taught Brund to tan hides. But it wasn't the same as these hunts, where he was alone, and only he could get out of danger.

There was something very clean about this: the empty night,

the dark blue sky deeper and somehow darker because it was full moon. And the moon sparking echoes from snow and ice.

This wasn't deep ice, but it was winter in Erradi, and a light coat of frost crackled on the grass underfoot and shone from the needles of the pines. There was snow in the shadow of the trees, from the last storm.

The apparent silence dissolved into a low cacophony of sounds. And the night smelled of pine, and cold, and incoming snow.

Eerlen took a deep breath. It was just him and his prey. There was no room for complex emotions, or for thinking.

He cross-tied his fur cloak. Instead of pinning it around his neck, as he usually wore it, he tied it across his chest, covering his left shoulder, but fastening under his right arm, giving him warmth still, but leaving his right arm free.

It was amazing he still knew the path to the lake that was deep enough to rarely freeze hard. And in this weather, it wouldn't be frozen at all.

Animals needed water.

He followed the way amid the trees carefully, looking for prints. And found the tracks almost immediately.

Not a pack of dire wolves. He was willing to face that, if he must, but he was probably too weak and wounded that he'd end up seriously hurt by it.

This was a lone dire wolf. Either a yearling, just kicked out of the pack by a stronger male, or an old male, dispossessed of his harem. In which case, the fight would be more even, Eerlen thought. But not easy. Not in his state.

In his mind, Myrrir flashed, with one of his lopsided smiles. Why can't you leave the animals alone, Eerlen? You don't need the pelts. What have they ever done to you?

Myrrir had actually asked him that after the last hunt, having caught Eerlen bathing, before Eerlen had had a chance of discarding his blood-crusted clothes. Myrrir had been amused, but Eerlen had given him a very serious explanation, involving this being close enough to villages, and the dire wolves being dangers to villagers, particularly children. And how cleaning the area—that night, he'd not been impaired by wounds, and he'd killed all four in the small pack—also meant more hunting for the villagers.

Myrrir had looked dubious. As he should have. It wasn't a lie, any of it, but it also wasn't true. Or at least that was not why Eerlen did it.

He did it when—he took a deep breath, gasping the clean, cold air which seemed to burn into his lungs—when he needed to stop feeling and to do something.

He followed the track a long time, in the dappled shade of the pine trees. And he had to stop to rest three times, which probably meant he fell behind, but he couldn't be winded and half-dead when he caught up.

Suddenly, he heard a sound ahead, breaking through other sounds of things rustling in the dark, and the sounds of something flying overhead.

What he heard ahead was crunching bones and tearing, and a sort of animal snuffling. The dire wolf had prey and was eating. Good.

Eerlen walked slowly, trying not to make noise. It would be best to catch the wolf by surprise.

The terrain rose suddenly ahead, and he couldn't see. He hesitated at the last edge of the treed expanse, but the only way to see was to climb to the prominence. So he did, slowly, carefully.

Cresting the ridge, he stopped, suddenly.

There was indeed a dire wolf: three times as large as a large human, covered in white fur, with massive teeth in his heavy jaws.

Only the dire wolf was dead, ripped almost in half by a huge claw. The owner of the claw, a large, tawny, feline beast, twice as large as the wolf the beast was feeding on.

Eerlen had never seen one like it. He'd heard—

In the moment of surprise, he must have made a sound. He caught himself midstep back. Too late.

The beast raised its head and made a sound somewhere between a purr and a growl. And Eerlen forced himself to freeze. He could smell blood from the dire wolf. His heart beat so fast, it deafened him.

Everything in him wanted to run. Run now. Run immediately. But if he ran, the beast would be on him in a moment. He would be dead in seconds.

He forced his breath to be almost imperceptible. Normally, he'd throw a shield and walk away under its cover. This was too much for the state his body was in. But—

But if he used his power, with power burn and shortly after

opening a portal, it would be the last thing he ever did, anyway. Though the beast might not eat him.

One day, brat, you're going to pull one of your monumentally stupid tricks and you'll die for it. I just hope I'm around to watch. The oily, gloating voice of Lahem Drahy, the archmagician before him, came to him out of the past. He minimally hunched his right shoulder. At least Drahy wasn't around to watch. That was something.

Thoughts of Brundar, of Lendir tried to intrude, but he pushed that out of his mind, too.

He took his lance in his right hand. The beast was still looking at him, eyes half-closed. Was the low growl in its throat increasing?

Everything in Eerlen wanted to run, or to throw up a shield.

He tensed before he realized that the animal's shoulders were going down, the back raising. It was going to leap.

There was enough time for a flash of fear, a wordless promise that he'd never ever again do anything like this.

And then it was gone, and his mind was empty. Empty of everything but the cat's movements as it prepared its leap, the lance in his left hand, smooth wood, metal tipped. And the cold air going in and out of his lungs. He had one chance. Only one.

The cat's head came up. He leapt. The leap would take him to where he'd fall atop of Eerlen. But Eerlen was moving, without thought, instinctively.

Running towards the cat, as the cat started to come down but before he did. Under the cat, shoving the lance upward with all the power of his right arm, then throwing himself sideways away from the cat, and rolling on the snow-crusted pine needles.

Before he stopped rolling, he heard the thud of the cat's body falling, and hoped that meant he'd got it, otherwise he was dead.

His heart was beating too hard. He felt nauseated. He managed to pull himself up.

The beast was dead, sprawled on the path.

Eerlen managed to stand on shaking legs. He should recover the lance, but he didn't even know if he could walk.

Vomiting surprised him, sudden. It barely gave him time to hunch over and keep it clean off his clothes. He didn't know how scared he'd been.

His heart was slowing, but there was a whistle in his ears, and for a moment, he thought he was dreaming the voice that said,

"Eerlen Troz, Emee, I don't know whether to congratulate you or tell Lendir what you just did and let him keep you chained in a safe cave the rest of your natural life."

But as Eerlen turned in the direction of the voice, he saw Nikre Lyto walking towards him. Nikre Lyto in full battle leathers, with his blue magician's cloak on.

"Nikre," he said, and managed a couple of steps. "I didn't... You didn't get pulled from shield holding? You?"

Nikre shook his head, which was a relief. Eerlen didn't know what had called Nikre or why it had, but Eerlen would never forgive himself if he interfered with shield holding.

His knees faltered suddenly, and Nikre was there, arm around his waist. "Emee, where is your damn line shelter? The one nearest here?"

When had Nikre last called him that? And how could he say it in such a stern voice? "Don't want to go there. Someone might be watching Troz shelters and—"

"Too bad. You've lost your choice in this. We can go to your shelter now, or we can go to the palace. Your choice on which is less dangerous."

Eerlen laughed despite himself. "The shelter."

"The shelter, Eerlen," Nikre said, and it took Eerlen a second to realize he was mind-speaking him. He gave Nikre the coordinates, then darkness descended.

THE ARCHMAGICIAN'S BUSINESS

EERLEN

Eerlen Troz was in deep darkness, pushing up and up and up. Little by little, he saw light filtered through the deep gloom, and then heard crackling and other sounds. Almost certainly a fire, and crockery hitting together.

He sighed deeply, and then the thought appeared, and he spoke it, in a hoarse voice, before even becoming aware he was talking. "The child!"

"He's fine." A calm, familiar voice. "And you are fine. I took the opportunity to do some healing. You're just tired. You should be tired, Eerlen Troz."

Eerlen blinked his eyes open. Nikre Lyto was standing close and bending over him. His mouth was creased in deep disapproval, but his eyes crinkled at the corner, adding to the amusement lines there. Since when did Nikre have lines at the corner of his eyes?

"Are you awake enough to hold a cup? Let me help you up."

Nikre pulled Eerlen up to sitting against the wall. Handed him a warm cup. Eerlen tasted it. Sputtered, "Cream with honey?"

"Drink up. It's the most calories I can get to you in a short time from the supplies you have here."

Eerlen moaned and muttered, "It's punishment, is what it is."

Nikre's lips turned up minimally at the corners. Eerlen sipped the cream. It was still revolting, particularly with the sweetness, but he could feel energy returning.

Nikre did something to the fire, then said, "Eerlen? Did you... Is everything well with Almar?"

Eerlen blinked. "Yes. We swore."

"I know. Ad Leed told me."

"Ad Leed. You didn't—"

"He hasn't done any other type of healing that involved pattern merging. And what I just did on you didn't involve it. But Eerlen, the ruby would tell you if the pattern were contaminated."

Eerlen drank. "I wasn't sure. In deep no-magic. But I see. I see my pattern is clear." He realized he was feeling the ruby, sensing it. With no pain. "Healing?"

"I healed the rest of your pattern burn and the physical damage. Eerlen, did you fight with Almar?"

"With Lendir? No. Why?"

"With Brundar?"

"Brund? Not today."

"The ambassador."

"Why would I fight the ambassador?" Eerlen felt genuine confusion.

Nikre turned around and sighed. "Then why?" He waved his hand. "This thing? Why?"

"What?" Eerlen felt uncomfortable. He remembered Nikre as a dirty-faced child, dressed in rags and beaten for existing, clinging to him and crying.

He remembered Myrrir insisting they adopt Nikre. To protect him, Myrirr said, but really because Myrrir loved the child at first sight. By pattern, since adoption, he was Eerlen's child, Myrrir's sireling, and you had to look deep and long to find his birth pattern. Which was a good thing, all things considered. It gave Nikre protection and the prestige of two of the ten lines.

He remembered Nikre, a few years later, allowed into Eerlen's room—after a disastrous birth where the child was born dead and Eerlen was left nearly so—tentative, tiptoeing, clutching Eerlen's hand and crying over it, and Myrrir saying that the child had been terrified of losing Eerlen.

"Nikre..." he said softly. Anyone else prying into his life would be courting a duel, but Nikre had family privilege. Still. The questions made Eerlen uncomfortable.

"Eerlen, I'm not stupid, even if I never said anything, because it was none of my business, but I remember the hunts after big fights with Myrrir. I remember being scared you'd get yourself killed this time. I remember realizing you'd left on a hunt and staying awake, and watching until you came back." He looked straight at Eerlen. "Myrrir knew, too, you know? He also watched for you. It almost broke him."

Eerlen almost said then Myrrir should have controlled his temper, but that was unfair. If Eerlen controlled himself perfectly, he wouldn't go hunting alone and unadvisedly.

The funny thing, Eerlen thought, is that Nikre's eyes looked very dark, partially because they were sunken deep beneath his brow, but when he looked up like that and met Eerlen's eyes, they were actually a golden brown. Attentive, observant. And right then, concerned. "Eerlen, I'm still afraid. Did you fight with Almar?"

Eerlen shook his head. "I did not. He's asleep. He's going to kill me."

"No. He's going to threaten to kill you, but then he'll just be heartbroken you risked yourself and the child." Nikre paused. "If he finds out."

"If—"

"If we can get you back before dawn, and we will, and if you send Brundar out to me so I can heal him, we can smooth this over. Blame it on me."

Eerlen made a face. "I shouldn't lie to my sworn."

"Will anything be gained by telling him the truth? Other than hurting him? That you risked yourself and his sireling."

Eerlen sighed. "Likely, no. But— Why did you come? How did you come? And should you be doing healing after shield holding?"

A chuckle. He realized Nikre had removed his battle leathers and the padded undertunic worn against arrows, and now stood in a linen shirt and long wool pants. He came to sit beside Eerlen on the cushion, against the shelter wall. "I never did shield holding. I was about to leave for shield holding when the ruby called to me."

Eerlen almost choked on the last mouthful of vilely sweet cream. "It what?"

"Um...sent a signal. I also didn't know it could do that. It... It came through the ruby, and I got the strong sense you were in danger. And coordinates. Did you know...did it ever do that before?"

Eerlen shrugged. "My accessing of the ruby memory is imperfect. Drahy... Something happened to the ruby in his custody. I've read references to the ruby calling for help to the archmagician, but I thought it was poetic license."

"No. It reached."

"Like a human?"

"I wouldn't say that. There was no...person behind it. Just a sense that you needed me. So I woke up three first circles and told them to hold shield. They're probably upset. They'll live. Healing you wasn't difficult. And I can heal Brund. But Eerlen? What possessed you?"

"I was very angry at Myrrir," Eerlen said, aloud, and said like that, it seemed ridiculous. Was he a toddler, killing beasts because he couldn't scream at Myrrir any longer?

"Yes. I understand that. I am, also. I heard of the letter. I knew he wrote to Kahre. All the time. Just...to stay in touch. But that letter— Yet, this is perhaps not the best way to...to disperse the anger?"

Eerlen felt suddenly abashed. He'd have preferred a stern scolding than this gentle tone. And Nikre probably could scold him, using the family license. Instead, he sounded concerned, and very sad.

"I think," Eerlen said, in deep thought. "That I fell back on patterns of ...well, you know? I think I fell back on the pattern of being angry at Myrrir. I couldn't rage at the king. Not loudly. And I certainly couldn't—I mean. He was the king. I was a guest in his home. And besides, he only... He worried for me. That was the cause of his anger."

"And the whole court would listen in and repeat it, yes," Nikre said. "Myrrir didn't even realize it, you know? Or at least didn't realize why you or I or anyone should mind being discussed that way. Privacy was foreign to the way he grew up. People gossiping about him didn't bother him at all. But...that time is over. And Eerlen, you didn't hurt the child, but if you'd gotten injured—"

"I know. I just... I was so angry, I thought... I felt invincible."

"You are very impressive, but don't do this again. Lendir would be devastated. Brundar needs you. And you're growing a child with archmagician pattern. If you don't care—"

A chuckle ripped through Eerlen's throat. "Of course I care!"

"I know, but even if you didn't, we need that child. You or even I won't last forever."

He squeezed Eerlen's hand. "Do you feel up to bathing and changing? I put clean clothes by the pool. I've cleaned the furs. Where did you leave the skis?"

"Where I came out of the portal."

"I'll collect them. Eerlen!"

Eerlen blinked. "Yes?"

"I put a shield on the two animals. Once I send you back, I'm going to go back, remove the pelts and take them back with me. I understand you're making a donation to The King's Children."

Eerlen blinked again. He had no objections, but— "I am?"

"You certainly are. Do you want to explain the pelts to Almar?"

Eerlen laughed. He felt...better than he had since the attack. The healing had helped. "I guess not. And it probably can pay for nursemaids."

"Cows. They've been wanting cows, to supplement feeding the older children over one."

"Well, then I'm glad to get them a small herd."

He washed quickly, dressed.

At the portal, Nikre said, "Remember the story. I came to the shelter, woke you, made you come here to heal you, and now I will heal Brundar, and then you'll send me Lendir Almar, who I understand is also wounded, though it's minor."

"We could wait it out, let it heal."

"No. I didn't want to tell you this, but you're not longer physically hurting, and Lord Troz, this is archmagician business: you must know that the attack you suffered wasn't the only one. There were Draksall agents embedded at the palace. Either Draksalls or people from the stars have been seen many places. With energy weapons. And Brundar's spies say that they are arranging to use them at the front in Erradi. You know what that means. Do you think our shields will hold a moment?"

Eerlen shook his head in mute horror. "I don't know how we can prevent it," he said.

"I don't know. But Eerlen, I'm not the one who should be in charge at this time. I need your help. We need Brundar's help. I understand why you can't be at the palace. But you can't be hiding where a mind touch can't hit you. I understand if you go back for the birth. I know Troz are born at Yanda, if possible, but—"

"But until then, I shouldn't leave it on your shoulders. I understand. And we should try to understand how to contact the people from the stars about their lost ambassador. I'll send Brund to you."

He took the warmth of Nikre's shoulder squeeze and his peck on Eerlen's cheek with him as he portaled to the deep ice.

FURTHER HAZARDS
OF ETHNOGRAPHIC
COLLECTION

SKIP

In the morning, after my expedition with Brundar, everyone in the shelter acted like they'd been to some midnight drinking party I'd missed. It was all monosyllables and eyebrows lowered over eyes. I wondered why, but didn't dare ask.

Fortunately, I was the first one awake. More than fortunately, since it took me forever to get my hair to be hair.

Look, I hadn't had long hair since...well...ever. Mother had a portrait of me taken when I was two, with blond hair down to my shoulders, but I assumed she'd made it up whole cloth, until my hair got grown out and it was that same puffed-out curly muchness as on that hologram.

And it had gotten all tangled overnight. And I plunged into the water without thinking. You know, hair should be easier to disentangle while wet, but somehow it wasn't. Fortunately, I could slowly comb it out with their equivalent of shampoo in. Getting it rid of the shampoo took forever, too. There was a lot of hair everywhere. I cursed softly and wished these people preferred shaved heads. Seriously, of all possible hairstyles, for a barbarized culture, why long hair? I suspected if I weren't living with the royal family, I'd be at risk of vermin and worse. And yet, barbarian cultures tended to love all the hair.

By the time I made it to the general living area, I expected them all to be up and about their business, but no one was. So I did what normal people do. Okay, no. I did what I do. I checked on the bit dough I was trying to make into sourdough starter. Yes, of course I'd remembered to bring it from the first shelter, in its small ceramic jar, and I'd stashed it in a warm corner near the fireplace. I removed the skin, stirred it, and hoped. I thought it had a little bubbling going.

Then I went to the stasis compartment to decide what to make for breakfast and was surprised and somewhat puzzled to realize someone else must have stocked up, besides the very odd shopping trip that Brundar and I had made. There were eggs, what looked like and at a pinch nibbled tasted like cured ham, cream, milk and some kind of melon that looked like something I'd never seen, being purple with giant pink polka dots. Sounded like a melon, smelled like a melon, but I left it alone, in case it was a dinosaur egg or a form of eggplant.

Instead, I made a cake—look, I like baking, and everything was so new to them—relying on well beaten egg whites for rise and honey for sweetening. Beating the egg whites till stiff was a heck of an arm workout, but no one was awake yet.

They still weren't awake when I took it, all fluffy and risen from the oven, which was too bad because of course it fell and wrinkled a bit. But it was still fluffy and beautiful, anyway, for something without a smidge of baking powder.

I'd finished cooking eggs—there really were a lot of eggs, probably three dozen—and ham, what I judged enough for all of us, which I judged from previous meals. I set it all in the shelf above the stove, to keep warm, and was making coffee Greek-style when Peaseblossom dragged in.

He'd obviously bathed—I could smell the liquid they used for soap and shampoo—and just as clearly hadn't made extreme efforts to make his hair presentable, which made me feel secretly pleased with myself. His hair didn't look tangled, but it looked like had been allowed to spread out in bramble form. I realized most of the time he must be braiding it, or tucking it under itself or something, because I hadn't realized it went all the way, well below his waist. It looked positively wild over the simple linen tunic, tied at the waist with a belt of the same fabric.

I brought the food out, and his eyes widened under the lowered eyebrows.

"Bad night?" I asked.

He glared at me, but then I realized he was glaring with the peculiar squint of people whose eyes hurt. "Nikre," he said, as if that explained everything. I remembered Nikre Lyto, but what did he have to do with how Brund looked? So I said, "Uh uh" and set food in front of him, and a plate. He found his spoon and used his own knife. One of these days, I had to talk to them about the hygiene of using the knife you stabbed people with to eat with, but not today.

"Coffee or tea?" I asked.

"Tea, please," he said. So I made him tea, just in time for Almar to join us, widen his eyes at the food, and help himself. Meanwhile, Peaseblossom had spread butter on my improvised creation I'll call breakfast cake, and took a bite, gave me a full-on smile, and said, "Good. Thank you."

Troz dragged in afterwards. Or, rather, didn't drag. For the first time since the break into the shelter, his eyes shone, and he seemed to walk with a spring, even if he also flinched from the light. He wished us all a good morning, a surprise since I didn't know that was an Elly custom.

He ate more than I'd ever seen him eat.

Afterwards, he sat down to writing something he called "brotherhood requisitions." I didn't ask, since the explanation would likely involve that magic thing I'd not had time to investigate.

Lendir Almar, meanwhile, sat down with what looked like a sewing basket and worked at something tiny and white. His pose, and bent head, and the way he worked by the light of an oil lamp made me think of a painting of a woman sewing, somewhere in old Earth's history, and then I had trouble getting the image of the giant in a bonnet out of my mind.

Peaseblossom, meanwhile, helped me clean, as was becoming normal, and while he dried breakfast dishes, told me, "Sorry. Nikre Lyto thought it was imperative that we all be healed last night, and dragged us one by one two portals away to a little used and secluded Troz shelter to do that." He grinned. "I went to Tarkross afterward and bought food from the... Okay, I might have pounded at the merchant's door. Then Lendir did the same, because he apparently went to get fabric from his cousins. So...there is a lot of food, but I daresay we'll eat it. Nikre says we can't hide forever, maybe another two weeks, a month, at most. Which is good, or I'd go insane."

I nodded at the flood, then managed, "What is the thing with dots? Dinosaur egg?"

He raised an eyebrow. "No. Most of those are blue."

I didn't have the nerve to ask him if he'd invented that, but he didn't give any indication he was joking. "It's a melon," he said. "A" and he made and untranslatable sound, "Melon. It's sweet and spicy."

So, of course, after the full meal, we ate half the melon. It tasted like exotic cuisine. Sweet, lemony, with an edge of hot pepper. I hadn't found anything like it anywhere in the worlds I'd visited.

I could see it becoming very popular in Britannia on High. If I got out of here alive, I'd go into the melon export business. Unless Mother demanded seeds for her orangeries, which she likely would, anyway.

With Peaseblossom healed, he decided, because of course he did, that we had to go out and do some fishing and maybe hunting. I started to suspect the king of Elly had too much energy for any one person, or any dozen people.

We went out to the moderate zone. I learned they didn't actually do much of anything in deep ice, and most nomad lines didn't have shelters there. In fact, Yanda was the only shelter that he knew of that far into the deep ice. He said, "It must have been warmer in the past."

Given the glassteel structures inside what appeared to be rock, and the sink where the faucet had broken off, but the pipe remained, and a dozen other things, I thought it was probably a scout ship either deliberately or accidentally buried and wondered what the rest of the cave was. But I wasn't going to try to discuss it. Not just now. I wondered what had happened to the engines. Left undisturbed, they'd last essentially forever, and give energy to eat and light a city or ten, but I'd seen no sign of any technology more advanced than oil lamps.

We fished most of the day, in an area that was only moderately cold. There was snow in shady spots, but it had melted in the rest, and there were beautiful crystalline streams, and fish I didn't have the name for, but one kind of which—when we cooked three very large ones that night—tasted like salmon.

There wasn't much talk, because apparently the custom of not alerting the fish to your intention to make them dinner extended to Elly. To be fair, I didn't think that Peaseblossom's low, rumbling voice would disturb them much, but for all I knew, the fish here knew Ellian and would understand our intent.

I recorded a new and interesting curse, "Amissar's belt," without having any clue why it was a curse, except that it related, of course, to Missa Mahar. Whose un-diminutived name was Amissar. And the curse was uttered by Peaseblossom when a fish broke the line and took off with the hook in its mouth.

We returned tired and more or less soaked from the waist down to find Troz and Almar cooking, but they gratefully accepted our contribution to the dinner table.

The next day, I was dragged hunting. Okay, maybe not exactly dragged. One advantage of Peaseblossom being healed is that we didn't need to use public portals. He assured me third circle and higher was fine for opening portals when not wounded, and took me through a dizzying succession of three portals. And I got to do a survey of the fauna in the temperate areas. There were elk, I think, or at least they looked like Earth elk. There was a flock of wild sheep that looked halfway like mountain sheep and like domestic sheep, and were probably some bioengineered cross. Mahar refused to hunt those because he said only the lambs were tasty and he wouldn't kill those unless we were actually starving. I thought he was being gentle about baby animals, but he explained that it was in his best interest to let little lambs grow and make more lambs. "Not that this is a heavily hunted area, but still, we should have seen other herds today."

He seemed disturbed by this as we hiked several miles. Enough that I was getting winded, and I was used to long hikes ever since the Academy. Mahar was carrying an iron-tipped lance, and I'd insisted he carry two blasters, which he carried as I did, with blasters through my belt. Like mersi characters.

We stalked an elk, which seemed to me like Peaseblossom having way more ambition than capacity. Did he mean to take it down with the lance? These things were huge. We'd used projectile weapons to hunt them on Earth.

But we stalked it, not talking much, until we were almost ready. But just as Mahar lifted his arm, ready to aim, from cover of an evergreen, a huge, unearthly thing came out of nowhere, jumped on the elk and broke its neck.

I didn't even see the creature properly, before Peaseblossom took a jumping start, ran at it, screamed something, and stuck the lance in its chest before it had time to look up from the elk it was eating.

The creature made a muffled growl and died, blood pouring out of its mouth.

Afterwards, I learned how to field-skin two animals and butcher one for what we wanted to keep. Not only was he amazing with a lance, he was very good at skinning animals and butchering them. "No reason to waste the elk," he said. "We just won't take the part where the dire Wolf bit and broke its neck. Not a lot of meat in the neck, anyway."

Oh, yeah, dire wolves. So the critter was white. Snow white, with deep, dense fur. I realized a lot of the furs I'd thought were bear were probably dire wolf.

"We kill them where we find them, if we can, because they are large and eat a lot the game, which means nomads starve. Not us, because obviously we have other means of sustenance, but poorer nomads." He talked quickly while cutting into the dire wolf unerringly, and skinning the fur away more or less intact. "Bitch to cure, but there's a curing room past the bathing pool on Yanda, so we won't have to smell it."

I looked at the beast. It was like something from Earth's past. Thing is, if these were native to Elly pre-colonization, it was the only place other than Earth with large mammals ever. Someone definitely had gone nuts with a my-little-genetics kit.

Why was unfathomable, but the whole situation was unfathomable. Including what had been done to the humans. Why? What kind of madman would do this?

He packed the meat and the fur, neatly, into impermeable cloth of some sort that he had carried out, apparently, in the satchel over his shoulder. He tied the cloth in such a way that we could carry the useable parts of the animals out as backpacks.

The same dizzying succession of portals back, and we were in deep ice, going into the shelter, in...triumph?

Neither Troz nor Almar seemed surprised at what we brought back, which gave me the impression that ice nomads were far tougher than I expected.

He put the food in an additional stasis box I hadn't seen before. "For long-term storage," he said. And then we took the furs, walking on a ledge along the bathing pool, along the small river that fed it, into a chamber that he said—and smelled like it—was the fur curing room. The river went on, and up there, in the darkness, there was a glow.

"What's up there?"

Mahar shook his head. "Eerlen never lets us go near. He says it's dangerous up there."

"Has he been up there?"

Mahar shrugged. "Could be clan lore."

It wasn't till the messy stuff was done, and we'd bathed and come out to the living and cooking areas to find that Troz and Almar had cooked dinner, that I asked him, "Why did you use the lance? You had blasters!"

He laughed, half-startled. "I did, didn't I? But I've never fired one in combat or hunt. I've seen you do it, but I never have done it. And I know how to use lances."

And that he did.

My Lovely Assistant

Skip

During the time I was at the Academy, when my father picked me up for a few days during the holidays and took me to cultural events and important shows and sometimes just pure fun ones, one of the later was a show with an illusionist.

The number that fascinated me in the set that turned out to be—though I didn't know it at the time, being very young—a fairly retro show of stage magic as practiced in the twentieth century, was one in which the "magician" made "my lovely assistant" float midair.

His assistant was a young woman in sparkly clothing, and with black hair that must have been past her buttocks. He floated her midair, lying still, with her arms at her side, and her hair trailing to the ground.

I remember his running a ruler under her and above her several times, to show nothing supported her in that position.

Later, Father told me a lot about how such tricks were accomplished at the time.

None of that helped when Brundar Mahar and I came back to the Yanda shelter after about a month of residence, and when Troz had made noises of moving on, to find this trick being reenacted in the common area just off the entrance.

To give the full background, we'd been out hunting, and both of us were sweaty, and probably had some blood spattered somewhere, though we tried not to. We also were carrying the pelts of two dire wolves, this time harvested with blasters, which we'd used liberally since I'd found out Mahar could refill the blasters by glaring at them. Okay, he said that's not what he was doing and chattered away about mathematics and formulas, but to me it looked like he glared at them.

The blasters, of course, made the harvesting of the animals much easier, but it was still impossible to skin the creatures without getting blood on ourselves.

So we came in, dirty and probably stinking, and talking loudly about something inconsequential, only to be greeted with a loud "Shhh" from Almar.

He was standing, legs slightly parted, and arms crossed.

Meanwhile, Kalal Ad Leed was floating midair, lying on his back, with his arms at his side. His black hair hung down to touch the floor of the shelter, in that case what looked like a well-worn red carpet.

Enacting the part of magician, except they weren't running a ruler under Ad Leed to show nothing was holding him, Eerlen Troz stood at his foot, and Nikre Lyto at his head.

We went past and past the bathing pool, to the tanning room, where Mahar told me, "Go and bathe, I'll do the first immersion in disinfecting solution, and then I'll bathe."

"What they're doing..." I said. "I thought Yanda was a no-magic place."

"It is. But it's an archimagician and someone at close to the same level. They can pull from the ruby for this, and it means if someone has tapped into Ad Leed's power pattern, he can't interfere."

It made sense, as much as this magic stuff did, which wasn't much. I rushed through and washed very quickly, because I really didn't want Peaseblossom to come out of the fur curing room and catch me naked. The weird look he and Nikre had got when I'd shown my chest, of all things, made me uncomfortable. And there was that whole thing about not wanting to do anything improper because I wasn't allowed to get involved with natives.

So I rushed through, dried quickly, and put on the loose pants and tunic we all tended to wear around the shelter and to sleep in. I was getting used to the hair down my back, though I now braided it before going to sleep.

I more or less tiptoed into the common room, and knit myself with the wall, in a shadowy place, staying quiet, hoping they wouldn't see me and that something I saw would give me an inkling as to what was going on.

The first thing to note is that, unlike that showman "magician" in my youth, neither Troz nor Lyto were doing this for my benefit.

This was obvious in the fact they were concentrating so hard on

Ad Leed and what the other was doing that they probably weren't even aware of my presence.

There were minute gestures, their eyes would lock, and one or the other would nod.

The feeling is that they were engaged in close and difficult work, and being very careful. I'd seen those expressions in two people who knew each other very well, working, jointly, on some delicate equipment or complex computer.

Ad Leed was wearing the same type of clothing I was, which was heavy for Brinar, from what I'd seen at the festival. More importantly, there was a fur cloak and probably other clothing neatly folded in a pile near him, as well as the blue cloak I'd learned was the distinctive mark of a magician. So they hadn't grabbed him and brought him here unconscious and there was a good chance he'd volunteered for this.

But I didn't know what this was.

Peaseblossom slid, silently, on bare feet, to stand next to me. He smelled almost overpoweringly of soap and the liquid used to wash hair. I leaned close and whispered as low as I could in his ear. "What are they doing?"

He tilted his head and twisted his mouth, with the appearance of deep thought, then leaned in. "They are examining his pattern. If it's clean, they will...uh...there's no words, but join with his mind. There needs to be two of them so they don't hurt him. When it's only one, you can...absorb the smaller pattern?"

Almar didn't shush, but we both felt his glare and stopped talking.

At that moment, as if on cue, Troz and Lyto must have decided that Ad Leed's pattern was intact or whatever, because they both nodded, then extended their hands. Not to touch Ad Leed, just either side of him. And each of them gave the impression or made the gesture of pulling a thread taut with each hand. It reminded me of the gestures Ad Leed had made while performing healing.

Ad Leed moved. Not much. Kind of like the little adjustment someone in deep sleep made to get more comfortable, then resumed being absolutely still.

And then...questions started. The first one was easy, asking him if he'd been romantically involved with a male Draksall and who it was.

Ad Leed's forehead wrinkled, and he gave a sort of vexed sigh.

"Yes. I met him in my palace. I mean, I realized he was not Ellyan. It's..." He blushed, and I guessed with startling clarity what that "realizing" implied. "He said he was in the royal family in Draksah and had escaped so he wouldn't be killed during the fights for succession." Another vexed sigh. "At the time, I knew nothing of the politics in Draksah. I didn't find out there hadn't been a fight for succession and the Emperor hadn't been replaced until—" Another vexed sigh. "He disappeared, six months later, and that's when I started investigating and trying to understand what had happened. I then started talking to people who know more about Draksah, and I eventually..." A mumble and he continued, "Mahar's spy corps, and there had been no such thing, and having seen the royal family in Draksah, I doubt my... I doubt Itarr could be one of them. Unless the son of a very minor concubine. Doesn't mean it might not have been... He could be the son of a very minor concubine, but be threatened by palace politics and run here, anyway, and made up the other story to make himself important."

Lyto and Troz stayed quiet for a moment, then Troz asked, his voice normal, but also oddly incisive. I was used to Eerlen Troz sounding...well, kind and understanding, but he sounded like righteous wrath incarnate as he said, "And why didn't you report it? From the beginning, really, but particularly after his disappearance?"

This time, the sigh was deep. "I did not want my power interdicted," he said. "Under suspicion of divided loyalties. It's not just...the battle front. My subjects, my farmers, my fishers need healing often, and call on me. I couldn't leave them unprovided. But—" A dark blush suffused his cheeks. "I also— After he disappeared, I felt like a fool. I didn't want to admit I'd been fooled so easily. I did tell Brundar Mahar."

Troz's face twitched, but he didn't say anything. This time, he sighed. "Can you concentrate on the image of... Itarr, is it? Can you think of him as hard as possible?"

Ad Leed, eyes still closed, gave a little nod. Troz's hand went to the ruby, and Mahar leaned forward, slightly, expectantly.

Something started forming, between Ad Leed and the wall against which Mahar and I leaned. I say something, because at first it was just shimmers of light in the air, then it looked like a tangle of glowing wires, with light racing over them very fast.

I'm not sure when it started looking like the figure of a person, seen a long distance away in fog. And then suddenly a man stood there, in the short tunic of a Brinarian, and sandals.

He was...about Ad Leed's height, which wasn't very tall at all for a male, not even in Draksah. And he was golden-skinned, and dark-eyed, with an oval-shaped face and not-unpleasant features. Oh, and no facial hair that I could see, which didn't impress me nearly as much these days. His hair was dark, very curly, falling over his shoulders. And he had an expression of supreme confidence.

It was the expression that got me. I was looking at him and thinking it must be good to be so self-assured, when I realized I knew that expression, and by extension that face. And when that happened, my memory dug out the image of that same man, with very short hair, and a carefully sculpted beard and moustache, walking across a—

"Oh, shit," I said.

And all hell broke loose.

BALANCE OF POWER
EERLEN

For an archmagician to be startled while metaphorically el-bow-deep in a third circle's power and mind was not the worst thing that could happen.

No, the worst that can happen was if, on being startled, the arch-magician panicked, and his pattern decided it was a life-or-death moment and absorbed the weaker pattern. The result of such a thing was death for the weaker pattern. Ugly, screaming death. At least if the weaker pattern were lucky. Because the other option was for the less powerful magician to be effectively locked inside his own mind and power, unable to reach the outer world and utterly isolated, while his body could do only basic functions such as eat and sleep.

Having once faced such a death-in-life as a result of a deliberate attack by Drahy, and been saved only by his sire's genetic legacy of an unreachable Draksall portion to his pattern, Eerlen was always very careful to set safeguards when touching his subordinates' patterns.

He had done that, this time, and also they were in Yanda, which helped mitigate the danger. Which was why Ad Leed survived Eerlen's sudden shock unscathed. And why Eerlen didn't scream.

What Eerlen did instead was pull all the probes of his power back into himself and the ruby, at the same time Nikre did the same, and drop Kalal Ad Leed on the floor, his power shocked by the sudden withdrawal.

And, of course, flushed, and—even through the tunic covering him—visibly aroused, one of the strange side effects of being power-attacked. It was pleasurable enough for the victim that some higher circles through the ages had used initiating an attack then pulling back as a form of seduction.

Eerlen pretended not to notice, which was the best he could do in the circumstances, to preserve all of their dignities. The side effect vanished quickly. Ad Leed blinked, then drew himself to sitting on the floor, looking bedraggled, pale and shivering.

It could be worse, much worse. For one, Ad Leed had been over a fairly thick rug, not rock. For another, he laid there blinking and shivering, not screaming like his mind had been breached.

Even so, Nikre and Eerlen concentrated on him. By the time Eerlen knelt by him, Nikre was already kneeling there, telling Ad Leed, "Follow my fingers" and moving them from side to side in front of Ad Leed's face. His eyes tracked fine, so the possibility of damage was minimal. He would just be in shock.

Eerlen asked, "What is your name and parentage, magician?"

Kalal snorted, and drew himself up, still shivering. "Kalal Ad Leed, sired by Tmart Almar upon Malin Ad Leed. My mind is intact, Archmagician."

Eerlen nodded. "Appears to be so. Do you know what we were doing?"

Ad Leed nodded. "You were mind and power-examining me. I am sorry I did not tell you there might have been a breach. I didn't know—" He wrapped his arms around himself.

"I know. Don't talk." Eerlen looked over his shoulder at Lendir. "Can you get Ad Leed some warm milk? Or tea. Warm is the point."

Nikre covered Ad Leed with Ad Leed's own fur cloak, dire wolf pelt, deep and white. Ad Leed pulled up the hood, a measure of how cold he felt. Or perhaps to hide his expression.

Nikre and Eerlen fussed over Ad Leed a while longer, aware of embarrassing him, but of necessity, until they'd verified his pattern was intact, and that he was in his right mind and had stopped shivering. By then, Ad Leed had managed to sit up and sipped at a cup of hot tea. Lendir hovered nearby, like a mother hen trying not to brood.

Eerlen had been aware, meanwhile, of the ambassador and Brund talking to each other, just out of his line of sight. After a while, they fell silent. Eerlen noted that Webson helped Lendir make tea. And dose it with honey, which was fine, as sugar would help with shock.

Once Ad Leed was well, or at least not shivering, Eerlen left him to Nikre's observation and stood aside, calling his presence and command as archmagician to him and assuming the authority of his command. "Milord Webson?"

"Yes, Lord Troz?"

They should never have given him the cosmetic change to make him look Ellyan, small though the change was. For some reason, it made him look much younger, and at that moment—hands behind his back—like a guilty child who'd displeased an adult.

Eerlen couldn't help himself. He felt his lips arching in a smile, and sighed.

"It's not your fault," Eerlen said. "It was my oversight not setting silence around us. Nikre and I thought we'd be done well before you and Brundar returned, and I neglected to put up alarms to warn me when you came in."

Webson nodded. He still had his hands behind his back, and was looking up at Eerlen, his face very impassive, conveying an appearance of attentive obedience, like a well-behaved Brotherhood apprentice.

Eerlen didn't believe it for a minute. If he were half that dutiful, he and Brund wouldn't have been thick as thieves these weeks. Brundar's friends ran to a certain type, and it wasn't gentle and obedient. But then he remembered that Webson had been trained in war, and the pose fell into place: he'd seen palace guard look that passive and abashed when Lendir dressed them down.

He cleared his throat. "I might have kept control of the situation but for the sudden exclamation. No, I'm not upset, but I do want to know: Milord Webson, what made you swear loudly?"

Webson shifted his weight from foot to foot. He frowned in concentration. "Milord, I recognized him. The image you conjured. I didn't expect to see someone I knew."

"Him?"

"The...the projection? Image? The man?"

Webson said "male," which was accurate and also came through as "male animal" because Ellyan language didn't have terms for male or female humans, obviously. But Eerlen thought it referred to the person the ruby had conjured from Ad Leed's mind. "The projection of Ad Leed's memory?" Eerlen asked.

"Whatever that hologram—" The strange word came out of Webson's lips and sounded odd amid the flow of Ellyan. Eerlen would assume it was the term for "projection of memory" in his language. He shook his head. "Whatever that projection was. How did it... Is that what it was? Was it from Ad Leed's memories? Ad

Leed's...friend?"

"Yes," Eerlen said, and avoided smiling at the fine shadings in the word friend. He'd heard the same careful phrasing from younger ones in the brotherhood when talking about someone sharing their bed, but where the status of the relationship remained uncertain. Then realizing that Webson sounded concerned and confused by the way the magic worked, he said, "It was a projection of what I saw in his mind, so the ruby could record it, and could remember it if I needed to. So it could be shown to other magicians, if needed. Someone else might have seen him. If he was a spy from Draksah, he might be trying to get close to another magician."

Webson shook his head. "I don't think... Not if the person I saw was... I don't suppose you could call up the projection again? If it's in the ruby?"

Eerlen was about to say that of course he could, when Ad Leed spoke. "I can do it. I probably remember him best." He pulled his hood back, to expose a face still pale, but now also blushing and waved his hand midair, calling up the projection of his memory.

Eerlen could see Ad Leed's pattern coalesce to form it, which shouldn't have been visible, but he supposed meant Ad Leed was exhausted. And, of course, there was the effect of Yanda.

The projection showed the person that Ad Leed had called "Itarr." Short, dark-haired, golden-skinned, he could have looked Brinarian, except there was something a little too square about the chin, a little too sharp about the nose.

Webson took a long, indrawn breath through his nose, loud in the silence. Brundar came to stand beside him as though afraid he might be needed.

"That's not a Draksall," Webson said. "He's someone from my...from Britannia on High. Lowell. His real name is Lowell StJohn. Earl of Allridge. It's a courtesy title. His father is a duke, though I can't remember his title, which is stupid as there are only maybe twenty dukes in the Star Empire. Wait. I remember! I met his father at the last party my parents gave before— His father is the Duke of Drakeford. I knew it would come to me."

Eerlen was caught by the flow of words, and stunned. The titles were odd, but he assumed that this person was a Lord of the Land in the place Webson came from. Which meant none of it made sense, and all of it made Eerlen's head hurt. "None of those are Draksall names," he said, feeling as though he'd stepped on a familiar path, only to have the ground give out under him. His voice sounded aggrieved and on the edge of whining.

Webson looked grieved and a little worried as he shook his head. "No, Milord Troz. I'm afraid this man is my compatriot. I last saw him when I was at the... In diplomatic training. I was surprised to see him there, as he was not an instructor, and he didn't wear the uniform of a student, but my...mentor, Mr. Crowe, said that the was not with the IDS but with an allied group. Well, at least I think it was an allied group."

Eerlen recovered just enough to say, "An allied group? To the diplomatic service? To...servants of your sovereign?"

Webson nodded. "Yes. They are scouts. They investigate discovered colonies...er...planets that come to the attention of the Star Empire and apply for admittance. Did Elly apply for admittance to the Star Empire?"

Eerlen shook his head. "Not that I know." It seemed absurd that such a thing could have happened without Eerlen's say-so, but all the same, he felt obligated to look towards Brund, who stood against the wall, looking as stunned as Eerlen felt. He was relieved when Brund shook his head, confirming Eerlen's response, because frankly, Brundar had a habit of making decisions and taking initiative on his own, and Eerlen wasn't prepared to swear he knew everything Brundar might have done. Though applying for admission to a kingdom in the stars and telling no one would be crazy even for Brundar.

Brundar shook his head. "No. At least no one in authority applied for admission."

Webson groaned. "I don't understand it. Because StJohn should only be on a planet he's investigating for admission to the Empire, as a protectorate. And he was here. And if he was here, there are other scouts around. Like, teams of them. Which would mean that Elly is under investigation for admission, but then surely the king and...and the other authorities would know."

"Well, the authorities are almost all here," Brundar said. "Save for three Lords of the Land. And I didn't ask, and neither did Eerlen. Is it possible to admit a world that hasn't asked for it?"

"No." Webson was rubbing the middle of his forehead. "We have—in the past—invaded, pacified and occupied worlds, but that's not a matter for the Scouts. We only do that to worlds

that make war on us. Which I very much doubt Elly has done."
Webson's face scrunched, as though he had a headache. Then, as
though it made perfect sense, he wheeled around on his feet, and
headed for the kitchen at a clip.

"Milord Webson?" Eerlen called.

"I have to bake," Webson said. It sounded like he said it through
clenched fists.

He washed his hands and started pulling out flour from stasis,
and eggs and got a bowl from the shelves by the stove. Brundar of
course moved towards him as if pulled on invisible strings. Eerlen
would worry, if he didn't know for an absolute fact that Brundar
was called to the mere thought of sugary food.

Brund whispered something to Webson, and Webson shook
his head. "No, none of it makes sense. Let me try to order my
thoughts." He broke eggs into a large bowl, mixed in honey, started
mixing the two vigorously.

Ad Leed removed his cloak one-handed and, holding his cup,
headed for the kitchen. Nikre stepped towards him, as though
afraid he'd collapse, but Ad Leed looked steady enough on his
feet. Eerlen frowned, wondering if he should stop the Brinarian,
but Ad Leed's power had shown no signs of control or corruption,
so it was unlikely he was doing something under spell or compulsion.

And Ad Leed as Ad Leed wouldn't do anything against Elly or
the brotherhood. He was their best healer, even if Ter was head
of third, and he was Lendir's beloved younger half-crossibling.
Whom he'd raised.

Eerlen realized he was chewing on the corner of his lip, worried, anyway. This situation was all new and unfathomable, and
though he trusted Ad Leed, he still felt as though Eerlen were not
in full control of the situation.

He couldn't even tell what made him so nervous, as Ad Leed
skirted Nikre and waved a negligent hand at Lendir, saying, "I'm
fine, Lendir."

Ad Leed walked to the kitchen and stopped on the other side
of the table at which Webson was working. "I need to know..."
He stopped. Sighed. "I'm sorry. I need to know." Ad Leed reached
across the table, and grabbed Webson's forearm just short of the
elbow. "Please, Milord Webson. You said Itarr...was really... Those
names you said. He was from your world? Not a Draksall?"

DRAMATIS PERSONAE

Skip Hayden – aka Publius Cornelius Scipio Africanus, Kayel Hayden aka Kaheel Trohem – Viscount Webson, First Year Ambassador from Britannia on High, The Star Empire and accidental plenipotentiary Ambassador to the lost colony of Elly in the 26th century, Earth reckoning.

Eerlen Troz – Erradian nomad, sworn to the late king of Elly Myrrir Mahar. Archmagician of the lost colony of Elly. Sire of Brundar Mahar, King of Elly. Adopted body parent to Nikre Lyto.

Myrrir Mahar – Late King of Elly, and magician of the third circle. Sworn to Eerlen Troz. Body-parent of Brundar Mahar. Sire of Guinar Ter, Lendir Almar, Kahre Sarda and adopted sire of Nikre Lyto.

Brundar Mahar – King of Elly, Magician of the third circle. Ascends to throne at the age of 16 when his body-parent is murdered. Sireling of Eerlen Troz.

Lendir Almar – Commander of the Royal Battalion. Commander of the Palace Guard. Body guard of the king and the heirs. Magician of the fourth circle. Head of the fourth circle. Half crossibling of Brundar Mahar.

Guinar Ter – Oldest sireling of Myrrir Mahar. Magician of the third circle. Head of the third circle of the Brotherhood of Magicians. Half crossibling of Brundar Mahar. Lord of the Land of Lirridar.

Kahre Sarda – Sireling of Myrrir Mahar. Magician of the first circle. Half crossilbling of Brundar Mahar. Lord of the Land of Karrash.

Nikre Lyto – Adopted/legal child of Eerlen Troz. Adopted/legal sireling of Myrrir Mahar. Adopted/legal full crossibling of Brundar Mahar. Successor in waiting to the Archmagician of Elly.

Parnel Haethlem – Second circle magician. Head of second. Lord of the Land of Erradi.

Kalal Ad Leed – Third circle magician. Lord of the Land of Brinar.

Kaheer Mahar - dead toddler body-child of Myrrir Mahar, sireling of Eerlen Troz, full, older sibling of Brundar Mahar. Murdered at the age of 2.

Lahem Drahy – previousArchmagician of Elly. Eerlen Troz'spredecessor.

www.ingramcontent.com/pod-product-compliance
Lightning Source LLC
Chambersburg PA
CBHW031939240626
47153CB00003B/795